ALSO BY JILL HOFFMAN

Mink Coat (poetry)

JILTED

a novel

JILL HOFFMAN

Simon & Schuster

New York / London / Toronto / Sydney / Tokyo / Singapore

SIMON & SCHUSTER
Rockefeller Center
1230 Avenue of the Americas
New York, New York 10020

Designed by Chris Welch
Manufactured in the United States of America

10 9 8 7 6 5 4 3 2 1

Library of Congress Cataloging-in-Publication Data

Hoffman, Jill.
    Jilted: a novel/Jill Hoffman
        p.   cm.
        1. Man-woman relationships—United States—Fiction.
2. Married women—United States—Fiction. 3. Artists—United States—Fiction.
I. Title.
PS3558.O345J55   1993
813'.54—dc20   93-28635
                                                            CIP

ISBN: 0-671-79518-X

For my father, Stephen L. Hoffman,
and for the memory of my mother, Pearl.

ACKNOWLEDGMENTS

With special thanks to Bob Asahina, Lisa Bankoff, Vladimir Urban, Matthew Schwartz, Esther Hoffman, Nancy Stiefel, Chuck Johnson, Jennifer Weidman, Irene Urban, Rick Schneider, and all the members of my writing group, including Robert Steward, Shelley Stenhouse, Doug Dorph, Alice Jurish, John Penn, Anita Lobel, and especially my daughter, Jennifer Belle.

"And don't you think seduction isn't very nice?"
John Ashbery,
"The Songs We Know Best"

1

CAESAR SALAD

/ / / / / / /

I once saw a woman in my building who was in heat. She got off on the twentieth floor. The walls were painted dark chocolate brown, the same color as her skin. I was standing at my open door when she got off the elevator at the wrong floor in order not to be seen, then ran up the flight of back stairs to André Black's apartment, right over mine on the twenty-first floor. She was already aroused. Her orange dress stood stiffly away from her skin, ready to be stepped out of, or pulled off. She chased herself up the stairs, as if he were chasing her through the spacious rooms of the apartment.

Today I am like that woman.

My mother named me Joy because she wanted me to be a

joy to whoever saw me, wherever I went. For the first time in all these years, my own name belongs to me again, I am worthy of it. I am a hair's breadth away from the socket—about to be plugged in.

"Beauty like that money can't buy," Carl Vaggio once said. I remember his first retrospective at the Whitney twenty years ago. We stood apart in a room. His name was on the walls. He was amazingly young. No one that age had ever had a retrospective before. He smiled at me shyly with his missing teeth, like a baby vampire. My husband was around the corner with my bosom friend, Marlena. I felt entirely safe. Someone snapped a photograph. "When will I see you?" I said. "What's wrong with tomorrow?" he answered. It was when we always met. "At twelve." He held my hand. The next day at noon we went to bed.

WHEN I LOOK in my mother's journal, I read, "Never go back to your past, warmed-over soup never tastes the same."

But can I believe her? She is talking about my father, whom she wants. She is ravenous for the past. She wants back what was hers. What she had.

She is consumed with longing. "I felt safe in his arms," she writes.

I WILL SEE Carl Vaggio again. I eat a Caesar salad alone at Walker's, a restaurant a block from Carlton Street, and Egypt is the napkin in my lap. The waitress comes and asks if I want anything else. "No Moroccan salad today?" She laughs, as if she knows that today I am Cleopatra, dreaming of Caesar. The years shrink to a sonnet:

All losses are restored and sorrows end.

The moths have bit stars into my long black jersey skirt. I wear it anyway, day after day, for continuity.

I sit a long time, scribbling with crayons on the paper tablecloth, lips, eyes, hearts, arrows, all pointing the way to this great happiness. My destiny. Arrows strewn on a battlefield, pointing me to Carl. All roads lead to Carl Vaggio.

2

WARMED-OVER SOUP

/ / / / / / / /

*O*nce I wore pale jeans, tall velvet shoes, platform wedges, multicolored like Joseph's coat. And an old satin blouse, faded to purple, with its pocket on its sleeve like a heart.

I was married and living on the twentieth floor, in seven large rooms with nineteen windows. Sun patterned the Persian carpets in the living room, in the master bedroom, in the corner dining room, where my husband, Douglas, and I had a double desk. It did not penetrate into the foyer, empty except for the green Buddhist prayer rug, a horizontal temple with peacocks and exotic blooms. Does this mean I was rich? Were these my riches?

I had an exquisite curly-haired daughter with great blue eyes in a pale moon face. Isabelle. Two years later, a boy was born, Benjamin, and two years after that Penelope, a coppery beauty.

I had an important job—I was a poet, I taught poetry at a prestigious university—and, with a doting husband and dazzling children, I was the center of the universe.

LONG AGO, I had mulled over and over the miraculous arrangement whereby a man who is a perfect stranger becomes more than a brother to you, sleeping in your bed. "My God," I murmured, as if this were the manifestation of my most hidden wish. In graduate school, in my rickety apartment on the edge of the gorge, I waited in a see-through nightgown.

Lonely, my voice breaking, I called my mother. She and my father were living on Madison Avenue in an empty apartment newly painted and carpeted in soft matching avocado green. They had just moved from a suite in the Oliver Cromwell Hotel. In the unfurnished living room were hundreds of beanstalks, avocado pits grown into gangly plants. They would eventually be left to die, unwatered. "You don't have to get married like everybody else," my mother said. "You can be like Emily Dickinson. There is another path in life for you . . ."

But Emily Dickinson never left her father's house. All her poems were bundled in drawers, tied with ribbons. Though, in a burst of triumph, she wrote:

> I'm "Wife"—I've finished that—
> That other state—
> I'm Czar—I'm "Woman" now—

she was only dreaming of a preacher who moved to California and whom she would never see again.

Unlike Emily Dickinson, I wanted to be published. My other talent was in bed.

When, at last, I told my mother that I wanted to marry

Douglas Black from Philadelphia, she said, "I don't think he's man enough for you."

HANDSOME, WITH NARROW shoulders and a sensitive face, Douglas came up the outside wooden back stairs through the kitchen door. His major was philosophy. He had red hair, wore black-rimmed glasses, a white shirt. He stopped at the sink. Reached into the cabinet where potatoes grew strange roots in plastic bags, and took out the rusty unused can of Bab-o. I respected stains; I did not touch dirt. He scrubbed the dark, scowling sink till it shone. The transformation amazed me.

After that, he drove all night from Ithaca to Philadelphia, from Philadelphia to Ithaca. He drove me to Manhattan. We stopped on the highway and almost had sex. "No, don't," he said. "We have so much to live for."

I had known him for three weeks. Coming up in the elevator on Madison Avenue, he pinned me against the Christmas wreath. "Will you marry me?" he asked. The pointy green holly leaves and red artificial berries caught in my long dark hair. "I'm not going to let you off this elevator unless you say yes," he insisted.

"Yes," I said, submitting.

I forgot his name the next minute when I tried to introduce him to my father.

He took me out for my birthday. I was twenty-four, trembling on the verge of overripeness. He bought me a pearl drop suspended from a gold-plated leaf, something you get when you're fourteen. At dinner, at Motel on the Mountain, he said, "You have spinach wrapped around your tooth." I felt vulnerable in my teeth (cottage cheese was the worst). I was gat-toothed like the Wife of Bath, with a space between the two front teeth, which was supposed to denote lechery. I appreciated his honesty, and his erection under the table.

The day that Kennedy was assassinated we went away together for the weekend. We lay on the floor. There were angels in my vagina. And so I married him.

I MARRIED DOUGLAS because it was clear he would never grow fat. He had articulate hands and so I married him. In bars, my small hands went up and down the shaft of his beer glass, and so he married me. We would sit together for hours in my parents' apartment, my speckled Vuillard housecoat partly undone, while Douglas insisted on the compatibility of poetry and philosophy. They were the perfect pair, he said, meaning that we were too.

"I wish you would marry Douglas already," my sister, Heidi, said. "I'm tired of always coming into a room and seeing him with an erection under his pants."

My mother called him a "weasel," because he had won me. It was a compliment.

Once my mother and Heidi and I were in my parents' king-sized bed, resting. My mother believed in bed rest. When she dressed up to go out with my father, in a tiered ruffled black sheath, she was as beautiful as a flamenco dancer holding a rose in her teeth. But now she was in threadbare pajamas from the year one, her coral-tinted hair awry, and Heidi looked greasy, her mouth stretched leering into a smirk. My sister's dark hair was oily, her features blurred and smudged. It was not a pretty picture. I was ashamed.

"What a picture!" Douglas said, with sentimental approval.

My mother always said that the right man would make me feel like a queen. I married him for my mother. I married him because I hated his mother. My mother had brought me up on a daily pabulum of praise. "Your bad is someone else's good," she always said. Douglas's mother had always taken the other person's side against her son. "Some mothers think their children's . . . is chocolate ice cream!" she would shout, silently mouthing the missing word.

Abe Black, Douglas's father, was a soap salesman who did

well by charging his customers more than any other salesman for the same products. "Service" was his chief commodity, his wife boasted. A tall, stooped man with a drooping nose (really the biggest hooked nose I had ever seen), he shuffled about, subservient to his wife. Authority was conspicuously lacking in him. I had expected something very different. I had expected admiration, applause, his sexual approval. Douglas's father was an immediate disappointment to me but, from the moment we met, his mother, Naomi Black, was my natural enemy.

The first time we met, she was wearing fake diamonds. She was short and aggressive with blue-white hair. She took me into the den and showed me a book of Douglas's bowel movements. It was the part of child-rearing she had liked least, she said, turning the pages, but she kept a careful record of it, three times a day. She read aloud, she forced me to look. "Amount: normal; color: reddish-brown; consistency: soft to liquid; smell: putrid."

She paid me one compliment. I was wearing a three-piece pants suit from Bendel's. "You're so well coordinated, I hate you," she said, boiling a large pink cow's tongue for dinner.

IN COLLEGE, I had a long affair with a professor. It lasted sixteen months. He was Jedd Swenson, an art critic, well known, pink and fiery, with an abundance of wavy gold hair. "You're playing with fire," he said, as we danced in a bar near campus. It was my senior year, I had just turned twenty. "You're playing with fire," he said, as we sat in his Volkswagen in the snow. He was forty. He wanted to leave his wife for me, but I was afraid of marriage. I only liked older men so I wouldn't have to get married. I wanted to make up to married men for how my mother treated my father.

Once, after I graduated, Carl Vaggio invited me to his studio. Carl and I were just getting to know each other, when Jedd Swenson unexpectedly arrived to collect me. Like my father. I was enjoying this "studio visit," but I didn't mind. I felt coveted, in demand. I felt popular!

Marriage was a deadly trap, like the one Jedd Swenson finally set for me. Before leaving my tiny apartment near NYU to go back to Annandale-on-Hudson one Sunday, he put black paper specks in my vaginal jelly. When he returned, he opened the tube.

The black confetti was gone. I had been unfaithful.

He cried; there was a brief skirmish on the bed. I was shocked; my hand was broken. He had broken my hand. I was in the middle of taking exams. I had to lie to my parents. I had to tell them I slipped in the shower. I permanently lost the shapely middle knuckle on my left hand.

Douglas gave me a ring. A flawed diamond with a good (bluish) color. It was over a carat. I told Jedd Swenson over lunch that I was engaged. I had not seen him since he broke my hand. Afterwards, I was meeting Douglas, I told him smugly.

After lunch, I had garlic on my breath. Douglas and I stood on a subway platform. I had garlic on my breath, I was afraid. How did I know I could be faithful to anyone? "What if I'm unfaithful?" I said.

"I'll tag along," Douglas answered.

Two lines of poetry haunted me: "Fain would I wed a fair young man who day and night could please me, / Who when my mind or body grieved had the power to ease me." I didn't want to get married, because that meant the definite beginning of your story. The beginning implied the end. But if I was not in danger of losing my husband, or of my husband's wrath, of ruining my life, how could I be afraid? I thought that Douglas was that fair young man.

As soon as we became engaged, Douglas slept over. He slept on a mattress in our empty living room. My bedroom faced my parents' bedroom. In the middle of the night I saw my mother walking in her sleep. She was wearing a pajama top and droopy drawers. That's how I knew she was asleep: she wasn't dressed for a rendezvous. Our eyes met, but she looked right through me; she was walking towards the living room with a little smile on her face. I watched spellbound from my bed. Was she going to try to sleep with Douglas on the mattress on the floor? Did this mean she liked him after all? That he was man enough for me?

I was her life. She lived through me. Her love for me was my self-love. Recently, for instance, when I had had a headache, she called the doctor, a nice young Dr. Giuseppe. While he was examining me, I left my bed to throw up in the bathroom. "Even perfection has its imperfections," he said. This diagnosis met with our approval. Afterwards, she fed me delicious cold peaches and sour cream, and I felt better at once.

Still, this was going too far. Her frustrated longing decked out in rags and walking like a ghost? It was grotesque.

She paused. Still asleep, she seemed to think better of it. She turned back. In the morning, nothing was said.

THE WEDDING COULD hardly take place, because Naomi Black had to know the color of the bridesmaids' dresses—pink, yellow, or blue—well in advance, and my mother could not decide on the color. In the end, Naomi wore a pink satin gown on her short, plump body and a glum expression on her white satin face, as if she were attending her son's funeral.

Afterwards, we found his family weeping together in a Mamaroneck diner. During the wedding, Abe Black had risen from his chair to bless the bread, but the honor had already been given to my mother's father. Douglas said, "I'm sure she didn't mean to insult you, Dad."

"Your father's very hurt," Naomi had answered.

MY WEDDING NIGHT was the first time that I felt a small dread before the act. I became seasick in the New Paradise Motel in Paramus, New Jersey, from the Magic Fingers massage, and black and blue, as if I had been sleeping on a pea.

By morning, in my white cocoon, which had been on sale at Ohrbach's, I had fallen into a coma—for Douglas had made me promise to give up diet pills forever—and I slept through our preliminary honeymoon, getting a bone in my throat at dinner and having it taken out in the emergency ward, like a rehearsal for our having a baby together, and I slept through the packing, which Douglas did, rolling my enormous trousseau into sausages to avoid wrinkles, and I slept through our bon voyage party and slept hurriedly through Paris and London and the long drive to Ireland, where Douglas was to teach, sleeping most nights in the new Peugeot.

In Bern, Switzerland, there were two bears in a pit. They were fornicating, clumsy and dogged about it. They kept trying for hours. The docile lady bear had a patient look on her face that smote me with envy. On my honeymoon, I wanted to change places with a lady bear hugged from behind by a persistent clout.

In front of Géricault's *The Raft of the Medusa*, I held the hand of a small dark stranger in the Louvre. He was alarmed. "Oh, I'm sorry," I cried. "I thought you were my husband," and fled, embarrassed, to Douglas's side. A few moments later, in front of Delacroix's funeral pyre of concubines, *The Death of Sardanapalus*, I took my husband's hand again.

Again the small dark stranger was alarmed.

WE RETURNED, AFTER our yearlong honeymoon, and lived idyllically in the country halfway between our two teaching jobs, his in Bronxville, mine at Bard College, my alma mater.

Married, we visited my parents. Their building on Madison Avenue had only two apartments on each floor. The other apartment on their floor was empty. I was up before Douglas, my nightgown up around my waist, fingering myself while my husband lay beside me. He had been out drinking in a bar with my parents' doorman the night before. After a half hour or so, I saw, in a facing window of the unoccupied apartment, which

I had never noticed before, a black man watching me with a white paintbrush in his hand.

WE MOVED FROM the country to the city when I got my big teaching job at Columbia. It fell into my lap. In spite of my huge belly. I went to the interview nine months pregnant and on crutches after our car accident, Douglas and my mother propping me up, one on either side. "You're kidding," I said to the chairman when he called and hired me.

Our doorman building on the Upper West Side, with its heavy wrought-iron doors and heraldic blue canopy, had its entrance on the hill leading up to Broadway. Charlie, the doorman, was a handsome, grandfatherly figure. Wally, on the alternate shift, always bowing and scraping, never left his armchair. Pressing the buzzer in his hip pocket to let us in, he would raise one cheek of his buttocks as if he were farting.

A student of mine from Columbia saw me with Douglas and Isabelle, wheeling a baby carriage on Broadway, and said, "Your husband is demonically good-looking." I was pleased at this corroboration, for I had almost forgotten why I had married.

FOR YEARS I was lost in the details of my husband's face. The cleft in his chin repeated under his bottom lip and above his upper lip. His voluptuous bottom lip and ascetic upper one; his frank teeth.

I looked at my husband and he looked at me and I did not understand the color of his eyes, which were light brown, reddish brown, not like my own. I did not understand him. I lay still and pretended to be asleep beside him in our queen-sized bed, waiting for him to masturbate. But he never once betrayed himself. He allowed himself to be smothered even in summer under my down quilt. He thumped openly with insomnia on the hard horsehair mattress that my mother had given us, but never furtively shook it. He was very thin and transparent, and I blamed him for this because I could not see into him very deeply, I could not see into him at all. We were one flesh; it had unsexed us.

"If p entails q," he said, "it does not follow that if someone believes that p, then he believes that q."

"He's womanish in the kitchen," my mother said.

"No, Mother," I defended him, "he's not a woman."

I held him from behind like the old moon with the new moon in its arms. He turned around and bent his handsome refined face towards me, the one curl right in the middle of his forehead. "I love you," he murmured, lifting the starched flap of his pajama top from between his legs to enter me. We did not kiss. I held him in my arms while he worked, his face buried in my neck, his sweat trickling into my washed hair. Twin meadows in the small of his back gradually filled with dew. "Darling, should we have chicken paprikash tomorrow, since my parents are coming? Do you think Pierrette will marry Claude? Did you pick up your shirts from the Chinese laundry?" Then jealousy of his orgasm took possession of me, and I climbed to the top of the small incline.

HIS MOTHER HAD taught him that it was a sin to go barefoot. When he was a boy he had broken a toe, and as he always had his white buck shoes on, it had gone unnoticed and hardened that way, curling under. It offended my eyes. I blamed *her* for the blemish.

Now when Douglas walked barefoot, his toes curled distastefully off the floor, curled up, even the one that curled under. As if he despised life from the very soles of his feet, as if he were not comfortable on this earth.

And soon Douglas began pushing out his bottom lip into a pout, like an English butler, as if he thought that made him very fetching. "Indeed," he said, in the middle of every sentence. Or, standing in the butler's pantry, "Indeed."

WAITING FOR THE elevator, we always saw our neighbor Earl Revo in his nightgown. It was Earl Revo's idea to paint the walls brown. He was an interior designer who lived across the hall in 20C. The building hired him. At his behest, the lobby was also done in chocolate brown, with fuzzy royal-blue wallpaper that it was fun to trail your fingers along. Visiting us at the beach one summer, Earl knitted, though his knitting was ugly, he complained, from the combination of the thin wool and his big hands. His wife, Lydia, had a benign tumor on the inside of one thigh, that looked like a testicle, which she refused to have removed for only cosmetic reasons. When they first moved in, she painted "I Have A Right To My Anger" on one wall. Lydia was an artist. They had known each other since high school. Why shouldn't they get married? they said.

There was one other apartment on our floor, where Gwen McMann lived, the Valium lady.

The McManns' apartment had been filled with concert pianos at first. One evening, George McMann came home from his IBM job and stood outside in the hall, pounding on their door. Then he rang our bell and asked to use the phone, afraid his wife had committed suicide. He was talking to the police when Gwen finally appeared, bruised, dopey, looking pregnant in her bathrobe. Her stomach swollen from wine. Two days later George was gone. He packed in the middle of the night and left. Soon after that, the pianos were gone too, like a herd of elephants, leaving havoc behind.

"I'm not afraid of living alone," Gwen McMann said. "My worst fear," she said, "is to wake up one morning and find myself in somebody's novel."

This was our extended family. No wonder we felt normal in comparison. No wonder we thought we were happy.

IT WAS A cold December morning. The night before, the street had been a bride, watched from the upper floors through coated windows that made stroboscopes of the neon lights from the cleaners and restaurants. We had watched the snow fall like New England on Manhattan, a wonderful simplicity visiting us, as if Vermont had driven down for the weekend to sleep in the living room on the comfortable pullout couch, had gone with us into the children's room to listen to the perfect breathing, and to stand with us at the window, our arms around one another, remembering the first snows of childhood, the sheer dotted-swiss curtain that had melted into real life.

And gradually, during this intermission in our lives, while Charlie, whose wife had just died, guarded the great drafty door in the lobby from the armchair, we slept. The soothing scrape of the shovels making a thin ribbon of cement plaited itself like love knots into my long dark hair. I woke up with my head full of last night's dialogue.

I was at a party. I had been talking to Marvin Grossnutz, the chairman of my husband's philosophy department. His belly impressed me, his bald intelligence.

"I should hate to find that I had to be unfaithful," I was saying with fervor, my large eyes unblinking and innocent.

"Why?"

"Because it would be the most unfortunate thing that could happen."

"Why?"

"Because of the word 'cuckold,' " I answered.

Marvin Grossnutz, known for his one polka-dotted tie and the hieroglyphics in chalk on the back of his Wallachs sports jacket, had a look of German pain on his face. Chin raised, lips drawn down in sensual arrogance. He was listening to a favorite jazz record of the host's.

"Beware the man who hears no music," he bellowed.

"I am such a man," I announced.

"Today is my birthday," I continued. "Douglas gave me a beautiful nightgown. It's black with tiers like a wedding cake. If you want to see my new nightgown," I added on an inspiration, "you can look on page three of the Magazine section."

"Taste this," Grossnutz said, handing me a long-stemmed thimble of some elixir. Our fingers met. It was a curious moment. Previous impressions—the rabbi, the homosexual, the pedant—flashed before me like three men in a tub, and drowned. My fingers were soldered to his hand. Finally, I pulled them free and took a sip.

"How old are you today?" he asked in an arrogant, personal voice, taking my other hand.

"Thirty."

"I would have thought twenty-three," he said, digging his nails into my left palm. I sipped again.

He brayed into the lily-scented air, "You close one eye like an old man drinking schnapps!"

I HAD NOT aged yet; I had grown younger. My hair was not in a bun, as it had been, to make me look older. It fell in a fur cape over my shoulders, which were bare, except for black spaghetti straps from the black birthday nightgown. I lay like a box of dark chocolates with a pink satin ribbon around my middle, unruffled by any intimacy of fingers choosing the almond, the caramel.

Slowly, I noticed Douglas's head on the pillow. The features were princely, the planes noble. His half-open mouth was filled with red light. On the surface, he is very pretty, I thought, except that his straight small nose is too sharp. When he touched me, his soft hand begged permission of my stomach, my thigh. I jumped with horrible tickles. I froze. It reminded me of my grandfather who molested me. My father's father.

"Uppy-time," I said, for I loved pumpernickel and butter and honey and coffee with milk.

DOUGLAS HAD HEADED the committee that hired Grossnutz, the new chairman, but he, Grossnutz told Douglas, would not have hired Douglas. I stood there dumbfounded, feeling helpless. It was only one sentence, which I was too petrified to challenge. One sentence that meant my husband was not good enough. The Persian carpet, the glass table on it, the precious children (one of whom had not been conceived yet), the maid's room with Pierrette, the live-in nanny, my secret sharer in it, our whole glamorous city life, could be pulled out from under me with one sentence addressed to my husband. "I wouldn't have hired you," said by Grossnutz with a certain swagger. But *I* was good enough. I resorted to my own powers (I was practically helping my husband to keep his job). I fell in love.

"GROSSNUTZ HERE."

"Will you come to see me?"

"Who is this?"

"Joy Frankel. Are you busy? Are you with a dozen show-girls?"

"Where is Douglas?"

"In Washington, for the protest."

The chairman arrived before I could even put Isabelle and the baby in their cribs.

"You're here so quickly," I complained.

Quickly, Grossnutz lunged. "Slowly, more slowly," I begged, a madonna with child pinned against the foyer wall.

"I don't believe in wasting time. Seize the moment." It was like dancing with my father at a bar mitzvah. "Don't you want *this* inside you," he pressed, his fascinating stomach upon me.

"No," I shouted. Grossnutz reached for his hat.

"I want you to see me undressed."

I took off my clothes and sat on his lap.

"Doesn't it bother you that that's the name of a char?" he said about my daughter's name.

"No," I answered, "it's the name of a queen."

"So you think you're hot stuff?"

"Yes."

"In fact you're beginning to bore me."

"Like fun," I said confidently, shifting my weight, putting my arm around his neck.

"Kiss my cheek," he instructed, holding a glass of Douglas's best bourbon in his effeminate hand.

"Tell me about the women in your life," I said. "What did you do this weekend?"

"I'm trying to forget," he groaned.

"Please."

"Well"—he groaned again—"last night the two women were very beautiful. One was seated at the piano, naked, playing Chopin when I arrived. . . . The other man wasn't as sexually imaginative as I. . . ." He would leave hideous bruises. I listened wide-eyed. "I have a yellow vinyl chair in my living room and a plexiglass—"

"Who takes care of you when you're sick?"

"Oh, I call up some old friend of mine who knows I won't marry her. 'Polly, put the kettle on,' I say." He glanced at his watch. "You've kept me fascinated from the moment I got here," he admitted, and was gone.

THE NEXT WEEK we met again.

"Waiter!" Grossnutz bellowed. Douglas winced, and I, under my scarlet dress, thrilled. "A friend of mine told me recently," he said, watching me for my reaction, "that when she thinks of me she thinks of avocado vinaigrette."

"When I think of you I feel like an artichoke with all my leaves pulled off," I replied.

Douglas excused himself from the table. "I'm going to watch the basketball game at the bar," he said.

Towards morning, my arm in Grossnutz's, the three of us wandered the cold streets, looking for an open flick. Then Douglas and I hailed a cab. There was a woman waiting for him, the chairman mentioned, in his bed. "I'll tell her I was out with a colleague and his wife," he said to me in parting.

THE WOMEN GROSSNUTZ spoke of were all wearing feather boas in my mind and velvet draperies from *Gone With the Wind.* He had had a rheostat installed in his bedroom, at great cost.

"What bra are you wearing?" he asked me, so that I imagined my hooded inquisitor wearing Nazi boots, holding a whip, his penis, which I had never seen, exposed. "Is it a good bra?"

"No bra," I answered meekly, sitting naked in the kitchen like melted butter. Longing for the sound of his voice, I called him from the kitchen when Douglas was in the bedroom and from the bedroom when Douglas was in the kitchen.

"Grossnutz here."

I heard him manipulating someone on his vast, dimly lit bed. I heard him swallow his pleasure between the two syllables of his name. I could tell by his amused effort in saying "here" that he was not alone. I could picture the moisture glistening on his double chins. "Are you alone?" I asked.

"Yes."

"Can I come over?"

"I have a cold."

I got ready, showered, shaved everywhere, dried myself with a monogrammed towel, dabbed perfume behind my knees, on my buttocks, on my thighs, behind my ears, brushed my aggressively clean hair, which fell back in an Egyptian helmet, and told Douglas, bent over his philosophy manuscript, minding his p's and q's, that I was rushing for a dancing lesson.

"Have a good time," he conceded.

Outside on the frozen street, people lay about like torn umbrellas, spokes jutting through their stockings and gabardines. I was carried uphill to B'way by the icy wind and, skating on my butter-soft boots, glided to a phone booth in the drugstore.

"I'm coming," I breathed, perfumed as spring.

"That won't be necessary," the chairman replied. "I have company."

"Who is that?" I heard Polly say.

"The sex-starved wife of a colleague of mine. I never mix business with pleasure," Grossnutz announced, and hung up.

I GROANED LIKE a table under delicate foods, a goodly table of pure ivory, all spread with juncats fit to entertain the greatest prince with pompous royalty. My cheeks like apples which the sun hath rudded, my lips like cherries charming men to bite, my breast like to a bowl of cream uncrudded, my paps like lilies budded.

The finality of it yawned under my feet with terrible jaws. Every inch of me was primed for his pleasure, and he preferred some tired old snack tray. So that was how it stood.

A neighbor stared in at me in my glass coffin.

"Sorry," I said. "Just trying to remember a number."

Then I got out more change and called Carl Vaggio, a famous artist. I had been introduced to him years ago, and he had always liked me.

"Grand Central Station," came a bored voice.

As soon as he answered I was saved. "Hello, Carl, it's Joy Frankel. I would like to see you."

"Why dontchu come down?" he said, his voice squeaking slightly, flattering me with its disuse. A rusty file he had just gotten out for my sake.

"Would Thursday be good?"

"What time?" he hiccuped.

"Anytime," I said, as after a head-on collision when you perceive that you are not dead and, though your eyes are full of blood and your bones are broken, you feel invulnerable.

He gave me the intimate directions as if they were instructions for making a bomb. "Long time no see," he concluded.

THURSDAY AT NOON I got on the Broadway downtown local. All the way there, I thought of my first love, Dennis Berg. Dennis Berg had introduced me to Carl Vaggio. I remembered Dennis's unpublished "Sonnet for Carl," in which he said: "Forget the Jewess you crave, whom I had / Once."

Dennis rarely published his poems; he didn't want to give himself away so cheaply, he said. Later he cut them to ribbons. They ended up no more than two lines.

Like the red-capped old peasant woman in an apron who thought her pies too fine to give away, who kept baking more and more pies, telling King Alfred, disguised as a beggar, to wait for a smaller one, and so was turned into a woodpecker, Dennis had turned into an art critic and wrote articles on Carl Vaggio.

Choosing lovers is like revising a poem. One word leads to another. You choose a word sometimes that rhymes with the word you crossed out, no matter how far removed it may be in sense, in meaning. In this case, actually, Dennis had crossed me out. But in my mind, Carl rhymed with Dennis.

He fit in the space where Dennis had been.

Long ago, on a train to Cambridge, I had sat next to Dennis on the edge of my seat, brushing my long hair—which had loosened its tortoiseshell hairpins and had to be re-coiled on top of my head—and apologized. He had always held it against me that he had been a virgin and I hadn't.

"I couldn't give you experience," I pleaded.

"That's an incredible thing for you to say," he answered, while the train vibrating under me tuned me like an instrument. For I had *been* his experience, his first experience, in his parents' home in Riverdale, where he had made love to me in his basement room with the Chinese scroll on the wall.

Dennis liked white bras, white nightshirts. I remember him using that white pencil on his face to stop the bleeding. His father drank, and he was ashamed of this. His mother was the strong one, who answered the phone when he called in the middle of the night, who taught him how to drive. She gave him a lesson to drive me home the first time I went to his house, where, as soon as I met her, I got a terrible headache.

I loved Dennis Berg. He was tall, with a big nose and narrow eyes. One fraternity at Yale said that he was the ugliest Jew they had ever seen; but to me he was Gregory Peck. He walked somewhat hunched, with an intensity that conjured all the dead poets I loved. Bees were attracted to him as they are to ripe fruit; dogs bit him. His friend Carl Vaggio, two years ahead of him at Yale, was the only non-Jewish person ever to set foot in his parents' living room, he told me. He hated the ghetto he grew up in, watching his grandparents like hobgoblins climbing the stairs to their second-story cave. He could never marry a girl who was Jewish, he said.

He left me and went to Oxford on a Fulbright.

I had not seen him since he had come back and gone to Harvard. Now I was unexpectedly going to spend a week during Christmas vacation with him in his new "flat." I packed Pretty Feet in my bag.

"What's that?" he said, seeing the small white bottle. I explained how you put the lotion on and rubbed away imperfections, rough spots, but he wasn't impressed. "No Feet," he called it.

On the train, I was overjoyed to be near him.

"Happiness is not the point, as I never tire of saying," Dennis said, quoting another poet, a perfectionist, whom he had met in Italy and who had taught him how to make love. Later she, the fleeing one, did want to marry him, but he had used what she had taught him to make love to someone else. Otherwise, there would have been no point, he said.

He didn't plan to screw me, though I nagged him like a poem that kept him up, hot, all night. Behind his shrewd stare, he was thinking of Ghislaine in England. How the mere Atlantic Ocean was between them. Him and Ghislaine. There was no room for another woman. He had known me before he was ready. I was unfinished business, a disheveled lyric whose last line he had failed to cement.

"Now you'll get to see all my secret devices," he said, meaning his biceps-building pulleys.

As soon as we got to his bare two rooms, he went out to call Carl Vaggio and his wife, Anne, from a pay phone on the corner. They had just married, because Anne was pregnant.

"Don't do it; it's wrong. Tell her you're engaged," they both told him. They thought our being together was "immoral." Dennis came upstairs slowly, like a husband carrying groceries, weighed down by all the things Carl and Anne had never understood. I was crying when Dennis opened the door, as if I knew he didn't love me, flattened against the wall in my tight brown velvet slacks like a leaf in the rain. He touched my elbow, and I gasped.

"Come off it," he scoffed. But the thrill stayed fluttering in the air like the corrugated ripples over a radiator in winter. He put his arms around me, and it started, what I had come for, the persuasive tongue of flame.

But I didn't have my diaphragm. I had left it in Ithaca, since I thought I was going to be staying with my parents in New York.

I went out to the drugstore across the street from him, to buy a diaphragm. I didn't remember my exact size, but the druggist showed me several and I selected one that looked right. When I got upstairs, Dennis had changed his mind. I was dismayed. To minimize my sense of loss, I tried to return the unused diaphragm. I went right back with it to the drugstore, but the druggist wouldn't take it back. It was against the law, he said.

Crying, I called my mother. "You're not going to meet anyone else in the next few days," she said, "so you might as well stay with him."

Then we were making love.

"Your waist is small as an insect's," Dennis said.

"Thank you," I answered.

"Thank *you*," he insisted. I was on all fours, and he was entering me from behind. "This is the way I've pictured it with you. D'you like it?"

"Yes. But I can't come this way," I stammered.

He turned me over, averting his lips now that we were face-to-face, like a medieval lady with her husband. "There's something I should tell you," he said.

"What?"

"That I prefer the male nude to the female."

"Oh," I gasped, edified. Then, "I'm coming," I gasped, half strangled.

"Thank you for telling me," he said politely, as once he had said, "This is a good spot," pointing to the underside of his penis. Like "the silver undersides of leaves" that he always started with when he tried to write prose.

He climaxed five times in a row, like a woman.

He told me the story of the French twin sisters as we lay together on his cot, with the smaller folding cot beside it. "Françoise had bled on *my* sheet at Oxford. I wrote that poem 'Hymen' on *her* typewriter. But then, I don't know why, I broke up with her," he said. "And the next time I saw her, I was walking through a strange part of London with a friend, about three in the morning, very full of ourselves, and we came across a young girl crying on some steps. It was Françoise. Then, six months later, in Spain, I ran into her twin sister, Ghislaine."

The name was entirely foreign to me. It sounded almost like Glenn, with a slight stutter. "How do you spell that?" I asked.

He told me. "It's a word like 'gazelle,' " he said.

"Do they look alike?" I asked.

"They're practically identical," he answered. "When I look at Ghislaine I see Françoise. It's very charged. She wore a uniform to school until she was sixteen years old. I can't tell you how exotic that is for me."

"Was Ghislaine a virgin too?"

"No." He winced. "In Barcelona," he continued, "we were getting on each other's nerves and decided to separate for the day. She was going to one museum, and I was going to another. I explained the buses to her and forced myself to stay away for the whole day. I came back late and saw her blue blouse on the balcony across the plaza. She couldn't have been bigger than an insect. That's when I knew, from the way I felt in the pit of my stomach, that I wanted her. . . .

"I can live in the aura of sex for three days," Dennis said.

Before I left, he taught me how to write poems. He tore apart my academic verses, which sounded like Yeats. He could "no longer read Yeats with pleasure," he said. Yeats, whom I adored! This sounded unbelievably advanced to me. He made fun of my line breaks. Under one poem, which ended, "Strange! Now / No breeze can move me to your side again," he scribbled a magical denouncement of me around my own name typed in the bottom-right-hand corner. It cast a spell like Rumpelstiltskin's dance. In black ink, he wrote:

> *Joy Frankel says*
> *I'm right when I attack*
> *her poems. Strange! Now*
> *She must write good poems.*

He had trembled in front of El Greco's *View of Toledo* when he was four; then fallen in love with the bare-shouldered girl pouring from a pitcher in Caravaggio's *The Four Musicians*, who turned out to be a boy. Ghislaine had boy hair and boy hips. He hadn't worn sunglasses even in Spain, he told me. He hated sunglasses. There was no doubt in my mind that he was a genius. Every minute spent in his presence seemed valuable to me, jewels gained painfully, like the pearls put in the little mermaid's tail on each birthday.

"There is a lov*er* and a lov*ee*," he said. "I want to be the lov*er*."

I wanted him so much, I even tried to mop. The kitchen linoleum underfoot rippled like the beach at low tide. "It feels different," he said approvingly, testing the ripples with his shoe.

The plane I took back to Ithaca at the end of the week had ice on its wingtips. Everyone was frightened except me. Like a terrorist in my despair, I looked around guiltily at the other passengers, willing it to crash.

From Ithaca, I telegrammed him once to say, in code,

using the word "menses" in a line of his own poetry, that I wasn't pregnant. He called, once, to tell me not to do that, not to telegram, that he had to walk all the way to the post office. After that, I never heard from him again. When he didn't call or write, I got up in the middle of the night and threw out his precious onionskin letters. Thin-skinned like him. Even the one with the drowned Shelley drawn in the margin.

I was taking a course in Elizabethan drama. In one play, there was a line that went: "Penelope filled Ithaca with moths." All that week, I watched Dennis's letters sit in paper bags on the curb, waiting for the sanitation truck. Typed gossamer pages occasionally blowing away, his masculine phrases, "Pushing up through the iron curtain countries," "Immense suck," beating their hungry wings.

Finally, I saw him again in Cambridge, from Douglas's car, hunched in the cold, pressing a half-moon of fingernail against his gum. We parked, and I was face-to-face with him, groping in the eclipse for my fiancé's arm.

Dennis raised his eyebrows at me without speaking.

THE NARROW HALL reeked of cat's piss. The stairs, rank as unwashed genitals, tested my courage at the threshold.

A crouching cat, patches of black fur missing, guarded the top stair. Carl Vaggio stood over him, smiling a toothless smile, his two side teeth touchingly like fangs. I was surprised at the sight of him, though he had not changed. He looked like an Arab assassin, a housepainter like Hitler, or a Santini brother. His hair was tied in a frizzy clump at the back.

My kiss landed on his neck.

"Sweet sweet silly mad goose." He patted my hair with his missing fingers. Then held me at arm's length to look at me. "I had a dream aboutjew last night," he said.

"Me?"

"That Dennis was here with Ghislaine. She came to my bed."

"What has that got to do with me?" I said coyly. "How *is*

Dennis?" I added. Just saying his name was like pressing a bruise.

"Which one?" Carl had named his son Dennis, after Dennis Berg.

"Your friend," I answered. But he smiled mutely; he didn't tell me. He served me a mug of Earl Grey tea, removing the tea bag with his passionate finger stubs. "You look happy," I said.

"That's because you're here," he answered.

"Don't girls chase you in droves?"

"I have an occasional cocktail waitress," he whined.

"Who are your friends?"

"I have one friend with a withered arm, who fixes me up. And Nicole and Orso Lombroso. I introduced Nicole to my friend Orso. They hated each other at first sight. 'Who is that fat old boor?' she asked me. He said, 'Who was that snobby cunt?' They got married."

"What does Orso do?" I asked.

"He drinks! I only cried twice in my life," he continued. "Once when Nicole told me she didn't love me, that I could only be a brother to her, and when whatsername took away the children. Anne. I didn't think that she would do that. . . ."

"What about me? Didn't you cry over me?"

He grinned at me, toothless with delight. "I don't go far for my women," he rasped, his sandpaper voice like a cat's tongue. "Anne came to my loft and got into my sleeping bag. 'You're crowding me,' I told her. She got mad and left. I made the biggest mistake of my life the next day when I said I was sorry I insulted her."

"You've changed—you talk more," I said cheerfully.

"I like talking to you," he whined, rubbing my back and neck, beginning to unzip my dress.

"Do you still love me?" I demanded. He shook his head, smiling his fanged smile. "I don't want to sleep with you unless you love me," I cried, covering my face with my hands.

"You don't understand—I'm too old for love."

I touched his smooth cheek. As if released from a spell, he put his hand down my loosened dress front and touched my breast. "I want you to be happy," he said.

A fire flickered in my abdomen. A thrill broke over my stomach like surf. His hand struggled at my back, fumbling, until the difficult stiff bra came loose. I had to hold myself back from helping him, though I didn't want him to see my human fallen breasts, which had once stood upright as Ben Jonson in his tomb. One of his rough trouser legs bulged down the side.

"Think of how happy you'll make me," he said, and led me down a winding staircase to his winter bedroom.

I lay on his low bed, surrounded by heaters. "If you really want to be my woman, you'd let the hair grow under your arms." He held up my legs and examined me like a racehorse. He was looking at my knee scar. "Very chic," he said.

I lay half off the bed, and he was on top of me.

"That feels wonderful," I said. "You're wonderful."

"I didn't do anything yet."

"Do you like it too?" I meant just the way it felt being together. The way we fit together.

"Yes."

"That's amazing, that we like the same thing! You have hair on your chest, you're beautiful."

"Shut up," he said gently.

His penis was a revelation to me, semisoft like Gouda cheese. He could put it in even without an erection. I suddenly had a sharp craving for Gouda cheese. "Do you feel guilty?" I whispered.

"Stop talking," he said. From the foreign weight of him, I peaked. Leaning on one elbow, he smiled at me as if he were a talent scout who had just discovered a star. I peaked again. He raised his eyebrows at me like Dennis; Dennis loitered in his face like a twin sister. I felt like Dennis, sleeping with Françoise and Ghislaine at once.

"Don't worry," I said, "don't feel guilty. I need you, I love you." It was a wonderful advantage I had over him. "I love you, I love you, I love you." I had my third, small, pinched orgasm. "Carl . . ."

"You're terrific," he said shyly, as though I had just won a race for him.

He went upstairs to eat a bowl of Haitian rice pudding. Then, downstairs on the street, he held my hand. My veins filled with Chanel No. 5. He hailed a cab and gave me ten dollars for the fare. "Pleased t'meetcha," he said through the cab window, smacking his lips goodbye.

3

TRADING CARDS

/ / / / / / / /

Once, when I was a child, I discovered a boy my own age across the street. I was a lonely child and he was the first boy I had known. In the lobby of his building he made a glossy fan of his trading cards, like a peacock spreading his tail of dark shiny Little Boy Blues. But my small hand with its ring of pink gold and winking rubies struck the cards. I watched his uncertain face as they fell to the floor, and I did not stop to grab them as I was supposed to do. I ran, and the boy vanished. When I went to Carl Vaggio, I did penance for the aggression that had brought me there. For cuckolding my husband. I submitted. I swallowed his sperm. I understood as if in the presence of the enemy team the mute signals indicating the position I was to take on my knees.

In my arms he would change to an angel, his skin glowing orange and gold and sienna. He was from Verona, where they slew women for adultery. I worshiped his veined penis, long, uncircumcised, primeval. Caught in the vise of his legs, I felt at the center of art history. If I said anything, even murmured, he stopped, disgusted. Or collapsed with pleasure on my shoulder. Long and blasé, usually half erect, his penis could do anything, go anywhere. Like a snake. I laid my cheek against his hairy chest like Eve returning to the garden.

"You're beautiful," I said.

"I'm ugly. I have a pinhead."

"Your eyes do something to me."

"They're snake eyes."

"Yes! When you look at me my own excitement excites me."

"Women are terrific," he said, and yawned. He had a harsh pointy yawn. "All this sex, I'm too tired to play tennis."

"Was Dawn here last night?" Dawn was his girlfriend who lived with him, with Wednesday nights off.

"There was last night and then this morning. She hung around till all hours this morning."

I asked, incredulous: "Did you sleep with her this morning?"

"Yes."

Live bullets grazed my cheeks. He saw their passage and, tender, gripped my long hair and rolled over on me. He made love to me again while the river of tears inside me churned hot. "C'mon," he said, "c'mon," his voice irritated, sandpaper, refining me.

"Schmuck," he cried out. It always hurt him the second time. "Schmuck!"

"You're most beautiful at the moment of orgasm."

"That's a good line, I guess," he said, smiling his fanged smile.

I sat at his feet and watched him watch television with an exotic Cuban cigar in his mouth. He took me out for lunch to have scrambled eggs and ketchup. He made me Earl Grey tea; he ate bagel and cream cheese for his ulcer. He was reading his second newspaper like my husband. "Do you love me?" I said.

"No."

"Admit you love me."

"No."

"Do you like Dawn better than me?"

"I like you all the same."

Our affair was a marriage of treachery and truth, compared with which other marriages seemed like child's play, husbands and wives like blindfolded children turning three times in a circle before they pinned the donkey's tail on the forehead, where the horns go.

"Did you have a good time in California?" I asked, worried for the first time.

"Yes. I ate a lot of humble pie."

He seemed different suddenly. In love. "What's her name?" I bravely asked.

"Valerie Rodriguez. Val."

"What is she like?"

"She's an unwed mother on welfare, her brother has gonorrhea of the mouth. I had to shake his hand," he complained.

"How did you meet her?"

"It was on account of Dawn," he said, smiling. "She called me to tell me she hated me or something, and I had to take a walk around the block. I met Val on the street."

"Did you make love to her?" I asked, my voice trembling a little.

"Yes, but she's no good," he quickly assured me. "She keeps jumping around. Women under thirty don't like sex. Besides," he added, "she has acne. I'd be ashamed to be seen with her."

"How old *is* she?" I said, beginning to be scandalized.

"Nineteen or twenty. She's taller than I am."

"You're very proud of yourself, Marco Polo. Why don't you marry her?"

"She doesn't like me," he said, his thin voice like gruel. "She says I'm negative and boring. Maybe I'll never get married, just to keep you around. You're like a cat that talks," he purred. "Look at his furry balls," and he held his black cat, Perfidy, upside down for me.

I MIGHT HAVE married Carl Vaggio, but my mother told me I could never marry anyone who wasn't Jewish. At our first fight, she said, he would call me a dirty Jew. The king of England wasn't good enough for me because he wasn't Jewish, she said.

Once I met a boy I liked and told my mother. "But I don't think he's Jewish," I said. "What's his name?" "Kenny Fink." Kenny was tall, with Brillo hair and acne. He taught my little sister Heidi how to play chess. That was how I knew he liked me. Later he rang the bell when I was playing at my fat friend Beverly's house, but she wouldn't let me let him in. We were playing sex. The irony struck me. Here was a real boy. She had a pink scarf tied across her chest. Her fat arms showed. I had to pretend to be the boy.

When I told my mother Kenny's name, she laughed.

"You're like a starlet," Carl Vaggio said shyly, as I fitted my body to his, grateful, as when the clouds parted on some birthday and my father's hand reached through, pouring thin brown envelopes of new trading cards from the factory in wholesale profusion into my lap, for he had gotten up at six in the morning to get them, to surprise me. To my surprise, not long after, a prisoner in my bedroom with a cold, I threw them out the window to the other children.

It was Tuesday. We lay in Carl's bedroom, with the garden he couldn't enter, which belonged to someone else, behind us, casting its leafy light. We had all the garden we needed in his bed. Other famous artists' paintings were on the walls. Frank Stella. Morris Louis. Mark Rothko. One had been leaked on from the ceiling. Ruined. He wasn't worried. It could be restored. Carl was the most famous artist in America. His greatness was a dazzling fact, testified to by remarks overheard in restaurants that I went to at night with Douglas, by catalogues with color plates from museums I had never heard of, museums even in Texas.

When we went to the Museum of Modern Art, Carl automatically got out his key.

My mother had always wanted me to marry a doctor, or she would mention the son of a rich pocketbook manufacturer. I would snap shut with scorn. I would imagine myself married to a pocketbook. Carl Vaggio was also the richest man I had ever known, and he had gotten rich by being an artist. But I could never marry a man with no teeth, I thought.

His wife Anne had just left him. She had moved into an apartment on the Upper West Side, near me, and taken their daughter, Cara, and their son, Dennis, with her. He was convinced that Anne had been unfaithful, that Cara was his but Dennis wasn't. "I guess Anne didn't think I should object," he said, "since he was the same religion as I was. I could have had blood tests done to prove it," he mumbled.

I thought it was the worst crime a woman could commit, having another man's child. I vowed never to do that. Besides, if I had another son, I wanted him to match Benjamin.

"Anne dressed like a man and talked like a man and ate like a horse," Carl said.

Dennis had introduced me to Carl Vaggio when he and Carl were at Yale. Then Carl graduated, and Dennis took me to visit Carl Vaggio's "studio"—a small, wretched room somewhere in Little Italy, with nothing in it but a huge black safe and the canvas he was working on. Carl told us he slept on the windowsill, because the neon flashing on and off all night scared the cockroaches away. After that, he sent me postcards and even called me at Bard once, but I was napping. There were only a few words exchanged. I came away groggy, unsure what had been said. Flattered, I went back to my dream.

Then I was getting a master's at NYU. He sat on my couch

with his thumb in his mouth; he rubbed my neck. After a while he said, "I'll say one thing for us—we're the touchingest friends I know."

I have a photograph of myself eight years later in a wheelchair, pregnant with Isabelle, wearing embroidered Chinese silk pajamas from my mother's trousseau. Carl and Anne were visiting us from the city. My leg was stuck out in a cast. I was distressed because my toes showed, purple. Carl and Douglas were on the lawn playing badminton. Anne said to me, "The hardest thing for you will be to get an au pair girl."

"How does it feel getting on the subway to get laid?" Carl Vaggio asked.

These were the best afternoons of my life. I went to him twice a week. Afterwards, I could live in the aura of sex for three days.

"Nicole is certainly angry at Orso," Carl said.

Orso Lombroso was a revolutionary filmmaker. His wife, Nicole, taught English at Douglas's school in Bronxville. She had green eyes and frizzy hair and made Carl take her home from parties when they were very young because it was raining out and her hair wasn't looking right. He had met Nicole right after I "turned him down."

"Why is she angry?"

"She caught him with an eighteen-year-old girl."

I lay naked in his arms, my vanity a suit of armor.

"She certainly is angry," he repeated.

"Did you sleep with her?" I asked.

"When?" he said.

"When she was so angry."

"Once," he admitted.

"Where?" I asked, my skin prickling on the royal-blue sheet.

"At her house." They had to climb a ladder, he explained, to the bed that was a sleeping loft.

"Who went first?" I asked, climbing to this new plateau of candor.

"Ladies first," he grinned.

Thursdays were ours, but the nights spent Nicole must be grand balls, I thought, beneath chandeliers, at which the conversation spun and and brilliantly changed partners.

I wanted to be friends with Nicole Lombroso, who was beautiful and dressed carefully. I wanted to look into her green eyes and see Carl pouring cans of paint one into the other. I wanted to possess him through intimacy with her. I wanted to be in their inner circle. I had met her once at Elaine's, where I had watched Carl touch Nicole's hair in greeting as if he were caressing their past. I had held hands with him under the tablecloth and fallen in love with her.

"Why doesn't Nicole have a baby?" I asked.

"She can't."

Nicole existed only in my mind and in Carl's rusty horizontal voice. I was certain that the heroine would have a baby.

"Take my word for it, she won't have a baby."

"Why not?"

"She's sick."

"What do you mean?"

"Well," he paused. "It isn't certain yet. It's confidential. You can't tell Douglas."

"I won't, I promise," I lied.

"No, I mean it. She doesn't want anyone at school to know." He sat on the edge of the bed, the hills of his stomach rumbling, his silken-fringed underarms smelling of mammoth art. I watched the hollows of his cheeks as he sucked at his parchment cigar with inverted smacking kisses.

"I swear I won't tell."

"Well, they think it might be leukemia."

I was too young, too happy; I didn't understand. It was as if my eyes had been closed at that moment and I hadn't seen what had been said. It became confused with my envy, with my longing, with the moist shuddering on my stomach moments before, a mare terrified beneath her rider, head thrown back, face turned to him, his warm testicles brushing my behind like demolition balls. I continued to ask, as one would ask the bedtime voice reading a fairy tale:

"When will they know?"

"Know what?"

"If she'll be all right."

"They know everything they're going to know," he said finally.

"Is she going to be all right?"

He didn't answer.

NOW I COULD face Douglas. Now when I met his gaze, my own was glazed with the knowledge of my other life. I let it hang between us like a thin Chinese screen, on which the delicate men and women in rich robes fornicated in positions that were unknown to him. I could face him knowing he did not know all that there was to my life. I lived like a cloud concealing the sun but bordered by its gold. He felt my radiance and let it rub off on him and ease him. For he had married me loving my self-love. I did not admit this, but I prized my chastity with Douglas. Since he had failed to conquer me sexually, to find me in my lair, which was hidden even from myself, I, according to rules that are passed on like brooches from mother to daughter, had never to relinquish the upper hand in the marriage. I could lord it over him. And it was desirable to be a slave with my lover and a master at home.

Douglas and I saw Marlena and Tim every Friday night. The lulling ritual of it sustained me. Marlena was forty when I met her, and the most beautiful woman I had ever seen. Her father had killed himself in Germany. Her mother, a doctor, had escaped with her to Australia. She was my confidante, my adviser; she was almost a mother to me.

Tim was redesigning the kitchen with Douglas, making it all butcher block. I was telling Marlena about Carl. I was crazy about him. He was a great artist and a great lover. I had never known anything like it. He was more "animal" than other men. I loved his razor wit, his sandpaper tenderness, his kind cruelty. He was my perfect mate.

"Yesterday was the most beautiful afternoon of my life," I said.

"Oh, definitely!" she agreed.

Marlena was very affirming. She entered swiftly into all my emotions. She knew more about my own life than I did. Yet when I suggested the possibility of marrying Carl who was each day becoming more famous, whom I was beginning to suspect that I loved, she pooh-poohed it.

"No?" Marlena said incredulously. "Two artists?" And then, in her soft veiled approximate English, "It would be too stormy, too tempestuous," she insisted.

WHEN DOUGLAS'S FATHER died, we went to Philadelphia. We slept in Douglas's childhood room, which he'd shared with his brother. The sheets were so tight I could hardly breathe. Douglas got into my twin bed. The funeral was the next morning. The combination of his father's death and the murderously tight sheets excited me. We fucked, as if to revenge ourselves on his mother.

Pregnant a third time, I lay in bed with Carl Vaggio, stomach swollen, proud. I turned over.

He lay over me.

My breasts hung down like firm melons. "Look!" I said.

"I know," he answered.

"My breasts have no feeling in them," I admitted.

"That's all right, they're just there for decoration."

From his bed, I ordered pork chops from Oppenheimer's on the Upper West Side. I gave my married name. The meat arrived at my apartment in the late afternoon wrapped in butcher's paper; Pierrette, the nanny, was there to receive it.

"Douglas's balls are cold," I complained.

"Refrigeration is good for making babies," Carl Vaggio said, always defending the underdog. "You're a whore," he flattered me, meaning that I was good in bed.

When the telephone rang at three in the afternoon, he put his hand, with one nail twisted out of the thumb stump like a claw, over my mouth and lied to his mistress, Dawn.

I COULD HAVE had Carl's child. Instead I carefully had Douglas's. I looked at her eyebrows when Penelope was born and joyfully saw that they were like Isabelle's and Benjamin's. I had not committed the sin of Anne, I thought sanctimoniously. I had not had another man's baby. I could admire my husband's terse white body through the clear plastic shower curtain, a satyr without hair on his chest, open mouth spouting; I could hand him the big striped towel, and choose his tie, and see Benjamin in the lean curves of his buttocks and Isabelle in his voluptuous bottom lip and ascetic upper one. Penelope had his red hair.

But then I would notice his strong chin jutting forward and the voluptuous bottom lip writhing and contorting and pinching itself inward as if with rage. And I did not like the look of his tongue on the perfect bottom teeth, a pink swimmer squashing himself against smooth rocks. I did not like the look of it. It looked like suicide. Self-hatred. Rage. Irrational rage, I thought. And turned my back on his irrational suffering. I did not want to kiss the hole that was his mouth. I did not want to be drawn in through it, I had no interest in the machinations of his jaw. I did not like what his face was doing when I looked at him, and so I didn't look at him.

Once or twice, when I came home late, coming up in the elevator after being with Carl, or feeling Douglas's darkness suddenly upon me like a floodlight on a criminal, I would lose control of my own image, as I sometimes did in the triple mirrors of department stores when the wrong face—a dark, frazzled woman I didn't like, Heidi—watched me from a side panel. So, sometimes my lies and excuses in the evening would catch me at an angle that repelled me. I closed my eyes, caressing my arms. If he touched me he would know everything. I opened my eyes and saw Douglas with his mouth open, jaw protruding a little, staring at me.

"What are you thinking?" I asked, alarmed.

"I was thinking," he answered, pulling himself out of the trance, "about the nature of moral justification." And then he added, after a long silence, "It's as if a machine were writing all of your sins on your skin." But I didn't wonder what sins, or comfort him for them, in the relief that they were his.

"Have you read *In the Penal Colony?*" I asked.

"Yes."

"Then they're not original sins."

ONCE IN THE subway on the way downtown, there was a sign. I looked up and saw, facing me, "Adultery: The Psychological Price You Pay."

When I came home, I saw Douglas was dwindling. His sighs and exhalations created a hissing music, like a teakettle with a spoon in its spout. When he scowled, I saw the devil facing me with a sharp nose.

In bed, he had not yet put on his drawstring bottoms that I could feel with my toes. He turned away from me, lying with his legs drawn up. I molded myself against him, absolved of my passion for another man. I put my hand softly on his still-enlarged penis, wishing it were always that size, for when it was small I felt helpless and afraid. My hand brushed his contracted scrotum, which was horribly cold, damp and cold as a dungeon. I must warm them, I decided, I must make them warm. I left my warm hand on my husband for five minutes. After five minutes, they were clammy and cold. It was like sleeping with a dead man, I decided. I took my sad widow's hand away from the cold balls of the corpse.

The next night I took pity on him. My hard heart softened. I sat on my husband's lap. "Tell me your feelings," I repented.

"I just feel as if I'm . . . losing energy." Douglas pulled his black turtleneck halfway up his face, so that he resembled an executioner, his fist under the black material covering his mouth.

"Don't do that."

"Sorry."

I looked at his exposed face, at the pretty cleft in his chin, at the deep suffering of his cheeks. "Did it ever occur to you that I might be responsible?"

"For what?"

"Your depression."

"How?"

"Is it your book?" I backed away.

"I'm not going to publish it," he said eagerly. "I've sent back the advance. Do you mind?"

"No, I think it's very brave of you. If you don't like it, why should you publish it? And if it's bad, it would embarrass me as well." I hadn't meant to say that. "I'm sure it's not bad. Why don't you like it?"

"It disgusts me."

"But of course you shouldn't publish it if you don't want to. It excites me that you won't."

"I love your body," he said, wistfully touching my breast. I clamped my arm to my side. "Don't you like me to stroke your breast?"

"No. I can't even stand the word 'stroke.' "

I don't love his body, I thought. The sadness of that thought overwhelmed me, impoverished me. His hips were too narrow, so that everything seemed to come to a point and constrict me. I could not get my finger *into* his rectum. I felt poor.

"I feel full of emptiness and perversion," he said.

"Douglas," I cried, my tears coming as easily as Milton's unpremeditated verse, "it's me."

"Why are you crying?" he began.

His softness angered me.

"I don't know."

"Wouldn't it be better to get to the bottom of it?" he said.

"But I know," I sobbed.

"Don't you want to know the truth?" he tempted.

"I already know," I hinted.

"Well, then, tell me. *I* want to know."

"You do?"

"Yes."

He held out his sword to me, and I rushed on it.

"I'm having an affair."

I waited for his curled lip and clenched, rippling cheek.

"Oh, you've had an affair," he said quietly, his ear warping the tense. "I don't blame you."

I looked up, confused. Could it be that I was invulnerable, that nothing could harm me?

"I think I want to be submissive in sex," he said.

"What are you telling me?"

"That I think the reason for my rages and depression is that I'm not getting what I need sexually. I've thought this for a long time, but I couldn't tell you before now. I didn't think you were ready for it."

I still wasn't ready for it.

"But men are supposed to be aggressive and women submissive," I insisted.

"My fantasies are all of strong women, who dominate me, who use me," he said.

"Do you want to make love to a man?"

"No. Why can't I want to service a woman?" he pleaded.

THE NEXT DAY I said to Douglas, "Don't you want to know with who?"

"With whom," he corrected.

"Do you?"

Douglas shook his head. "Not unless you want to tell me."

"Don't you know?"

"No."

"Carl Vaggio," I said, insulted.

"Oh."

"Had you guessed?"

"No." He laughed in his throat. "I know one thing I have more of than he."

"What?"

"Fingers."

"And teeth." Inessentials, I added to myself.

He stood at the glass dining-room table sipping black coffee, his eyes on the front page.

I had forced Douglas to befriend Nicole. To help get her tenure, because of her illness, without anyone knowing. We had all four gone out together, Orso and Nicole, Douglas and me. It was my doing. And Nicole had championed Isabelle and Benjamin (I was in love with the new baby, my copper Penny). She bought Isabelle books, *Eloise at the Plaza*, and then we had gone to the Plaza for tea, with Isabelle, who was always so adult but that day had a little fever and slumped at the table and finally even slid down on the leather seat, under the tablecloth. It was a disappointment to me. Before driving to Bronxville to teach, Nicole would stop at my house, and Pierrette would make her soothing tuna fish sandwiches to take to school. One day Nicole brought her childhood china tea set as a gift for Isabelle. Pierrette washed it so that we could have real tea. The beautiful figured teapot slipped from her fingers and cracked in pieces in the sink.

"Does Nicole know?" he asked.

"I guess," I replied in confusion.

"That upsets me," Douglas said.

NICOLE LOMBROSO WAS the perfect friend. The one I had searched for all my life as if from one end of a Shakespeare play to the other. My long-lost twin. Even during warm, clouded pauses while we sipped, our mirrors spoke, reflecting each other:

"You are the fairest one of all."

"No, you are the fairest one of all."

"Dawn is a dreary girl," Nicole said, cutting the narrow

portion of apple pie down the middle, sliding the smaller half for herself onto an extra plate. "Take my word for it, she's literally the worst."

"You say 'literally' as though you were saying 'Lionel Trilling' very rapidly," I said, and she laughed at my allusion to her former teacher. I was teaching her how to write poetry. Operating on her poems without anesthesia while she gave me grateful, loving glances.

We talked about Carl.

"I love the mirrors in his dressing room. They're so thinning. Did you notice?" I asked.

"Yes," Nicole answered, getting out her compact and gazing in the oblong at a crumb on her iridescent mouth. "That was Anne's doing." I watched the intelligent movements of her mouth and tongue, like a cat's at a bowl of milk, cleaning itself after each sentence, each carefully measured thought.

"But it's astonishing that Dawn leaves nothing around. How does he get her to take everything with her each time, I wonder?"

"Actually, that's a new development. It wasn't always like that," Nicole said so cozily that I barely heard the bitter grains like sand in her voice. Her being was upright as a wave, holding itself on the edge of a heaving ocean. Her eyes had an unblinking look. They dominated her face. Her eyebrows arched thinly over them.

"Your eyebrows are so thin," I said.

"I have them waxed or tweezed. I don't believe in filling up one's forehead with eyebrow."

"I envy you having dinner with him all the time," I said brightly.

"It's no treat with Dawn along, I assure you. They lean into one another as though they'd otherwise fall. And she embodies the worst part of him—his deadness. Do you know, she reads the obituary column the first thing out of bed?"

"Carl says he cried when you told him you could never be more than a sister to him."

"You must never tell him I said this," Nicole said, "but that was not the reason. He was a terrible lover. I remember one funny time, when Anne and I were roommates. Anne was making love with her first husband in the next room after she had divorced him, and Carl was making love to me. When he left, I heard them crying out through the wall. I was still so aroused I didn't know what to do. I thought, who can I call, this is ridiculous. And I must have decided then that I simply couldn't see him again, because most of the time I never got excited in the first place, so it wasn't a problem."

"It's funny to be lucky to be the last in bed with a man," I said.

We laughed over this as if our omnipotent laughter could dwarf all men. But I was thinking about her leukemia. Nicole's father was a doctor. She had been given prescription drugs that other children weren't. Perhaps that was why she got it. Or was it from being in Carl's studio among the toxic paints?

"He married Anne because she could hum," I mentioned.

"He married Anne because she was pregnant!" she corrected.

"And he's such a sexist," Nicole said. "I told Carl your poems were much better than Dennis's. And he said Dennis's had to be better because he was a man. He literally said that! We had a huge argument over it."

"I could never marry anyone without teeth," I said to Nicole.

"I could never marry anyone out of my set," she said to me. "That's how it is in England," she explained. "You're friends with the same set from childhood until you die."

There was exuberance in my voice, world-weariness in hers, each of us admiring the quality of the other while glancing secretly into a small hand mirror at her own.

"I brought some poems to show you," Nicole said. And when we parted, with delicate remorse, each wanted to find the other a cab before getting her own.

* * *

FINALLY, NICOLE AND Orso invited us to the Hamptons.

"It's not very grand, I'm afraid," Nicole apologized as soon as we got there. The tiny place they had rented for two weeks was made of tin, more like a trailer than a shack, yet I felt as if I had stepped inside a royal palace.

Orso immediately took us on a tour. "You should call your next poem 'Weekend at the Grave of Jackson Pollock,' " he said to me, as he turned the car into the gravel driveway of a tiny cemetery. In the back was Pollock's boulder. It was a plain, very large boulder. "Notice that it's unsigned," Orso said, leading us to a neighboring black marble slab with the signature of Stuart Davis chiseled on it. "I prefer the boulder," he said.

Back in the car, we headed directly towards the wealth, the oceanside. "Hear them," Orso said. "It's the geese."

Nicole cried out from the front seat of the Volkswagen. "I hear them, I see them." The low dark V came honking into view and settled down in the middle of a potato field.

"Shh . . . ," Orso said. Without a word, he left the car and walked steadily towards them until, reluctantly, they rose cackling with marvelous elongated necks that stretched forward and were gone. "They've become tame," he said with great scorn. "This land is dying, this is the last of it. It's being bought up for these atrocious houses. Are you ready to swim?"

As we drove along, we saw the waves through windows of great mansions. The windows gave onto other windows, which faced the beach. The windows themselves rose like waves that showed us other windows, other waves.

It was early June. Chilly. Orso was the only one willing to brave the water. "Don't ever turn your back on the ocean," he warned, then turned and marched into the breakers. We sat and watched his powerful, deliberate strokes.

"I love you in my bikini," I said to Nicole. After my third child, it didn't look good on me anymore.

"I'm proud of this," she answered, showing me the hairline

scar from a hernia operation she had had when she was only old enough to have been carrying too-heavy dolls.

"Why can't you have a child?" I asked suddenly.

"I can't tell you. You wouldn't want to hear."

"I do want to hear."

"I can't. Trust me."

"Is it leukemia?" I asked.

"Yes," she said in surprise. "Most people get terrified when they hear the word."

"But you look the picture of health! You're so beautiful," I said.

"It's my tan," she replied, "and your bathing suit. It's the English in me, and it's will. Because you know I rage every day. I rage and rage. That's another reason why it's hard for me to write," she confided. "Because I'm afraid that anything I write will be the last. I can't help thinking that if I do nothing, say nothing, no harm will come to me, and I'll escape."

"I want to be old ladies with you," I said. "We must be old ladies together in the end." Her laughter flashed like the mica in the sand. Sand was flowing from her fist onto the towel. An hourglass.

We lay on our towels and applied oil. We lay on our backs with our straps down and our eyes sealed. We were one flesh. A darning needle landed on my hip. I opened my eyes for a second and saw its prehistoric wings. It flew from one to the other of us. I wasn't alarmed.

"C'mon, get wet," Douglas whispered.

"No," I said. Nicole and I were sewn together with a strong summer thread. It was a moment that I never wanted to be broken.

"Now's a good time," he insisted. I opened my eyes and saw the small bronze-and-white form of Nicole Lombroso balancing on a wave. The distance between us glinted like a sword.

Then Orso and I went for a walk on the beach alone.

"If Douglas were a man," Orso said, "he would kill his wife

and her lover with one blow. Like twisting the necks of two pigeons. When I see Douglas, I see one thing: lack of energy."

I stopped on the sand and looked down at my small feet. "He wants me to be aggressive in sex."

"That's how I like it," Orso said. "I am in love with a nineteen-year-old Swedish girl."

"Oh," I gulped. "I feel bad for Nicole," I said to explain my silence as we walked. This is the way you are supposed to take bad news, I thought, in the English way, as if it were not happening to you. As if it were happening to someone else. We walked together in silence along the beach, which roared with ocean and sky and the blue of Orso's eyes.

"I will tell you the image I'm thinking of," he said. "When I was with her in Sweden, we were together all night, and then I checked in at my hotel about eight in the morning, and we arranged that at exactly eight-twenty I would go to the window and she would be riding her twenty-five-year-old bicycle past the hotel. And I did. And I saw her tall and blond in her old black pea jacket and long black pants on her bicycle, and just at that moment a flock of swans rose up over her in the air."

"Does Nicole know?"

"I told Nicole that I shacked up with a tomato," he said, "but that's different from being in love with—"

"A swan. I love Nicole," I said.

"I love her too, I have always loved Nicole. I think she is the only person I have ever allowed myself to know. All those other women are shadows, or, worse, bodies. William James wrote about tender/tough, but he missed the point. It's just very hard to be in love for many years. I am in love with this Swedish girl. . . . I will kill you if you ever tell Nicole." He smiled.

How could two evils be happening at once, I asked myself, how could Nicole be ill and Orso unfaithful? Walking side by side, culpably in step with him, slender and graceful at his side. "She writes me eight-page letters every day," he continued, "and I answer them."

We walked in silence, stopping for me to prod a stone with my toe or pick it up. "You know I've stopped speaking to Carl," Orso said. "It's over between us. I had a dream about him. I was in a room where a lot of young, beautiful men and women were wearing white gloves and standing around, like in one of those old German movies of the twenties. Carl was in the center of the room, straddling a log over a chasm in the floor. He didn't look up to greet me, he just kept working."

"I know what it means."

"I hope you're not going to say the log is a phallic symbol."

"It's a dream about work. There's a chasm between you, but Carl keeps working and you are stuck in an old movie, unable to work."

"I love work better than I love any woman," he agreed.

"WE'RE ALONE, THE children aren't here," I said, lying down next to Douglas on the narrow guest bed. Nicole had just gone to bed, wearing a man's blue shirt. I had said good night in my long orange nightgown. The Hampton moon hung like a tatter in the curtain over us. Douglas took off his octagonal steel-rimmed glasses and tucked them, folded, under the cot. His face was narrow and keen, his eyes flinching; the lower rim of the left eye trembled incessantly. I pulled on his steel-wool hair, the soft fringe of it brushing his forehead. A new feeling was beginning to climb down from my throat to my vagina. I was going to possess him. I pulled myself forward and kissed his mouth, and then I kissed his narrow cheeks, I found his throat and neck, his bare arms covered with freckles. I understood finally. He wanted to serve me. He wanted to be submissive in sex, to do my bidding.

"Lie on your back," I said. I rolled heavily on top of him. His penis was thick as a log under me. Like Paul Bunyan, I coaxed it into place.

"You feel so supple," he swooned.

"Do you love me?"

"Yes," he moaned, "oh, yes." The moan distressed me. I

lifted myself up on one elbow. He looked wan and handsome, like a gay waiter in a French restaurant.

"Why are you cringing?" I asked.

"I love you," he whimpered.

"Do you belong to me?"

"Yes, oh yes." He was my valet, I thought, half disgusted, while my body started telling him its secrets, pulling out all its drawers. I was a huge chest of drawers sliding open and shut for him to enter, closing him inside. And then, almost before I knew what was happening, my body was emptying itself in rolled garments into a suitcase for a long trip, telling me that I could not stop now that the arrangements were made and were being carried out. I could not change my mind, now that the train had started pulling out of the station; and while he served, impersonal as a porter under me, I flung myself on the tracks.

"Was it good?" his annihilated voice asked.

"Yes. It was the first time I've come that way. Like a man."

"You're a magnificent woman." The compliment was one that Douglas paid many women; it was his tone that molested me.

"Don't call me that."

"You're a handsome woman, then,"

It was asking me to subjugate him. "Why do you say 'handsome'? Are you by any chance homosexual?" He winced. I pulled him down beside me. But I did not know how to do it. I did not know the right words to say. I had heard only domestic commands: my mother telling my father to take back the fruit because it was bruised, it wasn't ripe, it wasn't a good buy. How could I dub desire over those grim tasks? His penis was butting out of the opening in his shorts. Am I a domineering woman? I wondered. How horrible. His penis was in my hand, it was ripe, it wasn't bruised, it was a good buy. I laughed. It was like holding a dog on a leash. "You are my dog," I said, and there was an immediate answering warmth in my groin. "I must get a leash for you," I said caressingly. His eyes reddened; and there was a mysterious tugging at my vagina. I could feel the lips of it purse and swell. I felt as if he were inside me already, as if I was having a premature orgasm. I quickly stood up and went to the suitcase on the wicker night table. I took out a striped loincloth we had bought in Rome on our honeymoon. I tied an effeminate bowknot around his neck, leaving some over. "Until I can get you one with rhinestones on it, like a poodle's," I said, "it will have to do. Do you like it?" I asked, jerking it slightly.

"It's very nice," he said in a strangled voice as I mounted him. My fiery nightgown covered his bare behind. He pressed forward under me on his hands and knees around the tiny room. Pain ceased to exist as I rode him, ignoring his.

"My pampered jade," I said, "make love to me. Do it well or I will make you wear the leash on the beach tomorrow with Nicole and Orso. Wouldn't Orso like to see you like this?" He was trembling with the excitement of this humiliation. "Come into me," I commanded. "But first take off my nightgown."

He eased the clinging material off me with the anxious fervor of a lady's maid. "My gigolo, my poodle," I sang, and the gods showered me with orgasms like trading cards. The small monastic room filled with the smell of brimstone, of sperm, and I heard his faithful, muffled cry.

4

THE AMBER ROSE

/ / / / / / /

I was eleven years old, reading in the dark behind the love seat. There were two rows of shelves with novels. Tall plants with tiger stripes that grew in the dark (I had seen them in the dentist's office) stood stiffly in a narrow box at the top. The other side of the bookcase, in the living room, was mirrored. I was reading a secret novel, *The Sun Also Rises*. But close to the beginning it said that the hero was impotent. I was dismayed, bored, as if by a hundred hard words in a row. There was nothing left that could interest me. I put the book down. I climbed out.

Another time I learned that the wife pretended in the dark that her hair was long and heavy and the color of wheat. I read all day.

I was always mainly interested in sex.

I always bring up the subject.

For many years I could not read Henry Miller because of the word "fart." He farted. His girlfriend, or wife, farted. I closed the book. Now it is my favorite word.

It is why I like living in New York. It is a noisy city. There are men conveniently drilling on the street. There is always a truck rumbling by, or a subway. You can fart in complete privacy. All noises obliterated in the general uproar, any bad smell unnoticeable in the general malodorousness.

I remember being in love with Dr. Joe in camp. Dr. Joe had just gotten out of the army. The two blond nurses were in love with him too. Sitting in the sun outside the infirmary during his time off, I used to scratch his feet. "I like my feet to be scratched better than sex," he said. The blond nurses were jealous. One day I had the good fortune to be sick. I had a stomach virus. I had to go to the infirmary. He examined me with the stethoscope under my pajamas, which intimate procedure was the closest thing imaginable to what I most coveted, when suddenly it was all ruined. He asked me a terrible question.

"Do you have gas?" he said.

"No," I answered innocently.

"Would it feel better if you could pass wind?" he persisted.

"No!" I protested vehemently.

I trembled on parents' day. My parents met Dr. Joe. I was afraid he would tell them about my huge crush on him, about how I scratched his feet, about what a great slut I was. "Your daughter is a real . . . lady," he lied.

WHEN I WAS a child I studied my mother hard, in all her ways, but sometimes I only remember the bare facts. I remember that I was hers, as my sister was my father's. That early in life I gave up having a father so I could be her love.

She made me a sweet sixteen party. That morning my mother told me to take my braces out, but I didn't. I didn't see any reason to. I was only playing at Emily Kamen's house, on the other side of the building. Her father always slept on a reclining chair, with one hand on his stomach inside his trousers. When I came home for dinner, through the scary basement, with Emily, who let me copy her French homework so that I never had to conjugate a single verb myself, my gray living room was unimaginably full of exotic teenagers. Most of them I hardly knew. I wished I had taken my braces off. But Jason Furst, my boyfriend, who was twenty-one and in the army, was missing. His leave was canceled. Someone in his barracks had misbehaved, and so every soldier was punished. Of the whole party, I remember most that he wasn't there.

Later he divorced his wife, he told me, because she wouldn't wear white bobby socks like mine.

That year I went to another party. It was in the city, in Greenwich Village. I don't know how I got there. I only know that I was standing in a corner and a short man was standing in front of me with his foot raised on a stool. Like a dog raising his leg against a tree, the moment, the position, was sexual. I felt cornered, aware of his penis. I liked that feeling. His name was Mort Sober.

The following afternoon I sat on my mother's bed. She was under the covers, confiding in me about my father. She was sensitive and my father wasn't. She loved art and he didn't. She cared about feelings and he cared about facts. He had called me a "slut" when I flirted with boys in the schoolyard and the word had hurt worse than a slap. I looked it up in the dictionary. I held it against him with all my heart—I would be one to spite him. I flirted with Harold Shoemaker. I wore a red silk scarf around my neck. I let him feel me up. His knuckled fist bulged out under my yellow sweater—red and yellow, catch a fellow—and the fall night crept before dinner into my camel's hair coat.

In that crepuscular room, what I said to my mother is gone. What she suddenly answered, what she said to me, is: "I have an orgasm when I make love with your father—nine out of ten times!"

I was mortified. I had thought *I* was her husband.

I sat there in silence and slowly did the problem solving I was so bad at.

If she had an orgasm when she made love with my father nine out of ten times, that meant: (1) she made love with my father, and (2) she had made love with my father at least ten times, and (3) I drew the obvious conclusion: she had a husband, a lover, and I had no father.

The next day I told my mother a lie that worked.

That evening, without a murmur, my parents drove me to the city, to Mort Sober's apartment. I got out of the car, thanked them. Upstairs, Mort unfolded his Castro Convertible. But we made love on the floor. On the rug. It didn't hurt. I didn't much like him. I knew that Mort meant death in French. He was tentatively engaged. Afterwards, he defrosted a carton called "Salisbury Steak." That was a phrase I had never heard before, the one that stuck to the experience.

WHEN YOU TALK about sex all the time, it means you were molested as a child. It means you can't tell the difference between what is private and what is public, what is inside and what is outside.

My father's father was a housepainter and he molested me. He perceived my lust, my yearning behind the love seat; the furtive sexuality that policemen in tollbooths had detected and winked at when my father had let me pay. He put his old tongue in my mouth. For years. I suffered his caresses, staring with inky eyes at my punishing father, keeping the secret that would hurt him. Until one day when Heidi was sick in bed. My grandfather molested my sister. Then the spell was broken.

No. That is how I remembered it all these years. But this is how it really happened.

My sister and I were in the kitchen, my sister was simpering, telling my mother something my grandfather did. "Grandpa touched my puupy," she boasted. (It was our private word, pronounced like "whoopee"—puupy.) My mother turned on her with rage. "That's a lie!" she screamed. I was shocked. Betrayed. I thought it was my potent beauty that had aroused him. I thought it was my fault. I thought he only did it to me.

My mother was about to hit Heidi. "No, it's true," I said. "He did it to me too."

MY SISTER WAS little and brown. My mother didn't like her because she had dark skin. When she was born, a neighbor had come to see Heidi and had said, "She's so dark! It's a good thing we don't have a colored doorman. People would talk."

My mother wept; my father played solitaire.

"She makes *me* feel ugly," my mother told my father. "She looks like *your* ugly sister."

"Oh, please, Rose," my handsome father said. "She has nothing to do with Eva."

My mother cried for six months.

There are many photographs of me, professional albums in an off-the-shoulder blouse. Braids piled high on top of my head, long cylindrical curls down my back. In some I have a bored, voluptuous look. None of her, Heidi.

Bela, my father's father, was Hungarian. He came here when my father was two. He was married to Matilda, who wore flowered dresses and was surrounded by platters of home-baked cookies, the kind with jelly in the middle, the top one covered with floury sugar. Sweet flour on your fingertips. Everywhere you looked there were stacks of small framed cardboard prints, whole small rooms filled with them: purple plums on a branch; flowers. Matilda died on the operating table from stomach cancer.

My grandfather didn't look like my father. My grandfather was not handsome. He had a thick accent, white hair, wide hips, a big nose. I stood between his legs and felt the soft rub of his testicles. When I was sick, he reached under the covers and he said, "Sweet, sweet."

IT WAS SUNDAY. Grandpa's visit. He came early. Mother went to Klein's, which was open Sundays. She brought back huge boxfuls of clothes that we tried on and that she could exchange for seven days. My sister and I were four years apart. She was five or six or seven. I had my braids coiled over my ears on each side. Grandpa sat on a chair between our beds. Heidi was asleep. The frayed satin border of her blue blanket touching her face. Grandpa touched me under the covers. It felt nice. Like velvet.

I pictured love as a grownup. He would beg to do what could only give me pleasure.

I would yield.

It was the promise of how I would be loved as a beautiful woman. The power and pleasure I would feel, the power and pleasure I would give.

Heidi sighed in her sleep. Her little body moved under the sheet.

ONCE MY GRANDFATHER had been kissing my fat friend Beverly, putting his tongue into her mouth. "That was disgusting," Beverly said. "He put his tongue in my mouth!" "Is she Jewish?" my grandfather asked, worried. Her arms were the size of my thighs. "Yes," I said. He was relieved.

HEIDI AND I insisted that our father was not to be told. We didn't want to hurt him. Then the lock in the door was changed. All the keys were different. My grandfather didn't come every Sunday anymore.

ABOUT INCEST, CARL Vaggio said: "It's not that great— you're too nervous." Carl liked Heidi. I had brought her with me to his studio once. He said, "I liked her. . . . Y'mean"— laughing—"I was the only one?"

Carl Vaggio was slouched at the table, reading his newspaper when I arrived, his hair was in a ponytail. When he brushed it out, his long hair stood around him in a thin brown nimbus until he gripped it with one hand and clamped it into the elasticized band. Then his head seemed to dwindle on each side of his forehead and come to a point.

His navy sweatshirt, speckled with paint, had a little pointed hood. He looked up, Smiley.

"I got rid of Dawn," he said, his sandpaper voice a cat's tongue.

"I thought she was already gone."

"She came back."

"How did you manage it this time?"

"Her shrink told her she deserves more than just to be tolerated. I could only tolerate her," he said.

He looked like a derelict with several days' beard darkening his meager face. Savage as the heartbeat of the world.

"I had a wonderful weekend with Nicole and Orso," I said.

"Oh yeah."

"Nicole told me."

"Toldjew what?".

"About her illness. I pretended I didn't know."

"Good."

"*Women in Love*," I cried happily, seeing the book. "Nicole and I are both reading it!"

"It's the maid's. . . . I feel really insulted," he said, changing the subject, "because Dawn said I wanted to keep her around just to make love to. I could hardly do that number. I only did it to be polite. Can I help it if I keep having fantasies of—"

He stopped before saying "you." He would not blackmail me with his need. I was, after all, going away soon. I entertained him, telling him of our race, Nicole and I on the wet sand, and our charley horses the next day. He paced over the antique Navajo rugs, faded from the ferocity of his moods. He stood at the center of one, repossessing his kingdom now that

Dawn had cleared out; he switched on a miniature color Sony that sat on a dais in the middle of the room. Under the sky-light, a soap opera blossomed in full color. A high-strung woman, a handsome man.

"What do you feel?" I asked.

"Lonely well-being."

"Really?" I admired him. A hermit in the middle of his fame, taking bread from my hand, not knowing that in the last episode I had been to bed with my husband. I had cuckolded my lover. "Nicole had to go to another doctor today," I mentioned.

"Yeah. I'm afraid she's getting to be a professional patient."

"Oh no!" I defended her. "They just make her go."

"I know," he agreed.

"You hurt Nicole," I said. "How could you do that? Why wouldn't you let her keep Dennis's poems for a while?" Dennis had had one slender book of poems published by a friend in England.

"If she thinks they're so bad, what does she need them for? I don't want anything taken away from me that's mine. Besides," he added, "that book will be valuable one day." The sane vision of his smile dwarfed the issue. "I think I would have forgotten all about Dennis Berg if it hadn't been for you," he confessed.

I followed him across the long room, into the sunny bed-room.

"Why here?"

"I like the light."

"I like the dark." His hurt fingers were fumbling with the fake buttons on my dress.

"They don't open," I apologized. He stepped out of his pants and left them belted, half-rising, in two columns on the floor. The fur back of the chair, antelope and chrome, tilted when I laid my light dress over it.

"What kind of a bra is that?" he said, looking at my flesh-colored harness, seamless, with wire underneath.

"What do you mean? I always wear this bra." I envied him his curious lapses of memory.

"You have to be really sexy to get away with that," he said.

MY MOTHER WAS a beauty of pearl and coral, with beautiful hands and a beautiful back. Her eyes haunted me, and her almost transparent teeth. Her breasts drooped. Her nose was pressed up against the bakery shop window, she hovered in the doorways of florists.

A maiden carved out of coral, always in bed.

She was always rushing into icy water, rough surf.

She taught me the ways of a courtesan, letting me live in her closet and try on the silver robe hemmed with feather boa.

When my mother lay down on the doctor's table for a biopsy, she was still beautiful, though her body had always been in a strange disrepair, with loose flesh that wrinkled like lava invading a town. She was an overeater. All during my childhood she had hidden her gluttony, eating while I slept. She had taught me to avert my eyes.

My mother flirted with the very old doctor, whom Marlena had highly recommended. He was tall, like Abraham Lincoln. He had to go to open his summer house on the Cape; he had a half-dozen sons, but no one, it seemed, could open the house except him. She had a "curable" form of cancer. Paget's disease. It showed on the nipple. The breast would have to come off. He had to wait for the biopsy results, of course, but he was sure it was Paget's. He recommended a "radical." All his girls had them.

"Think of your role as a grandmother," he advised.

SHE AND MY father came to dinner.

"How could you?" she screamed at me. "It's too salty! You put in too much salt!"

The spaghetti was ruined. I hadn't tasted it. It was Pierrette's day off.

"I can't believe my own daughter would spoil my last pleasure."

I sat down at the glass table next to my father.

"You have cottage cheese in your tooth," Douglas told me. I was dieting, having only a scoop of cottage cheese and peach halves for dinner.

"Is it gone?" I smiled.

"No."

I smiled again.

"Yes."

"What do you think, Douglas?" my mother asked.

"I think you should have a mastectomy. Certainly if the fasting doesn't work. You don't even have to have a radical."

"Never!" she shrieked. "I won't let them cut off my breast."

"Why? It's better than dying," he argued.

"I'm not going to die. I don't believe in lopping," she said.

"I agree with Rose," my father said. "Doctors are the most dangerous group of men in this country. They want to cut. And I can tell you, sight unseen, anybody who's been cured by surgery didn't have cancer in the first place."

"My mother had a mastectomy, and she's still living," Douglas pointed out.

Naomi Black had buried her husband. Then she packed her bag bravely like a girl leaving for summer camp and told all her callers, "I'll keep you abreast." Now her one breast fluttered softly near the middle of her chest like a third eye.

"Opposite poles, opposite poles," my mother said. "I just wrote your mother a very warm note, telling her that she's a hard act to follow."

Only now was the wedding friction demoted from the status of a battle.

"All I know is that you've got something they can handle, and you're going off on some lunatic binge to fast," Douglas said.

"That's enough! I wanted to discuss it. I didn't come here to be insulted."

"But you didn't want to discuss it," Douglas said, "you didn't want to discuss it." In his rage, words fled, or came in echoing pairs.

"Some person you are to give advice," she said, "with all that beer."

"Rose has promised me," my father said, "that if the fasting doesn't work, she'll go to Tijuana and take laetrile." He was like a gypsy beside his wagon selling a tonic to cure baldness that, it just so happened, he believed in, that he drank himself, by the bottleful, as a prophylactic. He was the lawyer for laetrile.

THE NEXT DAY my mother went to Pawling, New York, to a health farm, to fast. She was going to show the doctors they were wrong. "Fasting is surgery without a knife," she said.

My mother had always been ahead of her time. She nursed me when other mothers gave bottles and doctors didn't believe in nursing. In grade school, I hung on the refrigerator door and begged for a smallpox vaccination. I had gazed at lettuce-less sandwiches on Wonder bread that other mothers left wrapped in wax paper for after school. I had eaten my first Social Tea biscuit at Francy-Kay Iger's house and my cheeks had ached, my mouth overflowing with saliva.

She disappeared in my father's car, with my father driving. She made him stop every mile, at every fruit stand, he told me.

"How could she have used all that salt?" my mother complained. "Joy knew it was my last meal. It was like vinegar on a sponge to me. It was terrible. I was so angry about it. And him. He's got a few things to learn. All that beer, and that temper!"

The car filled with cores and pits.

"Haven't you had enough?" he asked. They were parked outside the gate.

"Yes, I'm fed up with you," she answered, getting out. She

entered the forbidding house where there was a padlock on the refrigerator and a guard at the kitchen door.

I called her every third day.

"I'm fine, I had a headache for the first three days. Withdrawal symptoms. Coffee and tea are drugs. . . .

"I don't even want a sip of water. . . .

"I am dreaming of baked potatoes. . . .

"Why, when your sauce is always so divine . . . ?" she said, still harping on her oversalted last supper. "I can't come to the phone anymore. I've moved to the third floor." I listened to her voice grow weaker and weaker.

"How is your breast?" I asked.

"The breast is the same, but I don't have headaches or rheumatism. I'm fine. Don't worry about me. Don't call."

After thirty days, we visited.

Our heads were bowed. "I'm sorry it's so small," she said. She lay in bed in the garret, which she had chosen to avoid a roommate, a possible smoker. "I have had revelations," she said. "I've seen my mother, I've felt her with me in this room."

Then my father and Douglas took the children out to play.

"Something incredible happened to me yesterday," my mother whispered as soon as we were alone.

"What?"

"My bowel movement. I have hit pay dirt! A terrible black slime came out of me."

"Mother!"

"It's twenty years of old toxins, toxins from twenty years ago!" she sang.

"Mother, I'm afraid."

"Don't you dare speak to my doctor," she said.

NOW SHE SHOOK off my father's health insurance. She shook off my father. After thirty years of marriage, she flew to Tijuana and divorced my father. I had advised her to do it! Still, it came as a surprise. She had arranged for my father to pick her up at the airport, and they came straight from the airport to us, to break the news.

The following Sunday my dad took us out to dinner in the Chinese restaurant on B'way. For the first time, she wasn't with him. Walking there, he said, "How's Mother doing?"

"Fine!" I was positively jaunty. "I think divorcing you is the one decision Mother's ever made that she doesn't regret!" To my surprise, he winced.

MY FATHER MOVED back in with her while he looked around to "find another place." Then, when she was ready to "take him back," he left her. He moved in with an old man named Jack in New Jersey. The divorce had been a mistake.

My mother had always wanted to be "rich enough to be eccentric," but now she made herself look poor. "I don't like her life-style," my father said. I could hardly blame him.

My feelings towards her had cooled when she didn't love my children as much as I did, as much as she loved me. After the first preliminary squeal of delight, she would ignore the grandchildren she had come to enjoy, her eyes sliding off them onto her gnarled hands which had been beautiful, onto the hanging flesh of her forearms, onto the clock to tell her when her next program would be, onto the overflowing ashtrays and half-filled beer cans, onto the three started sour creams. "I don't think my grandmother emotions are working properly," she would say, unable to stop cleaning the refrigerator, or warming leftovers, or peeling moldy cucumbers. Douglas said it frightened him to watch her peel cucumbers, as if she were whittling down the man's penis, making it the right size.

"Mother, why don't you come into the living room and visit with us?" I said.

"I can't. One minute. I'm resuscitating your old raisins," she replied.

I was cruel. I put her wide-brimmed black organdy hat on Penelope and gasped and laughed at how much better it looked on the baby.

She wanted to give Benjamin money for Halloween, but her hand would not relinquish the dollar. She ran into the street with it. He ran dangerously after her.

I am still angry at myself because one birthday she bought Isabelle a doll and I did not conceal my disappointment. It was not the expensive doll I wanted for her, Scarlett O'Hara in a straw hat and taffeta gown. It was a small rubbery doll with a face like a pig. You fed her water and she wet. I thought it was an insult to my daughter, that it impugned her beauty, her worth. I thought she would hate it. "See my baby?" Isabelle said to me, holding it in her plump arms, rocking it. "Isn't she beautiful?" "I think she looks rather like a pig," I answered.

Isabelle quickly held the doll away from her. "Yes, she does," she said and put the doll down. She never played with it again.

I had meant to hurt my mother, not my child.

"WE WERE CUT off," my mother said each day, for the sake of the listening operator. She had devised a way to call from the street without paying. "Can you hear me?" she asked, her voice declaring a disaster area.

"Yes, darling, what is it?"

"I was cleaning in your kitchen," my mother said, "folding and putting away the shopping bags from your counter. I thought I saw a piece of meat under them. It was my liver. I cleared away the bag and then I screamed. Hundreds of cockroaches were gnawing at it. I said to myself, 'I'm going to put it out of my mind and tell no one about it.' But somehow I haven't been able to shake off my depression since. Don't worry about me," she said. "I had another disappointing conversation with your father, but I'm coping. I took a little nap in the vest-pocket park right where I live. I lay down on a bench in this old coat and fell asleep. Then some boys came, and one of them threw a lighted cigarette into my coat while I slept. But you see, you don't have to worry about me. My nose saved me! I can take care of myself!"

* * *

"THERE'S SOMETHING I have to tell you," Nicole Lombroso said. We were in The Library, a restaurant on upper B'way whose walls were lined with books, unread books that had been bought by the yard, having one of our fabulous lunches. She was disappearing on the red leather bench; I was stuck up on a high bentwood chair. Then we switched. "It's not as good as it looks, is it?" she said, as I sank down in the soft red leather. She agreed with the Wife of Bath that women want sovereignty; I agreed with Nietzsche that they want submission.

Nicole, however, was married to a huge mountain of a man. An oppressor.

Green-eyed, with high cheekbones, she blended with her surroundings—the Hamptons, Orso's loft in the East Village, these books—and always for an embarrassing instant when we met, unrecognizable.

We had discovered that we had the same birthday. Only she was three years older. We were both Sagittarius, both born on December 13. "That's the best birthday present I ever got," I said, "to share it with you."

"There's no one I'd rather share it with either," Nicole said.

By now we were almost mirror images, in high heels and new summer clothes. I had the amber rose that Carl Vaggio had given me around my neck; she wore an ivory rose.

Her cool glamour enveloped me.

"There's something I've been meaning to tell you," she said again, separating the chives from her omelet with her fork (she had forgotten that she was unable to eat greens). Then she told me that she was having an affair with Carl Vaggio too. (He had mentioned that one time, when they climbed the ladder, but I thought it was only the one time.) She told me gently, couching it in her usual annoyance with him. "He does treat us all the same. He is the same with all of us. All four of us."

"Four! I only count three." There was Dawn, who was his

mistress and lived with him, with Wednesday nights off. And me—Tuesdays and Thursdays. And Val in California. Carl said about Val, "I have to have a girl for when I go there. I can't play tennis now, with my hip bothering me. I've got nothing else to do when I'm finished at the studio but waste my time with women."

I was happily distracted just then by a woman walking through the empty restaurant. "I could wear my hair like that," I said.

"Why should you, when your hair is so spectacular the way it is?" Nicole answered.

"But he said to me," I said, "that I had the best of him. And it made me feel . . . not jealous."

"He said the same thing to me."

"Not at the same time, surely!"

"At exactly the same time. I can tell you, for example, what book you left there on what day. I was there the day before, or the day after. *I'm* the fourth!" Nicole said.

"Why didn't you tell me?" I accused her.

"I thought you knew."

"No. I thought it was all in the past. But I don't believe it."

"Once I said to him, 'Joy doesn't know, does she, about you and me?' Carl said, 'No, I don't want to disillusion her. She thinks you're so perfect, in love with your husband.' "

For a moment I could not even manage to change the subject.

"He just goes from person to person, I assure you," Nicole continued. "It's not the numbers that bother me particularly, it's that he just *goes*. He is simply incapable of intimacy. In the fifteen years I've known him, he hasn't changed at all, or he's changed for the worse. His shrink is making him an emotional cripple, his shrink is *a bad man*. . . . "

She sounded awfully like my mother, who said my father was *a bad man*, her voice whipping.

"He's intimate with me," I said.

"No, he's not. That's not intimacy."

"I was there when you called," I said. "I thought you were just friends."

"I was there when *you* called. *He's* just not there."

"I love his body," I said, through my tears. "When I'm with him, I feel in some privileged place where I'm not missing anything—and everything."

"I liked it too," Nicole said.

"What is it about him . . . ?" I said. "His body, his fame?"

"Maybe his suppressed violence."

"Yes! You wait around willingly for weeks for some display of"—I lifted my long hair from my neck—"passion," I said, and a tear fell. It fled down her apricot cheek. The first I had seen her shed. It made me giddy. I was seeing depths I had never seen before. "So this is the conversation that we've never had," I said.

"Yes."

"I can't believe how lucky he was to have us both," I cried. "It really makes me respect him that he's had you as well as me."

"It makes me feel contempt, not respect. That's the difference between us."

My heart was strangely heavy, I noticed.

"I feel better now that I've shared the burden with you," she said.

"I feel very shaken," I said.

"Nobody likes being fooled."

"But I approve of his choice," I continued, high on the seesaw again. Till a cloud bore me down. "What must your feelings about me have been?"

"I felt ambivalent at first," she admitted.

"We were just side dishes," I suggested. "I was pickled cucumbers that he ate with his roast beef sandwich from the Jewish deli. Whenever he ordered a little dish of marinated cukes, that was me. Were you the coleslaw?"

"I was pheasant under glass!"

She laughed deliciously and we ordered one cheesecake for dessert.

"But what about Val?" Nicole said. "I've thought very carefully about what the requirement is for a woman to be desirable to Carl Vaggio."

"Jewish, with dark hair?" I said.

"No." She waved her hand back and forth in front of my face. "Emotionally walled off. If you had met Val, you'd see what I mean."

"Did she have pimples?" I asked.

"No! She was an extremely attractive young girl."

"Oh," I said, disappointed. "Carl said she had pimples."

"If she did, it was clear that they'd go away when she got a little older!"

Once Carl was going to see Val in California, and I was jealous and upset. I threw up on the street, and he soothed me. He stayed on the phone. "Think of all the three-letter words that stand for parts of the body," he said. "There are nine." I thought hard, I concentrated. I didn't want him to think I was stupid. Arm, leg, eye, gum, hip, ear, toe, jaw. I got eight. "And lip," he said. I forgot Val.

"You're tan," I said to Nicole.

"Yes, I'm losing it, I'm turning yellow," she said.

The cheesecake came, and we each ate our half. Then I came down with a bump. I sat awaiting consolation. "Now I have to leave; I have to see Carl," she said.

"I thought you had a hair appointment."

"I do. Afterwards."

There was time for flashback after flashback. They came like hot flashes to my grandmother's cheeks, as I looked at the chameleon face facing me.

"I told him one thing I liked," Nicole said. "I said, 'When I look in the mirror, I expect to see my own face.'"

She was my mother, he was my father; they were conspiring behind my back. I stood apart, assaulted.

"It was an odd moment for me just now," I confessed.

"I'm sorry. I'll tell you when I realized that I had been duped. When I saw your amber rose. Remember that I knew instantly where it came from. And I think he got the idea from me, from my ivory rose! . . . I'm going to tell Carl that I'm not going to see him anymore. I'm going to try very hard with Orso—to make it work again. That's what I want. And when I go," she said, "you'll have everything of mine. All my jewelry. Everything. But now I have to leave."

Before she left, I tried to hurt her.

"Did you have anal intercourse?" I asked.

"No," she said, startled, and was gone out the glass door.

5

ADMIRAL BYRD'S WIFE

/ / / / / / / /

After that, it was as if I had stepped into her shoes, I was inside her skin. I knew exactly how it was between them.

She spoke first.

"Cara mentioned something to me that you should know," Nicole Lombroso said, looking at Carl Vaggio, thumb in mouth, intent on his newspaper. "She doesn't like her room; she'd like to be alone on the other side. In the sunny bedroom."

He grunted.

"Why don't you ever talk to your children?"

With her he would have just been unhappy in a different way.

"And Dennis is too surrounded by women. Why don't you

play something with him?" He put his hand under her skirt. His eyes gleamed dully, still measuring his morning's work. "Well, will you let her have the sunny bedroom?"

"C'mon," he rasped. With her loosened clothes trailing, he led her across the vast space to the sunny bedroom, which was theirs, she thought, and Cara's. They passed photographs of Carl blowing smoke rings, of Carl with Perfidy on his lap and with the children at his drawing board.

"I'm getting fat," Carl complained under the covers. His own fat, he had discovered, was a wonderful subject with women.

"Where do you take Joy? Which bedroom?" Nicole asked.

"She doesn't mean anything to me, I told you. We're just friends," he wooed her. "Why do you two have to be friends?"

"It just happened that way, we just are. If she doesn't mean anything to you, if you're just friends, why don't you stop seeing her?"

"I couldn't possibly stop seeing her, we're very old friends, I knew her before I knew you," he said. "Why are women more interested in each other than in men?"

"Maybe they're more interesting," she answered. "I read Joy's manuscript about you."

"I told her she shouldn't bother to do all that typing."

"It was quite a shock, I assure you. I thought: Haven't I read this somewhere before? Haven't I had this conversation? You don't vary much, do you?"

"I vary a little."

"Yes, I know. I hadn't realized that you were still seeing your California friend. The 'lobotomized California girl.'"

"Why doesn't she keep her big mouth shut?" he said. "I'd take you to California with me but you can't get away."

"Maybe I can. I'm limping too," she said. She was beginning to think of taking a sick leave.

The phone rang from the floor near the bed. He picked up the receiver and put his hand over her mouth. She looked at him indignantly with her large green eyes. "Grand Central Station," he said.

It was very hard to be wrong, she thought. To have chosen so carefully and still to have made the wrong choice.

"Hi." His voice softened; he tightened his grip over her jaw.

"Okay. . . . What time?" He stared piously at the ceiling while he talked.

"Yeah. . . . Bye."

"Joy?" Nicole asked.

"No, Dawn."

"I thought it was over between you."

"I haven't spoken to her in three weeks."

"Well?"

"She wants to see me tonight."

"And you cannot refuse a woman, is that it? A damsel in distress?" She laughed bitterly.

"What d'you want?" he asked. "I want to give you what you want." He brought her body to life. Because of him she could do it. Because he would be there. He made her beautiful night after night. She would be wearing the right thing, there would be color in her face. She still needed his magic to keep herself alive. Frankly, she told herself, there isn't time to find another lover.

"Only love," she answered. They made love. Then that funny new pain in her groin. And afterwards, she thought: I'm glad it's time to go home. I can't wait to be in my own house again, alone, so I can feel like a human being. But he wouldn't let her go. He detained her. "How could you do this to me?" she said, weeping. "You didn't have to pretend to love me. I would have slept with you anyway. I made it clear that I was going to sleep with you anyway."

"I wasn't pretending," he said, "What d'you want anyway? You're the one that's married!"

"There is a smell in your house of cheap women!"

"Joy."

"No."

"It's the new maid, Jerri," he said. "A nice helpful hippie." The new perfume pervaded every room, sickening her. She thought of the revolver with hollow-point ammunition that Orso had taught her to use against her will—she hated sleeping with loaded weapons!—But she didn't want to kill him, she didn't want to give him the satisfaction. She would have to commit suicide, like one of her Russian ancestors. Indifference, that was what she wanted. She tried it on like a glass slipper.

"You want to make it real?" he said.

"Yes," she answered, taken by surprise. "I'm not going to call you anymore. You can call me."

His animal tongue reached into her mouth in his kiss that was not a kiss. He pressed one nail into her buttocks. He was the hunchback on her block, her vampire.

"Another triumph of geriatric sex," he said, at the humble end. She put back on her clothes—she had enjoyed dressing to take them off. Like a beggar, she smiled at him and left.

THAT EVENING NICOLE called.

"When I told Carl that I told you," she said, "he was very uncomfortable, very distressed. Not just that you knew," she said, sensing my satisfaction even over the telephone, "but because of me too. 'What did she tell you?' he asked me. 'Everything,' I said. 'Now you two can just go on without me, is that it?' 'Yes,' I said." Then she added, "If you knew how he wooed me . . . "

"How?"

"As soon as I got there, I told him exactly what I thought of him. And he said the one thing I wasn't expecting him to say. He asked me to live with him."

"What did you say?" I managed to ask.

"That I'd think about it. But I assure you, I wasn't one minute late for my hair appointment."

At that terrible moment I heard myself think: I would rather she die than that she marry him.

* * *

SHE WOULD NOT have told me if I weren't going anyway, to London, on a Guggenheim for a year, leaving her a clear field. And she wanted me to know. She wanted me to write the novel. "I want him to see himself in your novel," Nicole said, "to have it hold a mirror up to him in which he sees his own nature, his deformity, so that he'll tear himself in two. I want him to see that he is Rumpelstiltskin and tear himself in two."

I WENT TO the Old Studio for the last time. I was leaving for London. He stood with his thumb in his mouth and looked at his work. I asked him, on a hunch, if he was sleeping with Jerri—the maid.

"Yes," he said.

"That's awful. I thought you never slept with the hired help."

"It was a mistake. The housework suffers. She's lost all her magic energy. She's become as lazy as most women."

"You broke your date with Nicole yesterday, didn't you, to sleep with her?"

"Yes."

"How could you?"

He shrugged. "That's not all," he said, grinning. "There's another woman."

"You're kidding!"

"Charlotte, from Argentina. I guess it couldn't be more 'ironically cruel,' not in a million years. Not that I arranged it this way. It just happened. Nicole would just die if she knew this. Charlotte is pregnant. She has to have the baby because she has low-grade lymphoma."

I could see he was enjoying himself.

"Charlotte? I thought you only saw her one weekend."

"I saw her two."

"I thought you didn't like her."

"I don't."

I lifted my long hair from my neck. It was a hot summer

day. I started to coil it on my head. "Don't do that," he said. "You look nice with it down. You look almost young," he said. "From the back."

He led me to a pile of drop cloths in the corner. But, for the first time, he couldn't do it. "I just can't feel any aggression toward you," he said. "I want you to think well of me."

"Are you going to marry her?"

"I dunno. I don't like her in bed. She's not my type. We're not 'sexually compatible.' "

"What if the baby isn't yours?"

"It *is* mine. But it doesn't matter. She's a very nice girl. Anyway, that's the only way it seems I'm able to have children."

Nicole was furious, angrier than I had ever seen her.

"A thirty-one-year-old cocktail waitress whom his friend-with-the-withered-arm sends to his hotel room in L.A., who is a virgin, and who only slept with him once? Can you imagine?"

"Twice," I said.

"And who gets instantly pregnant and goes to her doctor and the doctor sends Carl a letter informing the proud father, who happens to be a rich artist, that the virgin from Venezuela has low-grade lymphoma and has to have the baby because it's her last chance, and he suspects nothing? Would you ever do such a thing, send such a letter? No!"

"And she's living with him," I said. "but he doesn't like her. I know he doesn't like her."

Nicole had been dying of leukemia and Carl couldn't stop seeing me. I still thought he liked only me. It was like with Heidi: I thought I was the only one.

WE DROVE TO the airport at night in my dad's old Cadillac. "All the comforts of home," my mother said ruefully.

Waiting for the group flight, which left at midnight, two children underfoot and a third in my arms, my mother said, "I met your Aunt Ida at the elevator and she said to me, 'Your skin is so yellow!' It's because she's jealous of me, that I'm not obese like she is—I can't believe this woman is my mother's sister!—but I went to see Dr. Fish, and I asked him. He said that maybe I should cut down the carrot juice intake. So I will. Meanwhile, I've been having some rheumatic pains, but he says he's delighted! The toxins are leaving. If I get a cold, he says it will be wonderful!"

"What does Dr. Fish look like?" I asked, for the novel.

"Oh, like Jesus Christ, Superstar, with dark glasses. He has one bad eye from a car accident."

At the airport, I called Nicole. The blood count was fine again.

IN LONDON, UNSETTLING weeks without a letter, and then a steady stream of them, all special delivery. "Dear Joy, Joy dear," came Nicole Lombroso's pastoral, seductive voice, and the mysterious silence in which nothing could be seen, only felt, lifted its curtain over the Hamptons. The news was there were more tractors now than cars, the sound of the wind in the trees (even in the warmest part of the day) was sharper and therefore more interesting. The fog was beautiful but insidiously damp and made the bronchial flu she had picked up feel less mild. Things had deteriorated from those happy summer days. It was all still achingly lovely to look at. But this was the dampest autumn she remembered.

Then she wrote she was home. The typing stopped and the green pen took over. "HAVE HAD NO CONTACT WITH OUR MUTUAL FRIEND," she wrote in Orso's small capitals. "THANK GOODNESS." Orso had gone back to the country where he said it was freezing and he loved it and saw a fox that morning rolling in the fields and enjoying the sunshine. "You must write to Orso separately," she wrote. "He is not a good sport about sharing. . . . It is Sunday and I am watching football, which I do with a little bit less ardor than Carl Vaggio, but then who could be as ardent as Carl Vaggio?"

"Your mother called me," she wrote. "She was very sweet

though nutty and asked me to eat raw vegetables and fruit and I didn't have the heart to tell her that those are the very things I am not permitted to eat!"

At the very bottom of the page, a scribbled afterthought. She would pass on one piece of gossip that she didn't like to think about—the Argentinian madonna remained, evidently more ensconced than ever, evidently more acceptable now as the bearer of "strange fruits," evidently as horrible as ever, *plus ça change*, perhaps he would marry her after all. After all, she was supposed to be bearing his child, which was all one ever needed to do for Carl Vaggio.

IN LONDON, THERE were months of record rain. A gray solitary dark closed us in. On the first Sunday the sun shone, we went to Hyde Park with Penny and Benjamin and Isabelle, who all had English accents. Douglas sprinkled their heads and outstretched arms with crumbs and took their picture covered with English pigeons. There were little wooden signs with the names of flowers in each flower bed: Pheasant's Eye, Dead Men's Fingers, Grace o' Sundays, Love's Breath, which I memorized to press into my letters to Nicole. At teatime, when we arrived home, a fatal telegram was waiting for us on the hall stairs, giving Nicole's hospital address and signed with the sinister message "Love = O + + ."

THE SILK DRESSING gown I'd sent gave her great pleasure even in its box, Nicole wrote. Orso had been marvelous, still sustaining, and their feelings for one another—corny as it sounded—sustaining. Carl's visits when she was first ill were very nice, very good times. Then he went to California and she became so ill that she had to be transferred; since then she hadn't heard from him much—it was hard to get through sometimes, and he discouraged easily—unlike Orso, his great energy was negative, his mode passive.

But in my last letter, there was a moment that upset her. She did not want to hear about the cancers of the clitoris or details of diseases. She had kept herself as ignorant as possible of details of her own illness. "It's like with Isabelle—she is not you—she is only seven—and I am not you—I am—hmmm—well—anyway—very sick—and I want to be protected a little."

ON OUR BIRTHDAY, a gift of silence: long minutes of transatlantic silence at each end. "Happy birthday."

"No."

I thought of a story she had told me. One day a boy came to her apartment after school to play. Her parents' small apartment on the East Side was crammed with foolish objets d'art, acquisitions, purchases. She went to a private school, naturally, but they weren't really rich. He looked around at the clutter. "Where do you sleep?" he asked in bewilderment. In a flash the answer came to her. "In the soapdish," she said.

"Well . . . birthday, then." Tears streaming down my face.

"Yes, birthday."

THEN ORSO WROTE for Nicole, whose right arm was tubed and pierced. Each morning, the London mailman brought the machine gun fire of his medical bulletins—the white cells turning blastic—his hard tone, his Hemingway sentences in which Nicole lay beautiful and knowing as much of her future as anyone, eating rather grim kosher meals. He taught her to avoid all but the most simple foods, he answered all her questions with guarded truth. He bullied and charmed. Carl had been decent and kind, if madly insensitive. I will always love you for what you and Nicole are about, he said. As far as her poems go, you are her sole mentor.

With the word "solo" over "dear, dear joy," Orso's letters would descend on the day like a helicopter, like a mourning dove.

Then, tragedy. Abrupt and butcherly. The animal had run its course, and all that was known about track conditions was now in *his* hands. All the biopsies, bone marrow, et al., were done, and the results were totally bad. Myelofibrosis was the name. It meant that her bone marrow areas were scar-covered and could not produce blood cells. Other organs compensated and took over, such as liver, spleen. *Spirit*. This, too, would become infected and it would end. Prognosis: two or three months without infection. Infection meant pretty instantaneous death.

No one could see Nicole, he assured me. Her oldest friend, Lila R., who lived in Paris was there in the Baroness's suite at the St. Regis, she had been there two days and unable to see Nicole. She didn't make a special trip: a gift from a patroness to the painter's wife. Something very poodle-like indeed.

He was more than blunt. He drove his points home. Neither he nor the doctors would allow me to see Nicole. Her deadly father, her zany mother, her plodding brother, and he were the only ones. And the first three didn't get to stay very long. And "Hercules Dante" simply would not do. Orso Lombroso would be much better. Joe Blow was a terrible name for Carl. Joe Bueno, yes. After all, he was a dago with a name as uncommon as Rumpelstiltskin and that was part of his charm as well as his making it.

I WAS SICK, gasping and retching over the edge of the bed, spitting up pearly foam into the salad bowl. The free doctor came. "That's not good, you know," he said to Douglas, "she's losing all her digestive juices." I raised a pleated brow to him and he staggered back a step, seeing a fiend from hell. "Come now," he said, "what's all this?"

I asked for a shot to stop the vomiting. It had been going on all night. "My friend is dying of leukemia," I said.

"Lithium is what I recommend," he said.

I refused it. "But that isn't convenient . . . for your family. For your husband. You have children, I understand."

"I am not a household appliance," I declared.

"But this isn't an appropriate amount of suffering, my dear! A drug would help you to feel . . . an appropriate amount. I shouldn't tell you this"—he hesitated—"because it puts me in a bad light, but I had a patient who . . . killed herself once, after a friend. She was married to someone I knew. The girl-friend committed suicide and a week later . . . I had no idea," he hinted.

"You mean she was a lesbian? Well, Nicole and I are . . . all *but* lovers. Will you excuse me?" I said politely, rolling myself up into a ball for strength before casting my long neck and long tongue out over the edge, while the doctor averted his eyes from the mermaid foam of my friend's life dancing at the bottom of the bowl.

"JOY LOVE," ORSO instructed daily, "do not come now." And he painted stark, discouraging bedside vignettes, with Nicole still too beautiful to get the attention she needed, the strain beginning to tell a bit. He supposed he hated anyone who saw a design where there was none. In grief as in anger there was an aesthetic. He cited Kierkegaard's brilliantly con-fused *Either/Or* as a case in point.

The first item on every letter was always "i want no theater." After that, when he said "i mean it," it was to say that I would be the first to know when anything happened, that he would do anything in his power to help with my book, with my stay in London. He had not read one word of the letters I wrote to Nicole. Nicole was the most private person he knew. She put them in the drawer next to her bed. He had no idea what I said. He consoled me for my writer's block. Did I know how long it took "evelyn w." to write one of those incredible pages? Orso had had a secretary with a first in Classics from Oxford who had roomed with a daughter of Waugh's.

They had to bring in an enormous machine called the Cruel, which of course no one but he could figure out. Cold water ran through coils connected to a blanket. It rather quickly brought her fever down three degrees. Nicole was brave and in good spirits. She was just being kept alive for one reason, he told me. So that she could come home and finish her poems. She was very tired, and her mother and father wore her out with brief Jewish visits. Her father cried, which made Orso want to open his skull for Xmas. He, on the other hand, could sit very quietly, read to her, let her sleep as he munched Carr's English Water Biscuits (from the tin, of course). Bath biscuits, much better, he informed me, were not available.

He wondered why he didn't break down. He sat there among her things—her typewriter, her picture, the picture of him she liked, my picture, my children's, her pens and music box. He would not let himself weep. He would not let himself go. The good doctors had become his friends and they admired Nicole for having lived through those first three days. It took courage. Like someone drowning, she could have surrendered. They had seen the surrender, that exhalation, that flutter of the eyelids. She verged and fought it with smiles and loving looks.

"I shouldn't do this," he would write, drunkenly, late, deeply pilled, 10 mg Valium, two Placidyl, and his mind running off the page as if he were already living in the dream that he had all the time of flying a very big propeller plane, with friends aboard, flying terribly low, through streets with houses inches away from the wingtips, and he was sweating but confident and somehow landing, but many of the passengers were no longer on board. And he would give me the name and address of an old girlfriend of his, now brilliantly married to some upper-class lush, she had been his girl when she was eighteen, now old, perhaps twenty-nine, who didn't like Nicole overly much, and he would write, the words running together, that he loved her, he loved her voice, which was such pure English sound not even the English could understand a syllable of it. He could. He'd beg me to call her, coach me on what to say, give detailed profiles of her entire circle of friends, which were the anti-Semites and which weren't.

He gave me constant advice about the novel, it would intrude embarrassingly in the midst of bad news about Nicole's worsening condition. He was mainly concerned with his own fictional identity, with his own name in the book. He did not want to be called Hercules or Dante. Orso Orsini maybe. No. He wanted me to use his real name. He wanted to be called Orso Lombroso. Many o's. Ercole was the Italian for Hercules, he'd add. But I would ignore his digressions and transgressions. His lively bursts of gossip. I saw only the love, the friendship, and the grief. My love to you and Nicole loves you, he always said, then censored and admonished. I must not write about cancers of the clitoris or any such. About poems, swans, novels, England, he instructed. Censor sleeps, he would conclude, signing his name "o."

SHE WROTE TO me one last time, a long letter, in her spindly green handwriting, sending me all of her love, all of it.

The night nurse had gone, the day nurse about to arrive to get her ready for breakfast. From where she lay, it seemed one of those perfect days when even the worst of New York's buildings seems justified by the cool light, the clear sky. But she was more removed than ever from that world—the world. Hers consisted of instruments so strange that one expected to see them only on a television rerun late at night. Sound waves had been used to make sure her kidneys were all right, nuclear medicines injected so that her whole body could be scanned and photographed; drugs of fearsome power poured into her; right now she was getting one that was literally brought up from the shades—it must be wrapped in brown paper and kept away from the sun. After, she became quite ill with chills that made her shake as though she was Admiral Byrd's wife without the proper clothing for the expedition. Then she got a fever that only someone with malaria could get. The Camille phase back at Beth Israel at the beginning, when she lay in white gowns with her hair spread around her like a Burne-Jones, was over. Her hair hadn't been washed in six weeks, but this week she could have a shampoo. Her hair was falling out anyway from the chemotherapy. Still—a shampoo. She could weep for joy. The rest of her was merely wasted as cancer was a wasting disease. None of this was romantic, she was afraid, or lovely and she rarely looked in the mirror.

FOR ORSO, TOO, it was a baleful season. Nicole was dying and bankrupting him at the same time. He would have it no other way. Her absence and pain and the eternal IVs sticking into her were more depressing than anything. The money part always brought about a mocking resilience rather than worry. Many friends had offered to help him pay, but he regarded that as dishonorable. Instead he planned to fuck Memorial Hospital. He was slowly going underground, moving $ around and beginning a series of high-toned shrills of outrage at Memorial, asking for detailed bills and explanations. Struggle made the right juices flow. All this no one knew about except Nicole, and she only a little of it. Verb. Sap.

He told me that my letters had meant much to Nicole and that he didn't know which poems of hers I had. He was trying to assemble a large enough batch so that a friend's secretaries on their special typewriters could type them very beautifully on bond paper with automatic spacing, etc., all according to my rather rigid directions. At least Nicole couldn't interpret my directions about presentation without what he felt was a certain rigidity.

When I mentioned her diary, he became agitated. "What diary?" he immediately wrote back. "If such a thing exists, I want to know about it immediately." I let it pass.

AT LAST ORSO wrote for me to come. He had always loved the fugitive and that which did not take root. All the better to see with—the *déraciné*'s virtue. And he was rather glad that he had literally pissed away tens of thousands of dollars on Dom Pérignon, Glenlivet. He said this now because anything that suggested duration did not wear too well with Nicole. She may have wanted it once. A complex web that he would save for our meeting.

*   *   *

FROM THE DOOR I saw Nicole. Her eyes were closed and there was a periodic noise coming from her lips. Her hair was braided on either side of her head, as if she were a child again setting out with her sand pail. A very small man, almost a midget, stood weeping at her side, next to a glazed blond woman in an armchair. A nurse stood in the corner. Orso was sitting at Nicole's left.

"Nicole has been allowed to slip into a coma that she herself arranged with the doctor," Orso said. "You're too late to speak to her. I want no theater," he said.

Nicole nodded her head yes. With every breath she nodded her head and managed a moan. I sat at her side and held her hand. "I was in such a hurry to get here I grabbed the wrong bag," the blond woman said.

"It's Cheyne-Stokes breathing," her father sighed.

"She's not getting enough oxygen. She can't hear, she has brain damage already," he said, blowing his nose.

Awakening, the stiff injured hand moved in mine. She had heard! But her hand moved away from me. An inch away on the sheet. Was she angry at me? Was she afraid that I would sleep with Carl? That I would marry him?

"Orso!" I cried.

"Nicole, Nicole, do you hear me? If you hear me, I want you to open your eyes," he commanded. "Do you hear me, darling? Open your eyes." Obediently, the eyes fluttered whitely open. The lids sank shut again. The shallow breathing continued.

The doctor came. He waved from the door. "I'm glad to see she's cozy," he said, and left, pursued by the parents. Orso strolled to the supply cabinet and stretched a transparent glove onto his hand like a strangler.

"I want you to go and get some rest," he said to Nicole's nurse.

She turned and saw his gloved hand. "Mr. Lombroso?"

"Just leave the room," he said.

"Oh, I can't, Mr. Lombroso."

"It's the right thing—don't you think?" he said to me.

"No."

"Do you think I'm being selfish?"

"No. I think *I* am. I want her to wake up and talk to me." That was what I had come for. To show her how much I loved her. To stop her from dying.

I looked coldly at his red-and-blue eyes.

"That's a little too selfish for my taste," he said, and removed the glove. Nicole's parents returned just then. In time to hear his disquieting performance.

"I have to call Carl to tell him the funeral is tomorrow," he said to me, and picked up the phone.

"The funeral will be tomorrow. No, not yet. I won't be there, of course. I have no interest in funerals."

"Now I won't have anyone I can call," Nicole's mother said. "She was my whole life. Now I will have no one to advise me. No one to call."

"You can call me," I said.

"Who are you?"

"Joy. Nicole's friend."

"Look at those cheekbones. Hungarian."

"I'm Hungarian too!"

An attendant came to give her morphine.

"Why are they giving her morphine?" I asked the private nurse, whose eyes never left the nodding form.

"The discomfort of being unable to breathe," she answered, "is the worst discomfort there is."

WE STEPPED OUT into the hall. Nicole had passed water. Through the parted curtain we could see her stiff blue body being turned.

"A Miss Vaggio," the nurse said, "is in the lobby."

"It can't be Carl," Orso said. "He's in Virginia. He had a baby. A girl. He was going to visit."

"Does Nicole know?" I asked.

"Yes. She knew yesterday. 'That's very funny,' she said."

Then Carl Vaggio, the mystery guest, appeared. Smiling, he leaned against the wall near Nicole's father, as if to pass the time of day. "He really loves her," Nicole's mother whispered to me.

"You have horses in Virginia," Nicole's father said.

"Seven," Carl rasped.

"I have one piece of advice for you. Never put money on anything that eats!"

"Hello, Carl," I said.

His eyes touched all my bases.

"She told me yesterday," the mother said. "She said, 'I think I've had just about enough of this.'"

"I HATE THIS chatter," Orso said. "I wish I were Jewish and could weep like Nicole's father. Anything rather than this ridiculous chatter." I saw the lids raise infinitesimally. Our private line went slack.

"I've given away her eyes. I've already signed for it. I'm going to turn off the oxygen," Orso said.

"Well, at least take off the respirator so she can breathe," I said.

Together we removed the respirator with its green elastic going across the cheeks. She was dead. "I want this, just this," Orso tugged, and the gold band came off; he bent to kiss the open lips that had turned ferocious. "Her lips are already cold with a faint stink of death. I knew she was dead from the relaxation of the sphincter—she wet herself," he said.

"I thought the sphincter was the colon."

"No, it's both."

Admiral Byrd's wife. She lay without the proper clothing for the expedition. Her tan had turned yellow. I kissed her warm cheek half in fear that a growl would come out from between her exposed teeth. There were three long hairs at the side of her mouth.

"Fuck God," Orso said.

* * *

WE TOOK A cab to the East Village, where they lived. Nicole's panty hose from months before were still drying in angular arrangement on the bathroom door. I felt her presence, the old excitement. "It's almost as if she were just here. How beautiful her stockings look!" I cried out.

"Are you crazy?" Orso said. "That's the Jamaican maid's work."

On her cleared desk I saw the diary. It was the first gift I had given her, from the time I was still pretending that I didn't know she would die. A child's five-year diary with a little lock and key. She was afraid to write anything, she had complained, because Orso would read it. The key was still in its plastic wrapping. I opened the small red book, fearing what I would find. It appeared totally unwritten in. The five years were a lie, I hadn't fooled her. She had had no future and we both knew it. I should have at least gone to Mark Cross on Fifth Avenue, I thought, instead of to the nearest stationer's on B'way; I should have bought an enormous book with a combination lock. I should have put more thought and effort into it. I turned the blank pages, feeling disappointed and at the same time reproached, when I came suddenly upon a single sentence. In the middle of nowhere one sentence in green ink. The sentence was about me.

"She lifted her long hair from her neck in a gesture so familiar that it brought tears to my eyes."

Then the phone rang, and I knew it was Carl. Carl on the outside for once, and me on the inside. "I want to be alone now," Orso said. And I knew Carl knew that I was there with him. Orso hung up the phone and turned to me. "I read all your letters to Nicole last night—and sent them to my archives in Wisconsin."

"I thought you never read my letters."

"That was before. Last night was a very different night. You wrote a novel's worth of letters. . . . " He unlatched a black jewelry box and sat down comfortably on the polished wood floor. The drawers opened in zigzag. They were almost all empty. "These are the gifts that Carl brought Nicole in the hospital," Orso said. "Nicole's mother has already been here. She already took all the jewelry."

The jewelry that was meant for me! Even her body was ransacked, I thought. Those green gems gone.

"Her vampire," Orso said affectionately, holding up an Art Deco mosquito. "I will have this as a souvenir of the year Nicole spent with you and Carl."

I sat beside him on the polished wood floor, Orso cross-legged like a Buddha. "What did you say?"

"I'm not stupid. He picked that ridiculous fight. And he liked Nicole. It was clear that he couldn't be my friend and her lover at the same time. I just can't make love to one woman over an extended period of time. It's a symptom of homosexuality," he twinkled. "Don't you think?" His erect penis appeared, a pink crescent over the dark planks. It was the same size as Douglas's.

"Hold it," Orso said.

"It feels very—alive," I said. Like someone shaking hands politely, hoping to escape, to beat it out of there.

He put it immediately away. I slept in my hat and coat on the couch. In the morning I left with an armful of Nicole's clothes.

The next day was her funeral. "It's like a department store," Orso said, coming out of the elevator. His foot was swollen with phlebitis. Her gold ring danced on the chain around his neck. He stood at the front of the jammed room and read the poem we had chosen of Nicole's with red eyes and an uneven voice. He made two mistakes. He finished and walked out. Carl had also walked out. He had gone to Virginia.

"THEY'RE TIGHT IN the crotch," my mother cried, trying on Nicole's plaid slacks. "I have such a funny square-shaped . . . I don't like to be reminded of my . . . sexual organ. I wish she were here to wear them. She was such a blossoming cherry tree of a girl, of a young woman. I wish you could be Bobbsey

Twins again and I wouldn't have to worry about you. . . . Just hold me," she said. "I don't want *him* to be at my funeral. I don't want him to be *the man there.* . . . "

Later, while she was preparing her endless meal—special-treat persimmons, cukes with a wedding veil of mold, unbleached nuts—waiting for my father to pick us up in the Bronx and drive us to the airport, I called Carl Vaggio from her bedroom to say goodbye.

"The baby was very cute. She was very pretty, everybody said."

"Are you happy?" I said.

"No, I'm not happy."

I could hardly hear over the noise of the blender.

"Well, good bye," I said. "I hope you're well."

AFTERWARDS, THERE WAS one radiant week of springtime, during Orso's visit, when the trees in pink blossom looked in at our balcony through the French doors. London opened its iron gates for us, its key parks opened. The albino peacock spread her tail in Holland Park. Orso sat on the sitting-room rug like Buddha and with his thick yellow fingers knifed through a portion of the manuscript that pertained to him. I had written it with Douglas. It was a "joint novel." He liked it. I told him that we were using his letters. He clapped his hand to his breast. "Me?" he said. "My letters?" pressing one hand to his communist-blue work shirt. I knelt at his side. He remarked on my memory, on the dialogue. He chuckled and smiled. I kissed his cheek. "I'm not sure about this, though," he said once, reading on. "I see the word 'torso,' " he blushed.

We returned to New York. It was finished. We presented it to Orso. Early in October I placed it on his lap, and he held it and said, "I will read *this* tonight." He had told me things he couldn't tell anyone else. Visions of Nicole. Cut to the exact end, she dies. Then he would wake up, not frightened, something quite worse, utterly alone, as he had been all his life, except for Nicole. Orso's new girlfriend was with him—she was an old friend of Nicole's—sitting behind him on the couch. He was excited. "Yes, this is me," he said, "this is mine. Yes, I wrote this—except for these funny words, 'Mimi' and 'Zeno.' "

THEN ORSO WROTE to our agent, he wrote to us. He feared it would come to this, and it had come to this. If it was published he'd sue. It would be published over his dead body.

"Did Nicole know what you planned to do?" I sobbed.

He made a little moan. "Of course not," he said. I felt a flare of satisfaction.

"You're either threatening or wheedling," he said, and hung up.

I HAD TURNED my back on the ocean. I was the grave of Jackson Pollock, crushed by the boulder of his weight upon my chest.

I called up a friend for a little sympathy. We taught together. She was a good critic, a "national treasure."

"Well, you just got mixed up with a couple of rough characters," she said. "And if you want my advice," she added, "I don't think you should let your mother in the house anymore."

"YOU MUST HANG loose," my mother cried. "We have a terrible connection. I'd like to cut off his balls," she shouted. "What?" she screamed. "I can't hear you. You'll have to talk louder—I'm in between trains. I'm on my way to an OA meeting. I have to keep moving, y'know. Hang loose! This too shall pass." A subway thundered by like the black winds in Dante that forbid conversation. "I don't want to go on this fast, but I am going towards life. . . . Stop that crying! Maybe this too is for the best. You must take one day at a time. Here's my train," she screamed and hung up.

6

THE DOORKNOB

/ / / / / / / /

"I have a broken blood vessel on my nose that is a wound to my vanity," my mother said. "It has begun to spout like a fountain. I am paying for this divorce through the nose! . . . I don't know whether to move, I want somebody to furnish for me—for one tiny room, one bandbox."

She had moved directly across town from me to an apartment I had never seen but pictured as Matisse's *The Red Studio*. All the bedding stained with blood. She bled from the breast.

I was silent during most of our talk. She said, "A few tomatoes at twenty-nine cents a pound . . . You know you can make a spinach salad, save a little of the bacon dripping and mix it with the oil. I couldn't get you a butternut squash, but maybe I'll get one yet. . . ."

The conversation switched to my father, whom I lamely tried to defend.

"Would you leave a bleeding child?" she screamed. "And whatever disease he had at the end, I would want to be part of. . . . He has no needs—he never had physical needs—he never knew that a man had to give a woman pleasure when he got married. He said so, he admitted it . . . I'm not the most chic person—I wear the same navy thing all the time—I'm getting to be known by the same clothes, but I don't care, what difference does it make as long as I can get there?—I incorporated this phone call in my dressing. I don't believe in clothes anymore. . . . It crossed my mind about Nicole," she said, "saying, 'Let go.' "

"IN MY DREAMS," my mother said, "I was looking for Dad, but there were no knobs on the doors. . . . Oh, the nuisance of having that door without a knob! What are they, breasts?"

"No. Penises," I said.

"They are?" she said doubtfully.

"Then I was beating on a man's chest—I think it was Daddy—saying, 'You're selfish, arrogant, self-centered.' I didn't think of it as my father until there were a lot of ladies around the room (OA members) and there was a big box of shoes—one man's shoes were like a big rubber—and he was letting other ladies sit on my bed and try on shoes. I was brought up that you didn't sit on beds. 'I come first,' I said."

I mentioned the problem of snacks for Douglas. I had to think of something for him to eat when he was hungry late at night. My mother was usually happy to talk about food.

"Snacks for Douglas? I'd like to bash his head in with his junk food. And how they wooed me! The Beech-Nut people. And I didn't want any salt used in your foods. I was ahead of times, so what did it get me? . . . "

My mother was my long hair; then my mother was cut off.

✳ ✳ ✳

ON THE PHONE, I take notes. I doodle. Later, on a peach-colored pad I find "disarray" written over one breast and "horrible" over the other. I've drawn a shapely female torso. In the romantic middle is written: "wedding-time / I didn't want to clean." The figure is cut off at the neck. In a coffinlike shape above her are the words "a home with a long glorious veranda leading to the sea."

This dream she's telling me, called "Getting Ready," which involves cleaning the drawers for the wedding ("I saw my mother clearly and my audience left and . . . "), gets mixed up, in the peach-colored pad, with the stark dream: "I found him in bed with another woman."

"What did you do for sex?" she asked.

"Sixty-nine."

"I taught you that."

"I knew it before."

"Then why did I have to starve all these years? He just lay there," she said. "I took a spoon and fork and I beat him and dug into him—I dug my own grave with this overeating—so maybe that's what it means. There is no happiness to be found at the end of a fork and spoon, I always say."

"IF YOU TRIED a sliver of mango—you'd go haywire," my mother said. "You are taking root, that's all I can say, you are putting down roots in the earth you need for your experience, for after. Nothing is lost. I want you to know that. Wait a minute—I have to go." In a minute the toilet flushed, her voice rising from the surf.

" 'Is that manly' I said, 'for you not to answer a letter that demanded an answer and a confrontation?' And your father said nothing. And I said that I wanted him to come here and to take care of certain bills. But not to come once when he has a key to this apartment during a long fast and see how I am? . . . I will be an asp up his ass! I dreamed I was in your kitchen high up over the gorge in Ithaca, with the back porch and sun in the kitchen sink, and I wasn't eating, and he was, but the table was cleared. I had gotten everyone their food and cleared up and there was a pill lying on a napkin. Your Aunt Ida, the wicked witch, used to have a pill on a napkin like that near her bed when I was a child and I used to think, 'What a waste of napkin.' Y'know, I love pits. When I get a peach pit I suck it until it is lifeless! A mango pit I can't get into my mouth it's so large, but I manage to suck on half of it at a time. It's life to me. Well, it was lying there on the napkin and I don't know why unless I thought it was a pit, but I put his yellow pill into my mouth and instantly there was excruciating pain and my mouth burned and was coated and crusted with white and I think I screamed out. And I woke up with the realization that your father is poison to me and that I must let him go or it will kill me. It was like feeling the hand of God on my shoulder telling me something. I will never forget the sensation of that pain. This nonperson is poison to me. . . .

"I would buy land in Mexico if they would let me, but they are ungrateful dogs—they come here and spread all over, but when Americans go there they very nicely slit throats. But I liked it. I liked the ocean. It made you feel the frailty of your being—you were here one minute, and could be caught and gone the next. I liked coming up against it. 'Nobody's going to get me,' it made me think, until I saw the helicopters over the water. They were out looking for their own people—strong swimmers, handsome, swarthy, strong men (polluting themselves with gallons of Coke on the beaches when they could be feeding on their own coconuts) who were lost, who had gone under.

"I'm sinking, but I'm not drowning," she said.

TODAY I WOULD swim, my mother promised me. A new pool was going to open very near us. I stood at her side in the sun on our hill. I was eight. I had a large folded towel under one arm; I wore my bathing suit. I stood still, taut with anticipation of the other children. My mother shaded her eyes with one hand, gazing into the distance. "No, the pool is still closed," she said, protecting me from polio.

AS A CHILD, I was secretly horrified by her big toe and used red nipples. Later, by the way she treated my father. I was secretly relieved for my father when she divorced him. "Why couldn't you make love to my mother?" I once asked him. "If there was a speck of dust on the coverlet," he answered, "she would object." I believed him. Now I was secretly horrified by the stink of her putrefaction. The doctors had told her it would come to this. But she knew better. When we went to a Broadway show together, A Chorus Line, there were two gay men in the row in front of us. "What is that man wearing?" she asked me in a very loud voice. "That perfume is making me sick," she said. "I think I should ask him to go into the men's room and remove that perfume as best he can." Her own smell was like the plague, like Auschwitz.

ONCE, I HAD lied to please her.

She lay in bed, coral. Her hair coral, her skin flushed coral after a bath, flannel pajamas.

"I took off my nice organdy pinafore," I told her, "and folded it very neatly during the rehearsal."

"You took off your organdy pinafore?" she repeated.

"Yes," I said. "I didn't want it to get wrinkled. I folded it on the chair when I had to put on my costume."

"You folded it on a chair?"

"Yes. While I was on stage."

"No, you didn't, Joy."

"Yes, I did. I was very careful. The first time it got messed up. But then I did it again. I made sure the ribbons were smoothed out also."

"That's very interesting," she said with a smile. "The organdy pinafore is sewn to the dress. Attached. It can't be taken off."

I looked down at my dress and saw the insidiously strong tiny machine stitches. I saw no way out.

"Just a minute—I'll be right back," I said.

I went into my room. The maid, Beulah, was there, ironing. I went into the closet, to think. I stood next to a navy-blue pleated skirt with suspenders. The shoes all stood in pairs at my feet.

Beulah was trying to talk to me. There was no time to be polite.

"I can't talk now," I said grimly. "I have to think."

"Why, I never saw nobody think so hard," Beulah said, ironing slowly.

What if another girl and I accidentally changed dresses— could I have had to take off my dress for any reason? to be measured for the costume?—and I put on her dress and she put on mine. My mother would want to know the name of the girl. Hilary, I thought. Sylvia Singer. But she would call the girl's mother. I could hear my heart. All I longed for in the whole world was a dress whose pinafore came off. Could the teacher from sewing class have taken off my pinafore then sewed it back on? Terror. A blank wall.

"You been in there a whole hour," Beulah said finally.

I came out of the dark closet. Thinking was useless. I decided to admit the lie. I walked slowly back to her room and stood by the bed.

She was turning the pages of the second, smaller newspaper, which my father had brought home the night before. I thought there was something sinister about newspapers, with all the news of what people had done, in black and white.

Never had she seemed to me more powerful, more terrible, more serene. "I'm sorry," I said, "I lied."

She wasn't angry, she was the image of repose. I knew I would never lie again. I would never again love anyone enough to lie to them. My coral mother smiled. "You're forgiven," she said.

*   *   *

MY MOTHER HAD her portrait painted in oils. She wore a black strapless gown with a pink satin diagonal ribbon under the lace, her small beautiful hands, in aristocratic idleness, crossed at the wrist and upturned in her lap. Her nose was not fixed yet. My father had just made the final payment. While we were sleeping, she took a knife and slashed it.

THE PHONE RANG once. I picked it up, dialed, let it ring three times, hung up. It rang again. I held it to my ear like a black snake. My mother said:

"I went to the supermarket and I said, 'Where's Max?' " Her father's name was Max. She went on, "I've known him now about two and half years. Is Max downstairs? No, Max died.

"He was saving me melons—he was . . . He had a heart attack." She was crying. "Scurrying, serious, his work had to be perfect, the seriousness, the commitment, the store, and he was only a worker. . . . I sobbed so in the store the manager, a nice young Jewish man, put his arm around me and said, 'I am going to have someone take you home—you are not going out of the store like this.' " She was crying for her father, I knew.

"Sadness and depression is a habit," my mother said. "Something strange happened. I missed a qualification at OA—you tell your life story and how you got hooked into food. Bonnie. A nice, wonderful girl—a teacher who can't teach anymore. Thirty-one, thirty-two. She 'qualified.' Her mother was there. There was incest in the family. The brother molested her and threatened her with murder over and over. She said I saved her life!

"My title is 'True Grit.' I look like a horse who is still running but who knows full well that the bullet is coming! A thoroughbred with one nostril flaring, who knows that her number is up—still running! A riderless horse! The only thing that rides me is pain. When a president dies or a general or somebody, do they put the boots on backwards in the stirrups? I have a cucumber connection—but I want to buy them Tuesday—I'll have to hassle it out. In my dream I was being x-rayed—cancer of the colon. We have a lot of dry drunks walking around in our organization—they go back. On Mondays I have one egg yolk instead of 2 ounces of nuts and to get it fresh and—I needed the food to cover up my pain. . . .

"I've told you how I feel, I don't think you should speak to this man ever, ever again."

"I can't do that, Mother."

Later I felt bad and called her. There was a busy signal. I dialed again and again, frantic to reach her. Even in the busy signal I smelled death, I heard the snake hiss.

IT IS OUR cooking Friday. From the bedroom window I watch my mother coming down the hill, carrying the two tired and worn-out Merit Farms plastic shopping bags with their horrible motif of little red chickens on a white ground. She is wearing many layers and has to undress instantly when she comes in. Her nipple bleeds from Paget's disease. She has tiny hanging breasts with red knobby nipples. She stains her blouse. At Overeaters Anonymous meetings, they call her 'bleeding heart.'

"Let me look at you. You don't look well," she says. "You need bed rest." She will not borrow my old green slippers. "Give me those," she says, grabbing two Baggies from the pantry counter. She tries to put them on her feet. There is an instant cadaverous effect. Finally, she agrees to wear my slippers and my long lavender beach robe, which has shrunk, with too-high slits on each side. She sits on Isabelle's bed for a moment in her brown stockings of layered cobweb.

"Why are you wearing those stockings?" I ask casually.

"Oh, they're comfortable, and clean, and I don't take off my clothes"—she pauses, coming to the incongruity—"except here. They *are* unattractive, aren't they? Here, read this," she says, handing me a letter.

It was a letter from an admirer.

"My darling Rosie," it began. "When I see you sitting in

your pain, bravely telling your story . . . " It was from a fat girl at OA who was now wearing hot pants, thanks to my mother. It was signed, "Your loving Joy."

"That's the other Joy I've told you about. She's very loving. People are so nice to me there. So many young people seek me out. I can't understand it. And my own daughter won't profit from my wisdom. Y'know, it ruins my day on Fridays?"

Working in the butcher-block kitchen, there is always a diamond droplet at the end of her nose. She refuses a tissue—then she will have to wash her hands. When she finally uses the tissue I bring, she crumples it up and tosses it casually on the butcher block. She does not like waste. She likes "making do." She says my name now with a betraying piety—as if she were lying, or killing two birds with one stone. She is really addressing the OA Joy.

She twists the necks of red peppers and drops them in the blender. She pours the raw livers clutched to her breast into the pan. I watch the pitiful pearl reappear at the tip of her nose.

"I have to carry as if I were a poor person," she says. "And I *am* a poor person. My father had a car. I was born into comfort. And now this! While *your father* rides around in a Cadillac!"

"Mother!" I say, and run my hand down the scrubbing board of her back.

"I am entitled to his services, after my years of hard work and all the meals I cooked his father—he came every Sunday for a meal." While my mother cooked, my father played golf, and my grandfather molested me. There is a horrible pause while she scrapes at a burnt pot. "I had to burn the pot for your sister," she says nostalgically. I remember that Heidi liked her string beans burnt. Or maybe she just said that to please my mother.

"I would have more pity for some cripple on the street. . . . D'you want to see it?"

This is the dreaded moment.

"Yes."

She unzips the lavender robe.

Something is missing. I suck in my breath. Her nipple is gone. As if consumed in quicksand.

Seeing the little door without a knob makes my heart pound.

7

LOVE NEST

/ / / / / / /

"This morning I had such a romantic feeling in my waist," my mother said. "You wouldn't believe what a romantic feeling I had. In my dream I had ordered a large fruit order, very large cantaloupe (an ellipse—very, very large—it looked like a small watermelon the way I used to serve them in boats with the tops cut off in a zigzag). The price of it was approximately three-fifty or three seventy-five. 'This is not a good melon,' I said. 'Yes it is,' they said. 'No,' I said. And then I thought: 'Maybe I'm crazy!' But then when we started to eat it, it had rottenness in it. It looked almost like a womb, I think. As far as the price goes, there are three hundred and sixty-five days in a year. Time! In my life I stayed to prove that I was right. And I was right! And I was vindicated! But I don't like this dream. To be right and to have something rotten? . . . The set is bouncing and dancing—I haven't one clear picture.

"But knowing that I'm ill, and knowing that I would need some help? . . . Do you know I still miss this man? I had a dream—a trip to the Caribbean—the brochure spread out against the newsstand, the whole vista—and Dad was there against the sea, and some carrots and greens and all my lovely food, . . . and there was a boy about thirteen years old—

"Who do you think the boy was?"

"Me?" I suggested.

"Or Dad? He was sort of a corpulent boy. And Dad said, 'Go out this door.' It was a balcony that had two doors. And so I went out and as soon as I did I said, 'Oh no,' and then, 'My God,' and I knew I had gone out of life—to my death. And that is why I must tell you, Joy, that I felt a moment of anger against you. I've had some angry feelings about you. To tolerate the cruelty of this behavior—not just to your mother, to anyone! I brought you up to be too soft. You don't know how to speak out. Then you won't speak out when you're hurt either, and I won't have done my job as a mother. The carrots were the sweetness of life, but sometimes they don't taste so sweet once I add the celery. In the blender, I mean."

I SPEND ALL day in the bathroom, smoking pot. I inhale deeply. When the little light comes on at the tip of the joint I am smoking, it's like the red showing on the tip of a dog's penis. The red excitement like a ruby.

> Thou by the Indian Ganges side
> Shouldst rubies find.

The mirror is the Ganges; I gather rubies by its side. I stand near the toilet and look out crosstown to Fifth Avenue. The little lighted awnings are as familiar to me as the buttons on my dress. All the drunks are dear to me, and the addicts. Every speck of mica. The garish stores, the squat church with a red

door at the bus stop, the traffic islands, the benches, the meager orchard in the middle of Broadway. The tar lake of the
five-and-ten's roof is patched and wrinkled with my harrowing
revisions, its black pools reflect the Dantesque flight of pigeons—on gargoyles and stone ledges, the female shaking the
male off.

From the bathroom window I look out on the Matchbox
cars heading left and right on B'way, on the tiny pedestrians,
one carrying a pizza in a flat white box, another in jeans with
the suspicious walk of my husband, his head ghastly silver.
The lady whom I always mistake for my mother has recently
passed by, frail black slacks sticking out of her ghoulish old
spring coat, gray hair, dark glasses bandaged in white on one
side, with a black patch over the other. A bag lady.

The old Russian from the cleaner's is passing like a sight in
Siberia, pushing a curtained cart.

ONE DAY in winter, walking the long boulevard home from
shopping with my mother, I saw far ahead a scene of puzzling
ecstasy, red, yellow, blue dots circling, enlarging, all grace and
agility. My mother in her felt hat let me stay at the rink and
walked down the hill and up and back again to bring me skates
with double blades. I skated. With what timid yet voluptuous
grandiosity I kept my balance. The maiden ice bore me in my
first illusions. As now grass does.

On the man's dresser near the bed (whose top is the height
at which Hemingway wrote his novels), I clean grass on a
piece of typing paper. Soon the paper rides on thousands of
tiny bearing wheels, the seeds. Scorched wisps of paper from
emptied roaches agonize like souls.

I smoke in the john with the door closed.

When I first smoked grass it went straight to my groin.

"Inhale deeper. Deeper," Douglas cried, jumping up and
down a little as he spoke. We locked ourselves in the bathroom.

Each morning there is one ring. I am just down to the last

intimate half inch of roach, which will scorch the amber spot on the tops of my forefinger and thumb (at first I feared cancer of the fingertip). I give the tiny joint a few futile kisses in parting and tear myself away from Johnny English, who follows the sun from one side of the street to the other and sits like the landed gentry near the hydrant that is his sexual plaything. It is early morning, and the street is sealed in shadow for the most part, and quiet, and refusal to breathe. The flight of a pigeon is miraculous—along the quietly reflecting tinted windows of the third floor in a straight line toward some mirror image of food? —and I wonder that he is not stoned.

I STOOD BEFORE the full-length mirror naked, accusing myself. I have eaten poetry. I have eaten junk food. I had two teeth capped on the left side by the dentist that Nicole and I shared—her childhood dentist—and he gave me teeth like the ones that I saw in her mouth when she died. It has made me look rather wolfish, I'm afraid.

In the book I lost that I valued more than any other, *A Child's History of England* (my father and I had left it on a curb in a carton at dusk and driven away), there were two color illustrations facing each page. The Protestant martyr Cranmer dipping his right hand into the flame because it was the part of him, signing the false and cowardly retraction, that had sinned first. And Queen Elizabeth on the same page alone in a ballroom, arms extended, one toe pointed under her stiff brocade, dancing for an admirer hidden in a balcony.

"Bend over," Douglas said. He had come silently into the bedroom and picked up the feather duster.

All my talents rushed to my skin. He gripped my long hair. "Down on your knees," he said. He looked too fierce, I was unconvinced. He grasped the flamboyant feather duster by its feathers and smacked me with the bamboo stick. I was on my hands and knees, naked in front of the mirror with my hair hanging over my face. My own rear view was a wonderful subject never before attempted in prose or rhyme. It was large and Rubenesque, on a small scale. And it was his property. I was on all fours, dimpled with proud humility, shaking my hair over my breasts and shoulders. He pulled my hair back. The feather duster sang cock-a-doodle-doo to my skin. The whole farm was awake with the pain of morning, with the dawning consciousness of earthly happiness.

There was a visible expansion of his shoulders and chest. The air about him swaggered. He pushed the feathered glory through my loosening thighs. He spread my legs.

All my parts lit up in obedient neon. I was vulgarly displayed: the one-hour cleaners on B'way, the fast-food restaurants, the florist, the shoe repair, the Fashion Discount Center decked with flags.

"You are my slave," he said. "You are nothing but a servant, and you will remember your place and behave as a servant. You are to be at my beck and call. You are to live to serve me, and wear a maid's uniform, with garters and stockings and nothing else. If I say 'lift your skirt' you will lift your skirt. Do you understand?"

In his hand, the feather duster's fire-fangled feathers dangled down. O the dangling down, the dangling down. I feathered into flame. We were blown like feathers on the wind, I on my hands and knees, he naked standing over me. The bamboo sang to my left buttock, to my right.

In the end he lost his erection. But I had lost my last virginity, I had become his. The feather duster lay basking in the sun. Its fire-fangled feathers dangled down.

I was nauseated for weeks and then I found out I was pregnant. I was thirty-seven, and the gynecologist said I could have this baby, but I was too old to have a baby after this one. He would perform the abortion but he would also sever my tubes at the same time. Heidi called from Minneapolis to say not to do it. "You will wake up the next day and mourn the loss of your fertility," she prophesied. I thought if I ever went back to Carl, I would need my figure, not another baby. My mother followed me on the cart all the way down the hall into the operating room, begging me to change my mind.

DOUGLAS DIDN'T GROW till he went to college. His mother's loud voice like an anvil kept him down. He realized this the first night we smoked grass together. A child psychiatrist with huge breasts introduced us to the drug. She came over for dinner. I served lobsters on the Royal Crown Derby red-and-gold plates we had brought back from Ireland. "Joy, you're the most infuriating person I ever met," the child psychiatrist said. "Even when you're high, you won't admit it." Her breasts like the bolster on a bed.

My long hair in the elevator reeked of it.

I suppose everyone knew.

In the hall, my neighbor Lydia Revo said, "Joy, do you have a tool-burning set in your house? There's always a strange smell that I remember from camp—when we used to make leather belts and burn designs into them . . . ?"

THEN I TRIED to go back to the past.

I called Carl Vaggio, and I said in a dark, aggressive voice like my mother's, "If I wanted to, could I come back to you?" I wasn't even sure he knew who I was—it had been two years—but in an instant he said, "I don't think so."

"Why not?" I demanded.

"Because I'm engaged," he said in his rusty voice that squeaked slightly. "Everything is in a mess here," he added consolingly.

"I cut my hair off and I thought of you. I have bangs."

"Oh yeah?" he said, "Cara has bangs too. She's here, visiting me, in the bedroom." (I had met his daughter once, when she was about nine. Dark-haired, olive-skinned, she admired my mauve-and-gray bulky-heeled shoes from Lord & Taylor. Then I lost track of her age.)

When we hung up I hung on to the word "mess." "Everything is in a mess here." I didn't like "mess." It was spring, a Saturday morning, 1976.

The next time I called him, in the fall, I heard his fiancée's voice. I thought she must be some young Puerto Rican girl. I was electrocuted by her happiness. I hung up and called his studio. He answered. He had just returned from City Hall; he had gotten their wedding license. "She has a beautiful voice," I said. "She sounds so young!"

"I don't know how *young* she is," he said.

Then he said the one thing I wasn't expecting him to say. That he wanted to be friends. But he couldn't see me until after he got married. After Valentine's Day. "And the reason for that is the maid isn't coming until then. I have to do all the cleaning myself."

And his wedding bells swung like wrecking balls, demolishing the hours, the weeks. My husband and I go to look at raw space midtown (I must have a change of view, I cannot bear to look out at the wasteland of B'way another minute). "Is this where you're going to build your love nest?" a little old man asks as we stand disconsolate among the columns in the awkward cut-off space. A love nest with Douglas? Impossible. My heart sinks.

My daughter Isabelle turns ten. Heroically I buy her a blue velvet dress, a gray Swiss coat. I call my friend Marlena from a department store: "I think today is his wedding day," I cry. I leave a long Italian kid glove in the phone booth. My last.

Tears in public. Mine. They flood small academic parties. I cry. I talk to an attractive man, and I cry. I talk to his cheery wife, and I cry. Later I tell the cheery wife that her husband has cheered me up. "Oh, he's very good at that," she says. "Did you say he chewed you up?" They drive us home and when I get out of the car, I have stopped crying. "Cheer up, Joy," she calls after me on the hard snow in farewell.

I HAD KNOWN nothing. My own story was not my story at all. Finally, I heard the true story from Carl Vaggio's own lips,

lips disguised and stretched over a terrible facade of plastic teeth.

I went to see Carl Vaggio again, the first uncomfortably warm day in April. He would not let me come to his house. I was to meet him at the studio. My digital clock jumped an hour and I was early, leaning against the door when he came around the corner, a powerful figure altered by a mangy fur hat, more square and rotund and—as I knew he would be— ruined by his teeth. He smiles more. He can't help it. So many years of grinding down every tooth in his head. So far it has cost him eighteen thousand and they are not cemented in yet.

The day before, I'd had a bikini wax. I had the first in London; he has never seen me this way. The way I have always wanted to be. The fine line up my stomach is gone. My crotch is a perfect triangle, my inner thighs baby soft. I am wearing jeans and new high-heeled brown boots, the jeans rolled up to the calf.

"A regressive grandmother," he said. "The boots aren't good."

"Yes, they are!" Inside, the leather is orange and says Dior. "They're beautiful and all I have."

"Pull them down." Obediently, I rolled down the cuffs. I looked better at once. He took me inside and everything was completely different and entirely the same. A few triangles stood around like indisputable broken-off fragments of time, but the rest was circles. Paintings on the floor, some coated with plastic ready for shipping. All dazzling. Cans of industrial paint standing around. Two broken swivel chairs like thrones.

He told me her name. "Heather Ogletree. She's a lawyer," he said proudly.

"How could you?" I cried, "when you were doing so well with Jewish girls?"

"You think about someone for two years," he said.

I was surprised that we were speaking of Nicole.

"When I saw your paintings, I didn't—" They had followed me to London, his fame spread everywhere.

"You didn't recognize me. That's what everyone said."

"No. I didn't see—Nicole."

"What's art got to do with life?" he said contemptuously. I thought he might surprise me with that violent tenderness and passion that she and I had talked of. The amazing lapses of his pococurantism, his Italian nonchalance.

"I was with her on the night she went into the hospital," he said. "I mean, I went home. And when I got home she called me. I didn't go with her to the hospital. Somehow I couldn't face that. . . . I have something for *you*," he said.

It was cocaine. I took some, up my nose. I felt nothing. We were standing. He was before me. I saw the Medusa's head. It was Nicole's, held in his hand by the scraggly curls, smiling and screaming at the same time.

He was telling me that he loved her.

I SAW HEATHER taking a drag, taking a toke. It was a vast space, it was Carl's loft, I realized. He was there, wearing the fur hat. He looked handsome. There were a lot of people standing around. I got closer to Heather, and realized she was sucking on her finger, not smoking a joint, sucking something sweet and gooey from her finger. Then I saw the cake, great and square on the table. There was a colored picture of his art portrayed on it. An isosceles triangle. And in giant script the single word "Labia." It was their wedding; I woke up with a start.

WHEN I SAW Carl Vaggio again, I said, "Do you know what you should've done when Nicole died? . . . You should have married me."

We sat in the larger and smaller swivel chairs, in icy weather, warmed by the tropical blast from the revolving ceiling heater, and Carl said, "Haven't you found somebody else to"—he said this with heavy irony—"love." I could tell by the way his chin quivered when he waited for my answer that he liked me. I was speechless. I shook my head no.

I had almost not come. When I called at eleven, he seemed busy. I said, "Oh well, this week is very perilous."

"Perilous?" he mocked. Then I knew that he wanted me.

"I was unfaithful to you once," I said. "I got pregnant again and had an abortion. I had my tubes severed, and I thought of you. So I can't have a baby," I blurted out.

"I don't want that," he said in his half whine.

I mentioned Orso's villainy. My book couldn't get published because of Orso's threats to sue. It had ruined my career.

"I know," he said. I felt safe once again, invulnerable.

"You can't stay," he said. "Levy is coming, and I don't want him to see you."

Avery Levy was his dealer.

"Why not?" I protested. "I'm nobody!"

"You've got a lot of . . . presence," he said.

It was the beginning of my long ecstasy. My gathering of rubies, my taking of cabs, my beginning the day in the barber's not knowing whether I would see him or not, my tweezing my pubic hairs.

"HOW IS PERFIDY?" I asked.

"Dead," he said. "He died a terrible death. He got something wrong with him—his kidneys—and by the time I got him to the vet it was too late."

I had the feeling I had arrived in the nick of time. We had both learned our lesson. It was not too late for us.

Carl put a portion of cocaine in his nose with a Sweet'n Low scoop. He had a dog with him, one I had never seen before. We left the studio and took the dog for a walk, I running to keep up, on my high heels. "That's not easy, is it?" he said.

This remark was applause to me. I loved the way he noticed everything, the way he appreciated my efforts on his behalf. It wasn't easy to be a beautiful woman, but it was certainly worth it. "Yes it is," I said, and I ran happily along beside him, stimulated by the challenge, proud of my boots.

Then he told me the story of Charlotte the cocktail waitress and the baby that was born on the day before Nicole died. "I had to put some money into a separate bank account for her. It was only a little bit of money, but it's been a tremendous nuisance all the same."

I was thrilled with his confidences, so happy to hear, at long last, his cherished point of view.

We got to his house, on a cobblestoned side street in SoHo. He got out his key. I had stood there so many times before. "Why don't you visit *me* sometime?" one workman drilling the street had said. "You're the seventh girl today!" It had four floors. The ground floor, his painting studio, now had a garage I had never noticed before. The second floor consisted of his drawing studio and a bedroom and office. The third floor had the kitchen and the round butcher-block table in a vast open living space with skylights, and two bedrooms on each side. The fourth floor was for guests, and where the maid slept.

We went to the second floor, so that the new maid would not see us. There in the middle was a great round couch, exactly like a nest. It seemed to be made in the image of the cheerful lint configurations produced by a family dryer. Clothing and scraps and rags partially formed it; blankets and heating pads emerged from it.

"My leg," he explained.

Surrounding the nest were dozens of tiny bottles of correction fluid in different colors.

"Why do you have colored Wite-Outs?" I asked.

"Sometimes I stay up all night and paint with them. The girl where I bought them said, 'You can't make that many mistakes.' 'I do,' I told her. 'I'm a terrible typist!' I showed her my hand." He held up his mutilated fingers.

He showed me their wedding picture. Wearing a Peruvian outfit of billowing white, bordered by Incan symbols, Carl stood smoking a cigar and looking at Heather. She was wearing a homely native skirt and jersey, clumsy sandals. She stood pigeon-toed, scowling at him. Her hair seemed to frizz from his gaze. I was envious, envious of his gaze. "It's wonderful how much she liked me there," Carl said sarcastically, handing me the wedding announcement in an unsealed envelope.

"I should have put it in the mail," he said, apologizing for a point of etiquette. He should have apologized for not marrying me, I thought unhappily. They had gone to Machu Picchu on their honeymoon before the wedding.

Then he was sweeping. "I'm cleaning so I can work," he said.

In the drawing studio was Heather's sewing machine.

He let me glimpse the bedroom. Then I had to stand and hold up posters—maps of New York—against the wall while he stood back and looked. He had gotten them at City Hall at the same time as his wedding license.

"I LUV YOU I luv you I luv you," he mimicked, "and what did it mean?"

I was astonished. He was chastising me. All my words were flat, meaningless things. I had left him and gone to London. His voice was like the gray sandpaper glove that my young mother wore to polish her legs, leaving them smooth, hairless, and covered with a fine white dust.

We sat in the swivel chairs as on a love seat. "Don't take off your boots," he commanded. He didn't want me to get too comfortable, to take off anything. I was ready to make it up to him, to get undressed. I was burning with love. He leaned toward me. A fountain sprang up of all our fiery afternoons like perpetual youth. We were in a Meissen arbor, shepherd and shepherdess. I leaned toward him. "Don't knock my hat off," he warned. He wore a Goodyear cap, hiding his baldness that I had never seen. We were alone.

The phone rang in the distance. I ran to answer it. "Tell him I can't speak to him now," he shouted. I felt as happy as any secretary in love with her powerful boss. When I returned, Carl was making a list.

"What are you doing?" I asked.

"I'm making a list of all the women I ever slept with."

On the margin of his newspaper, in pencil, their seven names. Only seven! He was Snow White in my eyes.

He was like a girl on the eve of her wedding, counting her past beaux. And I knew it meant that he would marry me, that I was the first and the last.

"I will be your reward," I said, and laughed because of my age. I was almost forty. He laughed his assent—dry, helpless heaves. "If you marry me, I promise to get younger," I said brightly.

I had found the fountain of youth.

"At least you're right on schedule," he said, meaning that I was a crazy middle-aged woman in heat. But with Carl Vaggio, of course, every insult was a compliment.

HE SMILED WHEN my poems were called "colorful." One reviewer said, "At their worst the poems are garish." His paintings had been called "garish." When I went back to him, he said, "One time, on a plane, I was reading an anthology of contemporary poets. I looked for you. But you weren't in it."

I wasn't in it. Exactly. I had lost my whole career. I couldn't even look at my own book of poems because Carl wasn't my lover anymore. He had been my gift, my gift of joy, of sexual fulfillment. It was too painful to endure. I had lost everything. Now just being in his presence, I was recovering some equanimity, some stature. He remembered my greatness.

I said, "Every time I passed a phone booth, I felt cut off— that I couldn't call you."

"You already said that," he said.

"I REMEMBER AN old aura," my mother said, "—when did I feel like this? I think. And it was the shingles. When I bought the distilled water in that pouring rain and I bought the Yahrzeit lamps, I had a feeling. . . . After three days the body wants to fast more when you're sick—if I can fast three days will I give myself a medal! God. Bananas."

My eyes opened wide. It was poetry. I wrote it down.

"I'm doing what nobody can do for me. The washing up and the whole thing was against nature. I feel my heart and my organs. You're vicious when you come to pepper. When you're into food you're into food, and if you want to buy Douglas something—he's a forager and a night eater— If you still like this little pot roast, we'll make this little pot roast. . . ."

AFTER RAIN, THE tar roofs have pools that ripple. The stores wear neon like my lip gloss. I cultivate the triangle of pubic hair like a gardener, using my tweezers days after a bikini wax. I stroke the trim goatee with one hand and smoke a joint with the other.

She gives me one ring. I am ready. I give her three rings, then she calls back.

"I wonder what images of me will remain when I go? I have four beat-up granny apples for raw applesauce. Samuel Johnson said whoever writes not for money is crazy. Poetry is sheer lunacy. My lunch is already late. Red Apple has some chicken cutlets. I don't know. Blood on a sheet, a sweater, the blouse, quilt cover. We had won a raffle, a pot filled with fruit. This call was only a token call."

ISABELLE COMES HOME with a little skinny friend from her class. I take one last drag out the window. She is screaming the words to a song, "love stinks." She sits on my bed in her rose Chinese coat, wild auburn curls, huge blue eyes, voluptuous bottom lip and ascetic upper one, voluptuous breasts. She is twelve.

"Love stinks!" Her friend giggles against the wall.

Grass stinks.

"TAKE THAT THING off your head and sit down," Carl Vaggio said. I was wearing a white hat with dangling strawberries that my mother's friend Margaret, from OA, had crocheted.

"I thought you would get tired of me always being the same," I said.

"No," he said. Immediately a state of timelessness ensued. It was like the room full of dazzling specks of color when I woke up in the night as a child. I could not grasp them in my fist. Rubbing the strangeness from my eyes increased it. Two of his helpers were in the studio. He was telling a story about his air-conditioning at home. The repairmen came, tried it, and said it didn't work. They were going to leave, he said. But he figured that they hadn't given it time to work. He gave it time to warm up, and it worked. He was talking to his two helpers and me. And then I did the smartest thing that I had ever done. I raised my eyes to his.

It worked. It started. The giant engine of our love. The fiery furnace.

"There was almost an accident," he said. "I threw my cigar into one of these cans. There could have been an explosion—"

"Would the paintings have been saved?" I asked coolly. They all laughed.

He was going to Florida to "lie down" for the weekend.

8

PERKY

/ / / / / / /

In the morning, my mother said, "Your sister Heidi is a strange bird. I always call her 'my gutsy daughter from Minneapolis.' I said to her, 'I want you to live each day like a man. Have your orgasm, and think, I have to make each day good for Heidi.' She's a hard nut to crack. . . .

"I dreamed of you and Douglas," she added, "an oddball dream—two soldiers in Vietnam—I think it was you and all you've gone through—but they were lured by somebody with a harelip and they had grasses of marijuana stuck through their lips. . . ."

That afternoon, she came over. It was our cooking Friday.

"Watch the bees," she said. We were picking fruit at the Korean place on the corner. The bees jewel the ripest, the sweetest. "Look at this head!" she suddenly cried out with wild enthusiasm, holding up a bunch of celery. "This is the biggest head of celery in the entire city!" I saw a neighbor smile.

I GOT THERE before him. The helpers let me in. I waited for him in the dark studio. Carl came in, full of news. His stride was more aggressive than usual. Peculiarly excited. "Heather has lupus," he said.

"What's that? Is that sickle-cell anemia?"

"No. Dummy. I married Heather because she wanted to have a baby. She had this 'anxiety.' Now I know why she was so anxious. She was sick!"

Once Heather had gone to the Mount Holyoke infirmary overnight for a small operation, he told me. "God knows what they did to her when she was out," he said, like an anxious newlywed.

"Did I tell you the big fight we had over sex?" he asked.

"No."

"She says that the few times I managed to make love to her, she was infertile."

My favorite game as a child was Statues. Someone spun you and then let go: in whatever position you landed, you froze. Now Eros spun me. Just being with him was the answer to all my dreams. I just wanted to stay where I was, sitting opposite him.

My amber rose dangled coyly from the top of my bulky hand-knit turtleneck.

"What do you want?" Carl Vaggio mused, almost to himself. "Money . . . ?" He reached towards me—I gasped!—to fix the amber rose. "No, it's the sex," he concluded, readjusting the chain and placing the rose flat on my chest.

When we had first gone to bed, in my young married days, when I had a brilliant career ahead of me and a husband who paid all the bills, Carl would empty his pockets of huge rolls of bills, fat rolls of fifties. They would lie beside us on a leather ottoman like loving couples, curled together amorously. They were exciting, like big cigars. They made me feel safe, the way my mother felt in my father's arms. Who can separate sex from money, the dancer from the dance?

"I sold my diamond to send Benjamin to camp," I said. He stared at the empty space on my finger. Anne had had an emerald. I could see he was considering what stone to buy me. A black diamond?

When it was time to leave, I said, "Will you make an honest woman out of me?"

"Maybe," he said, smiling. "Try not to be tacky."

"I will," I cried, overjoyed, and left.

I SAW MY father the minute I got on the subway. He was coming from court.

"Dad!" I said.

"What's wrong," he said. "Why do you look so unhappy?"

I couldn't explain that I was happy, that my face had been contorted with ecstasy.

It was like my wedding ceremony. It was an amazing co-incidence, like a blessing, to meet him. Yet I felt guilt, as if I were coming from the bed of my adultery—but I was coming from the hope of a better life that I could one day share with him.

We stood together at a pole. A beggar came by with a cup.

"Would you believe he's been doing that for forty years?" my father mused.

THEN HEATHER WAS pregnant.

But nothing else seemed changed. He still wanted to see me. Our courting continued, like badminton.

"How does Heather feel having your baby?"

"Unfortunately, she considers it *her* baby."

"How does Heather feel being rich?"

"She has her own money."

"What would Nicole feel about this?"

"Nicole doesn't feel anything anymore, thank God."

When I went to the dentist in my building, I found a free newspaper that reviewed Carl. I proudly gave it to him. He tucked it possessively under his arm. "I am your best historian," I claimed. He laughed.

OUR MEETING WAS for twelve. When I got to his studio, the door was unlocked. I walked in and saw him alone at the far end, reading a book. Daniel Defoe's A *Journal of the Plague Year*. I had come upon him reading it once before when I first knew him. It was the literary pose he struck. It was a sign he liked me.

We paced around the garage. I walked several inches above him on a cement curb. I had been ill with a headache and taken two Percodan, I told him. I had taken one and when it didn't work immediately, I took another. I threw up all night. When I mentioned Percodan, his ears perked up. "Where'd'ya get those?"

I told him that my mother had just been given them for her terminal pains. "I take Percodan myself," he confessed. "I started because of my teeth."

He told me what to do. "Empty the bottle. Take half. Fill the bottle half-full with aspirin. She'll never know the difference."

"That's terrible," I said, shocked, not knowing if he was joking or serious. "Of course she would know."

"I can't smoke pot," he told me. "I wish I could. One puff and my lungs close up. I choke," he said helplessly.

I TOLD MY mother. "Doesn't he know he doesn't need drugs if he has you?" she said.

I told her the whole story.

"He gave me five hundred dollars," I said. "He put them in the front pocket of my jeans. 'It's four hundreds and two fifties,' he said. 'You don't have to look at it.' "

"For what?" she said suspiciously.

"For the Percodan. For Christmas."

"Oh well, I like a big spender. I'm glad you have this oasis, Joy. . . . But I don't believe in men, I only believe in husbands."

AT THE END of her life, my mother said she did not want to pay for services. For someone to lift her in and out of a chair. That was too horrible, she said. She did not want to pay.

Before that she said, "You pay a price for every aspirin. The body pays a price, later."

On my birthday she wrote a horrible poem for me. "For My Firstborn on Her Birthday." It was about how I gave her courage, and reached out my young arms to her Auschwitz body like splints, and it was full of tendrils and vines, and how I made her want to stay longer at the fair. It was written in pencil on a ragged envelope. It ended, "I will stay longer at the Fair!" It was my birthday present. Before thinking, I laughed. There was nothing I could do with the poem to help it. It stank. I didn't want to start pushing for improvements when she was at her last gasp. I saw but did not think much about the pale shock on her face.

By now my mother was very ill. Her condition was deteriorating. She was all bones. The smell in her apartment only she was able to bear. It induced self-pity in me so strong, I forgot to pity her. Finally, two men came with a stretcher in an ambulance. I rode in the ambulance with her. She could hardly get to the bathroom before going with them. "Don't bother," I suggested. In her condition it seemed perfectly permissible to soil herself. Again she was shocked.

THE NEXT TIME, I handed Carl a big bottle of pink pills. "Oh good, I even have a headache," he said.

He had a Styrofoam box with him, containing a small painting on paper. It was like a stained-glass window, a butterfly, sky blue. "I stayed up all night to do this," he said. He scraped at the box. The air filled with white chips. He scraped at the painting carefully with a razor. "Let's make sure everything is right," he said. "We don't want there to be anything here that your mother could find fault with." He wrote on it, "For Rosie, xx, Carl." Then he put four holes in the corners to mark where it should be tacked to the hospital wall.

This was our intercourse.

"I wish you could meet her," I said.

"Why would I want to meet a crazy dying woman?" he answered, almost tenderly.

"Because she's my mother," I said.

"How's Perky, your Romeo?" my mother asked. "Tell him I like it," she said, pointing to his painting on the wall. "It's like a butterfly. Like I can fly away. Like stained-glass windows. The soul. I can't tell the time on this," she complained. It was Isabelle's watch I had lent her for the hospital. The face was clouded. "I'll never buy another Mickey," she said plaintively. She reached for some hoarded food wrapped in tinfoil.

"Please take these baked potatoes! Someone at home will eat them."

Nine brown persimmons were ripening on the windowsill. It was a horrible sight. They were entirely brown.

Suddenly, we heard a terrible scream.

"What is that?" she asked, alive to the drama. I caught a glimpse of visitors in the room across the hall. They were black, they were smoking pot. The TV was on.

"It's only television," I said flatly. "All mystery ends here."

After the visit, I left the four baked potatoes balanced precariously on the rail in the hospital elevator.

"How's Perky?" my mother asked. She lay in bed naked, her covers thrust aside. The red snake that grew out of her withered breast reared its head, hissed.

A last effort to expose herself. The exhibitionist.

"I had a dream," she said, "that I was going to heaven, and they told me that I needed a lawyer. And I knew that if I could get the right lawyer, if Daddy was my lawyer, I wouldn't die!"

"Men visited me," she said. "They were here talking to me all night. . . . And the sad thing is—I answered them! It's the Percodan," she said.

THREE TIMES A week I go to the barber. In case I see Carl, I want every hair to be perfect.

My friend Marlena doesn't understand this. "No, love isn't about how your hair looks," she says in her simpering European accent, "love isn't about hair." Marlena has very little. She always covers her thin hair with a scarf. But Carl Vaggio is so great, so exalted, that he deserves my hair to be at its very best. My passion is in every hair.

And Tony doesn't charge me much. I am his "favorite customer." I sit under a bib with my head backwards in a basin and my knees locked against Broadway. Anyone could look in and see me with my hair wet. Then Tony does it up in a towel, and I sit in the chair. His nose is red like Rembrandt's, his coffee steams with rum. My bangs are crooked. But he makes me look beautiful time after time. My hair curls under slightly in a cape. He shows me the back in an oval hand mirror. My silver hairs he calls "personality." He says, "You must keep ze face." (Face? Faith?) I go upstairs and dust myself with talc, and dress. I call Carl at twelve, and he says to come.

At twelve-five my mother calls. We talk for a minute, then she lapses into silence. The phone is somewhere on her body or on the bed. You can't hang up on your mother on her deathbed, I think. Then I hang up. I want to put loud, girlish music on the radio and concentrate on my makeup. I am seeing Carl Vaggio!

When I get downtown and go through the shabby door to the dark studio, the garage, I sense immediately that something is different. Something has happened behind the scenes. Electricity is everywhere, like static cling. Carl is dressed differently. He is bristling with aggression, with resolve.

I am on my knees. I feel as if I belong here. A tiny flag of kingly red silk, patterned with a scene from a hunt perhaps or something even more exotic, is sticking out of his open fly. His cock is washed. I have not seen it for four years. It is like meeting a European stranger. I am on my knees in my high-heeled boots. It is life-giving as my mother's milk. It is our first sexual contact in all these years. I feel as if heaven has opened again on my birthday and my father's trading cards pour down. The taste of his sperm is like the key to heaven, the key to the Museum of Modern Art.

Quickly, as always, it is time to go. Before I leave I have a few puffs of a joint, and then I take a cab to the hospital. The Hospital for Joint Diseases. It is almost a joke. Or a dream. Sitting in the back seat of the cab, on the edge of the seat, my mind radiant and blank as hammered gold, suddenly I am having an orgasm.

The cab explodes. It is more violent than any war movie. I am blown into the sky. The cab is flying. The driver suspects nothing, I never even stir. I am blown bodily into the sky. I try to fasten my attention on the back of the driver's neck, I search for any color, his cap, any clue, but I can find none. Nothing to remember this by. Nothing to take away with me. Everything is out of my control in a kaleidoscope of pleasure. Someone is holding it up to His eye and turning it.

Then I am returned intact.

Afterwards, the premonition that this was to be the peak of ecstasy. That it would never happen again.

When I get to my mother's room, the nurse is hovering over her; Carl's painting is on the wall facing the bed.

"Did he say anything?" she asks.

Four disparate words. She meant did he ask you to marry him. Her question puts me in a very bad mood. Always I told my mother everything. But now for the first time I hold back, I withhold my joy, my sadness. "No," I say, argumentatively, "there's nothing to say." I do not want to shout the intimate details of my affair with Carl Vaggio into the nurse's ear. I shake my head angrily. Then my mother closes her eyes and

I see her like a fish at the end of a line traveling fast down the stream to death.

She is jerked off, surrendering.

She can't stay any longer to hear if Carl Vaggio is going to marry me.

She goes into the coma from which she never awakens.

WHEN I WAS eleven, Joan Feldman, who was my age and lived in my building, called me and invited me to a hen party. I was ecstatic. I lived in the basement apartment, she lived in 8B. Every Friday, my family had cold cuts for supper, coleslaw. We sat down to eat. I soared towards 8:00 P.M. The walls collapsed; I was escaping. The phone rang. The party was canceled. I wasn't disappointed, I noticed. The thought of freedom had been so intense.

I was called at 4:00 A.M. by the hospital. My mother was dead. I felt the same sense of escape and freedom as when Joan Feldman had invited me to the hen party. The prisoner was freed! My suffering was over. I put on black.

My father and I choose the coffin. I favor thrift and haste. I quickly pick the cheapest. Barely plywood. The way she lived her life. He chooses mahogany with gold handles. "I think we can afford better than that," he says, "this one last time." We compromise on teak.

There are over three hundred mourners at her funeral, members of Overeaters Anonymous. Heidi insists on sleeping in the closed funeral parlor, staying with the body all night. She wears an unfortunate black angora sweater. Black wisps flying everywhere; like Medusa in *The Clash of the Titans*, which I had seen recently with Benjamin. I noticed the resemblance to my sister even then.

WHEN I GOT to the studio at noon, Carl wasn't there. He would be late, I was told. I sat happily with three helpers on swivel chairs. A black ribbon on my lapel. Then he came. He knew at once she had died. "You're mourning," he said. "I'm sorry."

I was skating with double blades. In all my brittle joy, gliding on the pearly ice of my oasis. The oasis that my mother wanted for me. Skating toward the explosion of happiness that would be like a mother-of-pearl staircase to heaven.

"It's just fake mourning," I said.

The real mourning waited for me underneath the thin, hopeful ice.

Later I would think of her happiness when my father visited her bedside. For once her attention was not on me like a spotlight. I didn't realize why she was so excited, so happy. I was thrust into the shadows. She was like a young girl, a teenager, beside herself with excitement, dying. "Try not to worry about anything," he said to her. Those were his last words to her. "Try not to worry about anything." And it would be like falling. The sensation of falling. Her unhappiness is a bottomless pit I am perpetually falling through.

After my mother's very first welcome-home visit when we got back from London, I found the word "toxin" scratched on the elevator door. She must have scratched it on the fresh black paint with a key. How could I have closed the door on her and let her stand out there in the hall waiting for the elevator alone, I wonder?

She sat on my couch at the opposite end from me, the room filled with marigolds from her sister's friend's garden. They disguised the stench. And she read me her writing, about my father. I said nothing. "It's good, isn't it?" she said expectantly. I could barely mumble "Yes." Now she is my sole mentor.

She is my mother tongue. When I read her writings, it is like finding a hoard of roaches, a jewel.

"Look at my breast," she said.

I fell to my knees. An evil snake hissed at her bosom. The stench was unbearable. The knowledge that she carried this with her and could not leave it, this death that I could hardly stand to look at for one moment. "Mama, Mama," I said.

She was carrying around with her her own worst enemy. She girded herself with the smell of fish shops, lingering there as she once did at florists. The smell that was unknown to her as the smell of grass to me. Wearing the unbleachable rag of the sorrow of my father's escape. "There's a lot of metal in you," her nutritionist once said. And once over the telephone she told me she had identified the smell.

"What is it?"

"Fish!" she said.

The shaping up of the material—blocking it like a sweater on a towel on a glass table—is good because it suggests that it belongs to my mother, that it was once my mother's.

Mama, I just made your cabbage soup. Hot and sweet and fragrant, I am perspiring as after lovemaking, my clothes limp and steamy in the lemon and brown sugar of your ethereal beauty.

When I open the trunk of old photographs I see her sitting in the gray surf with her back to me, looking at me over her shoulder in a half-familiar gray two-piece bathing suit. She is radiant. I look at her thighs. They are firm, tapering. The impossible has happened. All her skin fits!

"Mama, Mama," I cry. My face screws up in anguish. I am almost an infant, I almost bring her back. Mama darling, my love, my best friend.

My mother is the soothing balm on my fingers helping me to write. ("You don't ask a Hiroshima victim with scorched blistered fingers to pick up a pen and write," she wrote, "without first applying a soothing balm to her fingers.") I feel her style like the hand of God on my shoulder, telling me something.

I MET HIM at the studio. Everything was being moved. Carl was moving! I had known nothing about it. He could have vanished, I could have arrived and found the studio a garage again, the door locked, the place empty. Instead, Carl stood beside me surveying the last moments of his life there. I was included in his plans. "Now I have to say goodbye to everything that happened here," he said. I tugged at his sleeve. "C'mon," I said. I counted on the future. Nicole had happened here. His love for her. I stood near him and urged him to come away. The future was ours.

Parting, I said, alarmed, "I don't have your new phone number!" He stood, a famous artist, outside the cab and wrote the number in Nicole's little leather appointment book, which I still carried around with me.

9

THE NEW STUDIO

/ / / / / / / /

The New Studio took up an entire block. My eye fell on a gold rag on the floor. A mere rag, and it was richer than anything I had ever known. I wanted my children to play with that rag.

More than anything in the world, I wanted to marry Carl Vaggio. I had liked adultery, but now I was ready to fling caution to the winds. I was ready to try love. My mother had wanted me to divorce Douglas. Carl Vaggio was my "equal," she thought. I was fulfilling her mission. My mother would not have died in vain if I could marry Carl. My marriage to Carl Vaggio would cancel out her unhappiness. I imagined my happiness like the pot of porridge that never stopped overflowing, filling the streets; I would be like the children she told me about, who go to school spoon in hand, who eat their way to school. My happiness would be so great, I could never put down my silver spoon.

Carl said disparaging things about his own children, Cara and Dennis. But about mine, he was receptive. "They sound a lot better than my animals," he always said.

His retinue of helpers gathered around and, since it was the first time I was there, he formally introduced me.

"This is Joy, she's part of the work crew. One of the team." Then they left, to do their respective tasks. We were alone. I was awaiting the grand consummation of past, present and future. I felt that I was at court, at Versailles. At a distance, one young man stood gazing up at the ceiling, eating a sandwich. "I pay him eleven dollars an hour to do that," Carl said.

For each rendezvous, I dressed in the expectation of undressing. I was wearing Erace on my inner thighs to cover up the red spots left from tweezing. I hoped that today would be the time.

"I know one thing we could do if we were married. Make a porn film," he said.

I was a little uncomfortable at this suggestion but said nothing, prepared to overcome all my foolish qualms. If not for them, I could have been married to him all along, I could have had his children. In the past, I had let the most ridiculous considerations spoil my chances for happiness. For instance, I had been horrified by the way Carl allowed himself to be taken advantage of by merchants who came to his house with pre-Columbian jewelry or antique American Indian rugs. I thought he was too soft. He did not seem to want to drive a hard bargain. Also, Carl had mentioned once that he did not like to make love at night, when he—they—lay down to sleep. He did not think it was a very sexy time. "Maybe sometimes in the morning," he added. This upset me. I thought night was the perfect time. Also, the cat, Perfidy, had scratched his daughter Cara. "Her hair must have excited him," Carl said.

"He leapt from the stairs at her face." Carl just accepted it. I had not felt that my children would be safe with him and his cat. I saw how stupid I had been.

"I figured out how many times we did it," he said. He told me some gigantic number. (Probably he calculated that we did it twice, twice a week, for five years. Summers I had off, I went to Nantucket with Douglas and my children.) "I'll say one thing for us," he said, "we've had a lot of practice."

I put myself entirely in his hands. I looked at the floating city clock through the deliberately positioned porthole. I gasped in amazement. "I'm a good architect," Carl admitted. I gazed in awe at the ceiling. At the stately pleasure dome. I was in seventh heaven.

"I know one thing I'd like," he said, "watching you spend my money. Because I think it's against your nature."

This was intimacy, I thought. Nicole was wrong.

"THERE'S MONEY IN you, Joy," my mother always said. When I had gotten my first teaching job, at the airport my mother had kissed me goodbye on the lips. I was flying to North Carolina. Any man within a fifty-mile radius would find me, she said. But now I was unemployed. I had been "retrenched" after three years at City College due to the city's budget cuts. Poetry writing was not seen as vital.

"Get a job," Carl said.

"I can't," I said helplessly. "I'll work for you. Every morning, I'll wake up, put on a little uniform, and do things for you all day." With Carl I was about to get a *raise*. "I am very mindful of my 'elevation,' " I said, showing off my new English vocabulary.

There was a streak of fur past my legs. "Oh, you have a new cat," I exclaimed.

Another followed it. "They live here," he said.

"What's its name?"

"He doesn't have one."

"Poor cat," I said.

"Why? To live in this"—he gestured grandly—"with his mate?"

"To live without people, without regular habits," I explained, trying to make him want me. To make him picture living with me. A cat can look at a king, I thought.

I HAD JUST been to the barber. I saw from the sudden worry on his face that he was looking at little black cracks across my cheeks and nose. The devastation was only a few cut hairs. And then I saw Carl's mind brush away the cut black hairs and I was restored to him, whole, perfect in his eyes. And that is how I came to know he intended to marry me.

It was pouring. We climbed a ladder that was totally vertical to the high second floor. Rain fell. We were climbing behind a waterfall. We reached a secluded grotto. "I will make this nest for you," he said, tearing the new insulation out from the unfinished walls and ceiling, then lying over me. "You have such a look of complete abandon on your face," he said gently. He raised himself over me, fully clothed, on the pink and silver bower. "Sweet baby, sweet baby," he said.

I was too grateful to be disappointed that it didn't go further. That nothing more happened. I knew he was nervous. "Anyone could climb up here," he said, looking down at the men in overalls.

"Then you'd just fire them," I answered.

Besides, I shrewdly told myself, the very fact that he didn't sleep with me now meant that he intended to marry me. It meant that his intentions were honorable. If he wanted only to sleep with me, then he would sleep with me now. Like me, he wanted more. It was very old-fashioned. Almost medieval. This heightened chastity was more erotic than anything I had experienced. While I was not undressed with Carl Vaggio, I could remember so perfectly every detail of when I was. He could remember. My body was more perfect now than ever. We could afford to wait. It was a slow dance. A minuet.

* * *

A WEEK WENT by. "Fancier and fancier clothes," he said. I glided in in my high-heeled boots. Fine red wool pleated skirt from Bendel's. Incredibly subtle tight dusty-pink top also from Bendel's a year before. I wore my mother's amethysts on a long gold chain around my neck, each faceted amethyst imprisoned in a gold band. "I don't see why you don't buy some hiking boots," he said.

I bought new jeans that had no pockets. "Can't you do anything right?" he said. Tender mock scorn. "Now when the look is supposed to be 'all pockets.' "

"When we get married, we can get off drugs," I said.

"I already did that," he said, "with Heather." I was crest-fallen. "I thought you'd be glad." Heather had lived next door to him. I had met her on the street once when I was walking with Carl. She was with a young bearded doctor, his white coat and stethoscope flying. Her hair was a tawny bush; she was pigeon-toed. Orso said, "When Nicole and I first met her, years ago, she was a dish! But she's not a dish anymore."

"I could never be glad about anything you did with Heather," I said.

MY FATHER MARRIED Ruth, his secretary. I went to the office; I saw him writing a law brief, his lips pursed tensely in concentration. I saw her sitting across from him at his desk. I knew at once. From his aura while he concentrated, working. I called her the next day to say how happy I was that she and my father loved each other. "I don't know what you're talking about, Joy," she said. Six months after my mother died, he married her.

"How does your father like banging Ruth all the time?" Carl said.

I ARRIVED AND Carl was wearing red satin boxer shorts. Under the red satin, his testicles showed. Like my father's when he sat in boxer shorts in the lime-green armchair in

Riverdale. Large untidy tumors protruding at one side. A long time ago, Carl and I had been in bed and he told me that he had just read an article in *The Village Voice* about lesbians. "They can come fifty times," he said shyly. Then he mentioned "penis envy." I had penis pity, I told him. He laughed. "That's a good idea," he said approvingly, "your *best* idea."

I had penis pity now, but I didn't think it was a good idea to mention it. Instead I said, "What I miss most is . . ."

"What?" he said. I could tell that he really wanted to know, but I feared words might keep it from happening.

"I don't see why I have to ruin *everything*. . . ."

"You're not ruining anything. What?" he reassured me.

And so I said it. "When we lay on our sides and you entered me from behind."

"Oh, I do that with all my girls," he said, "with all the girls I sleep with."

ONCE IN THE summer when he was mysteriously absent for two weeks, seeing him again at the New Studio, I said, "I thought you had been taken hostage." It was the time of the hostage crisis in Iran. "I should *be* so lucky," he said, in a New York Jewish cadence that hinted at worse troubles. He was almost a Jew.

Once I didn't call him when I was supposed to. It was the time I went to the Playboy Club in New Jersey with my father and Ruth.

"I thought that just as I was on the point of possessing you," he said, "you disappeared. You vanished."

"I had to go a long way for this tan," I replied. "All the way to the Playboy Club in New Jersey."

He had just come back from Brazil, and smiled.

ONCE I ARRIVED after seeing my father at his office. "How's Ruth?" Carl asked.

"Fine," I said. "She was wearing a pink pants suit." Carl was with his helpers in the vast new blond space. He had to go to the bathroom, he said. There was no bathroom. Only a urinal. He held up a gaudy section of one of his paintings for a shield, and peed behind it. Like Henry VIII, I thought. His stomach also was huge, like King Farouk's. He sent me for a Blimpie for him.

IN THE FALL, on Veterans Day, he said he would marry me. I looked at him with reproach, not believing my good fortune. We were sitting in the New Studio on two swivel chairs on the second story. "At first I thought it was—unlikely," he said.

"Unlikely" seemed a terrible word.

"But now it seems like a better idea."

My luck seemed boundless. "But now it seems like a better idea" more than made up for it.

He leaned towards me and we kissed.

It was our first kiss in all this time. A solemn pledge. It seemed like majesty.

I still could not believe it. Our short interview was over. I ran out on the street. I was carrying Nicole's green Chinese parasol. Some construction workers on the corner started to talk to me. Waiting for a cab, I glanced over my shoulder at them, these innocent bawdy witnesses of my newfound America, my empire. And there was Carl. He had come out after me with a dog, a Shar-pei on a leash. I ran to him. "Goodbye, I love you," I said.

"I love you too," he said shyly, "more than anything—in the world."

Again, early in November, he said he would marry me. Early in December he said he would marry me—soon. "I'll marry you next year," he said.

WHEN HE DECIDED to marry me, I saw what he was thinking—the funny cruelty. Heather would accuse him of leaving her because she couldn't have a baby. He would laugh—dry, helpless heaves—he was leaving her for someone who couldn't have a baby. My severed tubes! That would be his defense.

Then Heather was pregnant. If she died in childbirth because of the lupus, he wanted me to bring up the baby, he hinted. I held on to my happiness. I closed my mind to the fact that Heather had not gotten pregnant by herself. I was drowning, but not sinking.

Then Heather miscarried.

I am in my glory. The future opens its peacock tail for me. I ride triumphant in a convertible to Douglas's sister's pool. Isabelle has just gotten her first period. She won't be able to swim if she doesn't use a tampon. In my hard joy, I make her try at least eight slender tampons before giving up.

I think that there are a lot of pools we will be swimming in!

In the spring, Heather got pregnant again.

As soon as I got to the New Studio, he told me. "Imagine me fucking you when Heather is six months pregnant."

"No!" I cried.

I ran out. I walked in circles, suddenly getting into a cab and going to his home. It was about half past one. I was terrified that I would miss him. I remembered I had said, "I would like to run Heather and the baby through the belly with a bayonet." When we were almost at his house, I saw him. He had just bought two papers; they were folded under his arm. I burst out of the cab. He took my arm and steered me toward the studio again.

"Why did you do that? Why did you leave?" he said. "I put aside this time especially for you."

As we walked, to distract and calm me, he read aloud from the desperate personals.

When we were opposite his studio, its entrance open-windowed and inviting like paradise, I slapped him hard across the face. I was looking steadily into the eyes of a stony-faced woman—who was hoeing her garden—as I did it.

*   *   *

AT HOME EACH moment was unbearable. I needed a Valium. I went next door to Gwen McMann, the Valium lady. Her ceiling was falling down in tatters like a wedding veil. Ms. Havisham. Her large bedroom was peopled with thousands of pill bottles. Her new lover was a druggist. The sight cured me. Just to look was an overdose.

In the middle of the night, I woke up in despair and smoked sinsemilla that Carl had given me. He had bought it for Heather but she never touched it. "I mean *never*," he said.

The next day, I called him at home. To my amazement, he answered.

"You just caught me," he said. "I was almost out the door. I'm on my way to Europe for a few weeks—to think about whether I want to be involved with someone like you."

For two weeks my thoughts are sanguine. I relive those chaste moments, first freezing in his old studio, then rained on in his new, which was the Taj Mahal but still unfinished, crawling with construction workers. The thrills broke later in my stomach like surf. I see the canvas covered with highlights, certain moments. My face cracking in little black lines when he looked at me after a haircut; climbing a ladder under a waterfall in the midst of the men in overalls; the nest that he made from insulation that he tore from his own half-built studio. His "mausoleum" he called it. He spread his peacock's tail.

I see him framed against its rainbow.

Glorious. Male. Triumphant.

"Sweet baby, sweet baby," he whispers.

I cannot forget how he came up from behind and surprised me when I leaned out a front window looking for him; or his rapacious glance across the ballroom of his work space. And especially the time we lay on the new blond floor during his lunch break. He was taking a nap, to get an idea. He had to get, not a good idea, that wasn't good enough, it had to be a "great" idea. I curled against him, the way I used to in bed, while he hid his face in his hands. It was too much like a dream, I had a terrible foreboding—a premonition—and I didn't know that he was weeping as he pretended to sleep.

AS SOON AS he returned from Europe, I called. "Why don't you get a hotel room for us?" he said. "I'm tired of making love to women who are half dead."

First Nicole, and now Heather. He had decided he deserved me, after all.

I called every fancy hotel in New York. They were all filled. It was the first weekend of spring, they explained. Finally, I got a room in the Biltmore, under my name. The day arrived. I put on my hot-pink dress like a tent, designed by Brigitte Bardot. Pink stockings and green high-heeled sandals on my feet. I stood in front of the full-length mirror on the bathroom door for an hour that way.

I called Carl at twelve. He wasn't there. I called him at home.

"I'm sick!" he said.

"What is it?" I said, all concern. This was a very ominous turn of events. I was afraid that my luck had failed me.

"The flu."

"Oh," I said, pretending to be relieved, "that's nothing."

"It's amazing what it's done to my intestines," he said. We talked a little more. He was obviously sick. I sounded tortured. My happiness was in mortal danger. I was afraid that Heather was there, nursing him. Finally, he said, "Just cancel the reservation. They won't mind—if that's what's bothering you."

I went to my father's office.

I was wearing my pink bridal tent. I told him about Carl Vaggio and me. To make it real.

"Oh yeah?" my father said. Just like Carl Vaggio.

10

THE HORSE FARM

/ / / / / / /

*A*fter Carl said he would marry me, I relaxed. Douglas dressed up as a woman. "Remember when we went to that Halloween party?" Douglas said.

I remembered that I wore my father's hat, a black smudged mustache. I lost my headache. Douglas was a woman, wearing his rolled black socks in a large bra we borrowed from Pierrette.

"I liked that," he confessed.

He was wearing a green-and-white-figured hostess gown that Marlena had given me. He had squeezed into it, forcing the zipper up the back. He had squeezed into it in the closet, with amazing tenacity. His determination excited me. It didn't close all the way. I saw the white V of his back, his lips with my red lipstick on them. As a woman I loved him, I understood him. He was strangely beautiful. Clumsy, touching. I was looking at someone who had already experienced the ultimate disappointment. I felt the rush of power, the plush swelling of the groin. I felt what it must be like to be a man. I thought of having his broken toe broken again and fixed, so that the sight of his white tapering toes would please me, and my Chaucerian change purse swelled. My nether lips.

He was my wife. His being my wife meant I was a free woman. I was free to marry another man, to marry Carl Vaggio. This was my wedding night.

"How can I be your wife?" he whimpered.

"Dolores," I said. "Dolorous Dolores." For he is gloomy, meditative, his lips drawn down always as if there is a bitter taste in his mouth. I make love to him in my grandmother's gauze apron, in my mother's black lace mantilla, in garter belt and stockings. Once he had asked me to darken my areolas with lipstick; now I ask him to.

"My mistress," my husband said. It is the language of a dirty book. One I haven't read. It means he is my servant.

It lasts a week. Afterwards, when I hear him say "hello" on the phone, the word all drawn out, distorted—in a phony deep voice—"hallew"—like a butler—I get sick.

"Indeed," Douglas says. The more defeated he feels, the deeper his voice gets. "Indeed," he repeats, in a fake British accent. His pretentious butler's voice. My own clothes in the closet, my makeup, my lipsticks lined up on the sink, are all ruined for me.

I TELL HIM I want a divorce. We are waiting impatiently for his rent-controlled apartment to become available on January 15. It is practically no rent in the Village. He is almost looking forward to the move, to being a bachelor again. He has been dating other women. One night his mother called and I said Douglas was out on a date. "He shouldn't be!" she yelled. I was amused. Douglas even took out a little divorcée in the building from the third floor who had two adopted children and had once called Isabelle "supercilious." *That* I thought was disloyal. Douglas had decided that he would date well-to-do women, who could pay for tickets to the opera, and that he would save money that way. I didn't interfere with his plans. It had been our joke all along that he didn't mind if I was having an affair with Carl Vaggio, as long as Carl paid for the children's shoes.

He had told me that he wanted to be submissive in sex. Even though he told me, I had no idea what he meant. I thought that you were either gay or straight, that all heterosexual men wanted to be the aggressor. We had gone to a sex therapist my gynecologist recommended. When Douglas was on top of me, I cried, I didn't feel that I was *under* him. I climaxed; he didn't; but I felt no sense of regeneration. It was a wasteland. I felt like a ballerina being lifted in the air by another ballerina. Where was the handsome prince in tights?

Douglas told him that he liked big women with big feet. I sat weeping, looking at the little feet that were my pride and joy. The doctor said: "Then what did you marry *her* for?" Douglas had no answer.

I had not gotten a divorce because I didn't want to bring up three children alone. I had not gotten a divorce because I thought I was too perfect to have made a mistake, too perfect to have married the wrong man. My mother had made my father impotent. I thought I could make any man a man.

I changed my mind when it came to marrying Carl. Marrying Carl was like marrying the Prince of New York, a chance to restore the kingdom, to improve everyone's lot. It would be better for Douglas. The children would come with me, but I would leave him the apartment. He would return when I moved to Carl's house in SoHo, and everything would be kept intact—my mother's Persian lamp and matching glass beaded bowl in the living room, the candelabra on either side of our bed, the glass table in the dining room, the Persian carpets, the children's rooms. The children would visit their father weekends. Carl Vaggio would pay for their shoes. Everything would be the same as before only better, a million times better.

It was a great extenuating love.

In the words of a Shakespeare play: Jack would have Jill, naught would go ill, each man would have his mare again, and all would be well.

It was only when I saw Douglas in Marlena's half-zipped hostess gown with the green-and-white picnicking couples going from shoulder to floor and my red lipstick on his lips, that I could admit to myself I had made a mistake.

It was then I told him I wanted a divorce and we decided to separate. We waited for his apartment. We went to bed.

Douglas whimpers in his sleep. He protects his groin with one hand. All weekend I had disliked him for his bitter expression, and for his silence. He can't speak. "We've said it so many times before," he says. He laughs and throws his hands up. He does crossword puzzles. But I had tricked him. Knowing I was going to marry Carl, I had subtly encouraged him to reveal his true nature. And he had succumbed. Like Achilles disguised as a woman spinning, who is shown a spear and betrays himself by reaching for it. Then I turned the new knowledge I had of him against him. When he was most vulnerable, most sexually honest, I asked for a divorce. And I had promised to love him forever and to leave him only in death.

Suddenly, it is a horrible picture of myself that I see. Suddenly, I dislike myself so much that I say:

"Do you want to do it one last time?"

"Can't you see I have to be alone?" he answers.

I am up all night crying.

"Indeed."

DOUGLAS AND I went to the Thalia to see the fifty-year-old film *Napoleon*, by Abel Gance. I thought I saw Carl in the front row. White shirt, sleeves rolled up, gold wedding band. I knew it wasn't really Carl (Carl had no white shirt, no wedding band), but I willingly suspended disbelief, I let myself think it was. The man in the front row became Carl; and Carl merged with Napoleon: the artist and the strategist merged. I was Jospehine. That night Carl's father died.

The Wednesday before Christmas, when I saw Carl again, he told me, "Something happened to me when I saw my father lying there with a tube coming out of his penis. I didn't know how I could go on. But I said to myself, 'You've made a life; now live it.' "

I was sorry that his father had died. Anne had hated his father, he told me. "She thought he was so terrible. Well, she was right about that," Carl said. But I knew I would love his father, that his father would love me. I did not know that when Carl saw his father lying there with a tube coming out of his penis, it would make him want children of his own even more.

"At the funeral," he said, "they made him out to be Jesus Christ."

He was going away, to his mother's, for Christmas. We were to meet December 26.

I called the studio.

"Carl can't see you," Roy, his helper, said. "But he walked all the way over here to tell me that. To tell me to tell you," Roy said, as if impressed.

Douglas moved out in mid-January.

IN FEBRUARY, I heard from Orso that Heather was pregnant again.

The last time I called Orso, a year after Nicole's death, he had told me he didn't want to know people who no longer had anything to do with his life. "I never called you," he pointed out. "You have always called me."

Now I broke down and called him again. Orso said, "I took an exotic journey a few Sundays ago. To Carl's horse farm in Virginia. We went in two cars."

"Like a cortege," I said wittily. But it was my own funeral.

My mother taught me to read one day when I was home

from school, sick. I was in bed holding a book—when horses started galloping across a field. It was as if the book didn't exist, only a field of wild horses galloping into my mind. It was so private! Horses! I loved horses.

"Was Heather very pregnant?" I asked nonchalantly.

"Yes. And so were all the mares."

"And does Carl *love* Heather?" I asked.

"I don't know about that, but he was very 'up' that day! He's having a big show in Sweden that he feels very good about—and she was pregnant and all his mares were pregnant."

I pictured the green fields filled with his virility, his pregnant mares. I pictured it as if it were a page in a book about things I would feel and think and know and see only in my mind. A book that would be closed to me forever.

"I think you should be realistic about this," Orso said. "Carl is very interested in that baby. He's going to be very involved with Heather for a long time."

But I couldn't be realistic. I had always loved horses. One summer in camp I had loved Johnny in a white shirt who worked at the stable. He had black hair and a piece of straw in his mouth. I was meant to share Carl's horse farm. Horses meant so much to me. I loved a horse I named Florimell, a big white mare, who liked me back, her ears turned back toward me as we rode and I recited poetry. I was the only one she didn't try to wipe off her, on the corners of barns, the sides of trees. I wanted to buy her and bring her home to my parents' apartment on Madison Avenue. When my mother had visited me in Ithaca I had taken her horseback riding. My poor mother was wretched on her nag, her behind was sore afterwards. It was dusk, I had no mercy.

When I was having Penelope, my stomach was a huge mound on top of me. The skin was jumping. They put the stethoscope to my ears. "Do you want to hear the baby's heartbeat?"

It was a herd of wild horses. Galloping.

Once, when Carl and I were leaving the New Studio, I forgot

something, I had to run back. Always there were great distances to be traversed. Then I ran towards him. Carl Vaggio said, as I approached him, "You almost whinny like my mares."

I was his mare.

I CALLED CARL at the New Studio. Gloria answered. "He's here," she said. "But he's upstairs, working. I'm not going to interrupt him," she said. "He's very serious about what he's doing. . . .

"He's not that great," she added strangely.

One woman to another. To comfort me. But I knew better.

I was sitting on the kitchen stool, weeping. Twelve-year-old Isabelle came out of her room. Pierrette was gone and Isabelle had moved into the maid's room, with a beautiful green marble scalloped sink that Douglas and I had installed the last summer I expected to be married to him, the summer I thought I would marry Carl. I had been weeping for months. The children had seen me, and so I told them. I didn't want them to think I was crying over their father. That I wanted him back. I told them I was in love with Carl Vaggio, who was very famous and rich, that I wanted to marry Carl Vaggio. That I wanted us all four to live together with him in his big four-story house in SoHo.

"What's wrong, Mom?" Isabelle said. She was very tall on roller skates that were white with red trim. She was beautiful, with thick curly hair and fair skin and red cheeks. I told her. I couldn't call his studio because Carl wouldn't come to the phone. I couldn't even call him anymore.

"I'll call him," she said cheerfully. It wasn't a bad idea. The phone trick. I was almost hopeful. Isabelle was an actress. Whenever she dialed Information, she used a Southern accent. She was very good at it. I dialed for her, almost smiling, almost feeling happy, triumphant, and I heard her say, in a glittery theatrical voice, "Hello, is Carl Vaggio there, please?" Then Roy, or someone, asked who it was and she said, in the same grand voice, very slowly, "Su-san Stras-berg."

In an instant, he came to the phone.

"Carl," I gasped.

"Hello. I missed you, you stopped calling," he said.

I couldn't believe I was hearing his voice. His voice was what I needed, the excitement, the energy in it, like a transfusion.

"Why won't you come to the phone?" I demanded.

"There's nothing to say," he whined. "It's all been said already—that's the trouble."

He meant he had promised to marry me. He had given his word.

"I've had to defend you to so many people!" I cried.

He laughed. "Don't bother," he said.

"Maybe next month," he said, as if waiting for Heather to miscarry. "I'll talk to you later." He hung up.

His words were like golden apples to me, they spilled in my path, I ran after them. He was busy sitting with Heather in their love nest now but in nine months or nine years or so I would hear his voice again. It was a distinct promise.

"What did he say?" Isabelle asked.

"He said, 'I'll talk to you later.'"

"I love the way people say that when they don't mean it," she said. I was suddenly depressed. I thought that he had meant it.

DURING THE FIRST transit strike my mother received a proposition in Key Food. She rang the bell on top of the meat counter as usual and the butcher answered. She inquired about certain chickens; flanken. He said, "There's a transit strike, you know. If I can't get home, can I stay with you?"

His apron was stained with blood.

All those Fridays she had rung the bell, shopping for meat for me, the butcher had thought she was flirting with him. Her, a vegetarian, a radical vegetarian. She ate only raw greens!

"Oh, you'll get home," she said.

Even during the first transit strike, I had thought it would be better if I were married to Carl. I had thought adultery could prove inconvenient. Now I am desperate. On the news I see long lines of cars again waiting at gasoline stations, with people not able to go anywhere, with no gas to be had, with people suddenly not able to afford gas. There are reports of delays; rumors of no cabs.

I go downtown—hitchhike partway. I get into a guy's car. He talks to me. I don't tell him I am going to see my fiancé, who doesn't want to see me, who won't talk to me. I make conversation. I ask him what he does. He works in a body shop, he says. That sounds suggestive, obscene. He takes me halfway. He tells me to drop in anytime. I get out. Then take a cab. Carl's studio is locked. I go around the block to find the back entrance. Can't. I call Isabelle from a pay phone on the corner to tell her not to go out without leaving her key with the doorman. I've forgotten my key. I haven't smoked and I notice that my mouth is very dry anyway. I stand there upset. I dial again. The phone rings once and Carl answers. "Carl," I say, strangled. His voice is irrigated. A garden with fountains. He is utterly composed. "I'm sorry but you have the wrong number." He hangs up. But it isn't the wrong number. It's exactly the right number. I have Nicole's green Chinese umbrella with me. The last time I had it, he said, coming out after me on the street, "I love you—more than anything else in the world." The baby in her belly: it wasn't "in the world" yet. Did he have that reservation in mind even then? It is raining lightly. I am wearing the amber rose. I groan aloud and try to be calm and think of what to do. It feels like a long time later, but it may have been at once. I call back. Even though I know of course from his answer that she is there. But he could have handled it differently, as he has done many times. He could have said, "Call me later in the studio." Was he coming to the studio, I wanted to know. I simply needed to know.

"Hello," Heather said. Being downtown, I feel very close to her—in my bedroom, in theirs.

"May I please speak to Carl Vaggio?" Now she has heard the voice of my absolute agony.

"Who is this?"

I said my name and the agony was undisguised. She shuffled off, obviously pregnant, scuffed comfortably off to call him, calling "Carl." She returns to the phone. "He can't take that call now because he's—in the shower."

"Oh," I groan. *That call.* I feel as if I have swallowed rat poison. I want to tell her before I die, I want to share the burden with her, as Nicole shared it with me. "Carl promised to marry me right before you got pregnant," I want to say. "Thank you," I say and hang up.

I have to go home and face my daughter. I have ruined my chances—and hers. All of theirs. I had thought he would buy Benjamin a horse. I try to pull myself together. I groan aloud and hold my stomach. The woman who sits next to me in the cab stiffens. She thinks I will throw up all over her. She thinks I am not someone you would want to share a cab with. At Forty-second Street we are stuck in a traffic jam. And I think, I have not ruined my chances. I can face Isabelle. I haven't lost anything that I had yesterday. Yesterday when he was at the studio. When I called him at the studio and he wouldn't come to the phone.

AGAIN I TRIED to see him. I went to the New Studio. It was entirely shuttered. The gates to paradise were closed forever. A military guard, one of his helpers, peered out. I penetrated the fortress. I ran in, past him, and up the stairs. It was clean and empty as a ballroom. On an enormous table in the center of the room was my latest poem. The envelope was gone. Carl had read it and left it there for the others to see, out of pride. It was my best poem. I went away satisfied. Afterwards, I realized that his workers had opened the mail and left it there for Carl, unread.

Anyway, the poets lied. No one's love was ever gotten with a poem.

* * *

I CALLED CARL at the New Studio, distraught. He wasn't there. Roy told me Carl was in the hospital. To rest up. I could tell that Roy had been instructed to say nothing, he had let that slip out. I was alarmed. "No, it's definitely nothing serious," Roy said. "There's a lot of guys around here who depend on him for their jobs. If anything was wrong they'd be very upset. He doesn't want anyone to know about this," Roy stressed.

Later I found out why: I saw Carl on television. It was a morning program, "The Artist in His Studio." I was in bed drinking coffee. There were crumbs. Carl put his hand to the back of his head and touched his hair in a gesture so familiar that it brought tears to my eyes. He was not wearing a hat. The camera focused on his nervous, mutilated hand. When he turned around, I saw his lost hair. It had grown back.

He had gone into the hospital for a hair transplant!

I DIALED. HE answered. He had to clear his throat. He said hello again in a clear voice. It still rasped; maybe the lisp was gone. (Because of his new teeth.) Then she picked up a phone and said hello. He said hello. "Are you talking to me?" Heather said. "I guess so," he said. "Since no one else is there," she said. Her voice sounded nice, cozy, sensual. Did she know I was on? Did he know I was listening? "I'm going to look for my keys a little longer," he informed her. He was ease. Energy. Composure. "I had them out there when we were watching television. I'll come upstairs in a few minutes," he assured her. For my sake? First he hung up. Then she hung up. Then I hung up.

I AM ON the verge of tears all the time, the blurring of my eyeliner inconvenient, my palms hurting in their secret way. Something I discovered as a child. If my feelings were hurt, my hands would ache with a thrilling pain like hidden sex.

I called Douglas at school. I thought it might be the ultimate infidelity to go back to my husband. He was glad that I called. He was interested. "Oh, life just seems more pointless than before," he said sadly. I said he could come over after work. I got into the shower, I shaved my legs. Through the plastic shower curtain I could see Fifth Avenue. I could have back what I had. What was mine. But by the time I dried off, I didn't want it. I called back. I canceled.

I HAD GOTTEN Marlena a job at NYU, running the Holocaust Studies building. Now that I needed her, she was working. She was in her office. In the middle of our conversation, if someone came into the office, she would unceremoniously hang up. Without saying goodbye.

"Don't roll those things over and over," Marlena said to me, in her strange exotic English, "because no new light can come from them."

For a minute I think she is talking about marijuana. I am holding a joint I just rolled between my fingers. Before I can reply, someone comes into the office. She hangs up.

It is Friday. I cry all day. But that night, luckily, we have a date as usual. Marlena and Tim are coming over at seven. My whole life is such a mess, it will help just to see them. They will sip wine out of the same glass, puff at the same cigarette, hold hands. Marlena will tell me that it would never have worked. "If he has a big belly," she will say, "then he wouldn't be good in bed." They will help me figure out how I can survive. Then Marlena calls. She cancels. "I have to arrange my scarf drawer," she says.

I FIND IT is counterproductive to go to bed with other men. Always they offer up a pale flickering candle next to his blinding flame. His fame. His grandeur. His cruelty. His *sprezzatura*. The changing sorrows of his artist's face. Nevertheless, I do it.

Marlena told me to do it. I will never forgive her for this. "You think I should just sleep with other men?" "Yes, I do!" she said. That meant the end. I am trudging along on the dark waters of the months when suddenly I lose faith. I sink. I am swallowed up. My future miscarries. And Heather's holds fast.

I WAKE UP beheaded. I have turned into my mother. A bag lady. I feel as if I bleed from the breast. I look down to check. I inspect the sheet for blood.

I call Ruth at my father's office. My father's new wife is the only one who has time for me. I talk about Carl for an hour, explaining his silence, explaining why I still have hope. "Joy, I don't know about this guy," Ruth says.

I CALLED THE doctor—a mutual friend—who had treated Nicole until her leukemia. He had an office filled with Carl's prints, signed. He came over at once. He drove crosstown in a heavy rain. There was something in my voice, he said. He was a trained listener. Something that worried him. We sat near a window in the same restaurant on B'way where Nicole had told me she was sleeping with Carl, too. We had to shout over the Thomas Hardy rain. His wife had died of a pinpoint of cancer that they couldn't find. He had had bypass surgery a year before and it was still painful, he said. I had planned to sleep with him, for revenge, but it was impossible. His face had wrinkled like a baked apple. His car was flooded in Central Park on the way home.

I AM HOPEFUL in Key Food. "Maybe next month," he said. The date on liquids—the hopefulness of March, April, May on containers of orange juice. I have an army of lovers to gain a moment's peace. I take two Anacin. I forget I have taken them and take them again. I take them again and again.

When you are jilted, it is with a jolt. You fall off the balcony of your dreams and land on the cement, the concrete sidewalk is covered with his cruelty. You can't go back to sleep. Sleep has no miracles up its sleeve.

I take half a Valium to go back to sleep and dream I am playing all my records piled one on the other, scratching them, ruining them. The records are my loves, my feelings, which will scratch if I pile them promiscuously. I invite a young poet over. Frank Wood. A poet and art critic. I tell him about Carl. "You don't believe that he loved me, that he said he'd marry me," I say.

"It's pretty realistic with all the paintings around," he answers.

He can't understand why I am so depressed. "Why don't you just put your feet up and read a book?"

An hourglass inside me empties and fills continuously.

He borrows twenty dollars and leaves.

I CALL THE studio. A new voice answers. "Is Carl there?" I ask pleasantly. "I don't know," he answers, and calls to someone else, "Is Carl here?" In the distance I hear Carl's voice. "Who is it?" Fierce, unshaven, angry.

"A lady," my helper answers softly. "I don't know—I'll find out."

I am confused.

Then Gloria's voice, which sounds somewhat like Heather's. Bossy. Charming. "Hello. Oh—hello—Carl isn't here. He hasn't been here," she volunteers, "for a long, long time." This is uttered heavily, as if it were intended to indicate the end, the end of the story. But I just heard his voice. I know he is there. It means he has decided to stay with Heather. There is nothing he can say to me. She is trying to discourage me from ever calling again. But I know he's there. I have seen through the wiles of Gloria to the presence of Carl. I have outwitted him!

Just to be sure, I call his home later. Carl answers. "I'm sorry. You have the wrong number," he says.

I thought his strength was in my hair.

FRANK WOOD, WHO doesn't understand why I am so depressed, persuades me to come to him downtown. He calls in the middle of the night. He is whispering into my ear on the phone in the middle of the night. This is his wooing strategy.

He promises he will find me a cab afterwards. Isabelle is sleeping in the maid's room, Benjamin and Penelope are asleep in their beds. The doorman is in the lobby, asleep in his chair. I leave. I have to pass the dark shattered warehouse windows along the waterfront where Carl and I parked, sat in his black Jeep. I make the cab go past Carl's door. A delicate fawn wineskin swells between my legs. I arrive, I see the young long-haired poet sitting on his stoop. We go up six flights; sock drawers bulge open at the door. A girl has just gotten out of his bed. I promise him Carl Vaggio's money. I say I will marry Carl and have an affair with him. His cock seems truncated, it is half the size of Carl's. Afterwards, he borrows another ten dollars. It is Carl's daughter, Cara, who has just left. He has not told me he is seeing her.

He thanks me for my slip.

"No, really," he said. "I haven't seen anything like this for a long time." Fingering it. It is a plain long beige nylon slip.

Then he falls asleep. I have to get my own cab. Now there are no more paid-for cabs, no more franking privileges.

Later he married Cara. Carl gave them a huge wedding. Everyone who was anyone was there. "What was Heather wearing?" I asked one friend.

"Oh, children," the artist replied.

11

SYMS

/ / / / / / /

Douglas's lawyer called me. Douglas wanted the books. I said he could have the Freud but not the Dickens (which I had not read). "He wants the set of Jane Austen," the lawyer said.

"No," I declared emphatically.

"Why?" the lawyer said, "What have *you* to do with Jane Austen?"

"I *am* Jane Austen," I said.

I walked with my dad in the snow. Icy slush entered my old Frye boots. He was my lawyer for the divorce. I was going to be "financially examined" by Douglas's attorney. I got eight hundred dollars a month alimony and child support. I was still unemployed. I had once been offered good jobs out of New York, but now, since I was retrenched, I couldn't get anything.

By the time we got there—somewhere on Madison Avenue—my feet were painfully numb. In the lobby was a large, a very large, Vaggio. His shaped canvas. His garish colors. His omnipresence. It towered over me like the executioner's ax. I felt like Anne Boleyn on her last day. What had made me rich now beggared me. What had exalted now beheaded. It couldn't have been more "ironically cruel" if Carl Vaggio had planned it himself.

We went up in the elevator to the lawyer's office for my financial examination. I was shaking and painfully thawing. My dad was nervous too. When he was the most nervous, I knew, he acted the most nonchalant.

Douglas's lawyer looked at my checkbook. "New York Ballet? One hundred and thirty dollars? Do you enjoy the ballet?"

"No. That's just classes for exercise," I said.

My father sat down in a leather armchair, leaned back, closed his eyes, and pretended to be asleep.

AT HOME, I called Carl. I said, "Carl!" "Yes," he said, knowing at once who it was. I was mild, relaxed. "I need to talk to you sometime." "There's nothing I can do," he whined. His thin voice didn't excite me. Maybe the magic was gone. "You don't have to do anything," I said. "You could help me just by talking." "Yes," he said. A tiny, an infinitesimal pause. "Well . . . bye-bye," he said, and hung up.

WHEN I WAS first married, maids were the main thing. Now Pierrette was gone. Alma, our next housekeeper, had a retarded daughter and an abusive, violent son. She sewed a beautiful print cloth book bag for me, with a flowered cloth lining. Carl Vaggio had taken it from me and put it over his shoulder the beautiful day we climbed the ladder in the rain in his New Studio. My mother called her "Almie." She couldn't say "Alma," I realized, because it contained a sacred syllable: Ma. So she said "Almie," the way religious Jews said "Jahweh" or wrote "G-d."

After Alma, there was Marta, who had a pretty grown daughter, a size six. When Carl said he would marry me, I gave her my tight-fitting Valentino coat trimmed with black fox for her daughter. I emptied my closets, I gave her all my clothes.

Later Marta saw me crying. Alone in my tower. She told me about the other women she worked for in the building. The one alone on the seventh floor with two small boys whose husband had moved in with another man. "How *she* is crying!" Marta said. "Your husband, he is all right?"

Then Douglas came to the apartment for some papers. He took the filing cabinet into the dark hall and stood looking through it near the elevator.

Later she admitted, "He is so—skinny."

I WENT CRAZY when I had to sell my apartment. The views had become part of me, like my limbs. I thought the little cars double-parked in rows going crosstown were the buttons on my dress.

"It's as if you were in a cab with the meter running," the lawyer explained to me. "It's not your cab. It belongs to both you and your husband. You have to move."

I CALLED MARLENA. "Tim and I were just remembering how boring Douglas was—so self-important, saying the same thing over and over with a solemn tone, as if he were lecturing."

"Yes," I agreed, somewhat pained. I looked at my shriveled past life. I saw it sitting on the long couch.

At a party, to a perfect stranger, I once said, "My husband wants to be submissive in sex." I remember my shock that I had told, that I had committed the extraordinary impropriety of confessing my disappointment. And later some dinner guest, in my apartment, in the presence of my husband, said that someone we both knew, someone I had recently met on West End Avenue, asked, "How does Joy feel, being the stronger one?"

ONCE, WHEN NICOLE and I had a joint birthday party, her other friend named Joy, Joy Gelt, called me up and asked me what color my bedroom was. She was buying me a gift. She was very rich. I looked around and saw no unifying scheme. "Purple," I improvised. I was amazed when I opened her gift, and found six lavender pencils.

When Douglas and I separated, Joy Gelt asked if she could fix Douglas up with her plain cousin. "Sure," I said. I had avoided Joy Gelt for a long time when I was mourning for Nicole, but now we were friends.

When Douglas met the plain cousin, Joy Gelt later told me, Douglas introduced himself, saying: "Hello, I'm Douglas. I like to be submissive in sex." Joy Gelt told this story for years. With undiminished glee. She never tired of telling it.

I HEARD THE good news and the bad news from Orso.

First the good news. The baby was born dead. Heather had to carry it two weeks knowing it was dead before she could deliver it, he said.

"Poetic justice," I thought, flooded with joy.

A clean slate. A new beginning. I moved downtown.

Then, later, the bad news. Carl's child was born. Another child. The awful thing had happened. The image of my grief. The reason for it.

"They spend their evenings at home, looking at the baby," Orso said.

The scene a creche. Domestic bliss. "Is he happy?" I asked.

"He's ecstatic," Orso said.

I GO INTO Syms. An educated consumer. I have a Ph.D. I have gray hairs. Silver venerable hairs. "It's always lovely to see you," the tall security guard says. I had come before. He recognized me. I smile a coy smile. It doesn't surprise me to get such a royal reception. I should have been in Bendel's, not Syms. I should have been rich, not poor. I should have been married to Carl Vaggio.

I go into the shoe section. It is summer. I am wearing sandals. I take one off and try on a black pump. It is 6AA, my size! I try both on. I put my worn sandals away in my bag. I choose some rich garments from the rack and carry them into the dressing room. Inside the curtain, the distracted salesgirl is separating a tangle of hangers. Without pausing, I walk to a mirror and hang the things. She glances at my shoes. I undress without taking them off. On one of the shiny soles is the price. It is high. I try on the clothes and stuff my own into my bag. At last I am wearing new clothes. I look in the mirror for a while, select among shoulder-padded tops. I keep the best outfit on, tear off the price tags with my bare right hand. The salesgirl is carrying merchandise out. I put my empty hangers inconspicuously among the rest. I carry my extra garments over my arm as if to take them to the cashier. There are long lines at the cashier. I change my mind, return them to a rack, and approach the door. I think there is a different security guard. I walk wearily out in my elegant ensemble and high heels and smile at him.

"YOU'RE SO LONG," I said admiringly.

"I've seen longer," he answered defensively. "In California."

I said nothing. But it wasn't the length only, it was him. A great artist, in New York. He was everything.

"There were a lot of blond boys there," he threw out at me like a lure.

I had no interest in California. I was already hooked.

I GO INTO Syms. I have a chance of getting a job. I need a suit to wear to the convention for an interview. I try on three black suits. The skirt of one looks good with the striped jacket of another. The third has a peach satin blouse.

The dressing room is very crowded. Nobody notices my strenuous standing still before the mirror. My impassioned dressing and re-dressing.

I wear my jeans skirt over a black straight skirt, a huge black sweater over the striped jacket over the blouse. I put on my raincoat and leave the store.

"THINK OF HOW happy you'll make me," he said. "Relax." I relaxed the muscles. Slowly his penis crept into my behind. His hand was under me, in front, touching. I was doubly coerced. He entered with amazing stealth. It no longer hurt. He had the mien of the molester. Then suddenly he stiffened. The molester disappeared. I became totally an object. He concentrated on his pleasure. He came. Seven hours later, in ballet class, the come would come out in a tiny attack of diarrhea. The dark message of the day's pleasure, my secret.

I GO INTO Syms. I put on a beautiful dress. It refuses to come off. A mother and daughter are quarreling in the cubicle near me. The daughter is dissatisfied, the mother huffy. Money is the issue. I look around. Everyone is as much in want as I. I see the fallacy. What if everyone took what they wanted? It would be anarchy. The end of society. Still, I bundle my old clothes on top of my new and leave, invisible.

I REMEMBER ARRIVING one noon and glimpsing a physical therapist in Carl Vaggio's living room. She was just leaving. She wore a nurse's uniform. In bed, Carl told me, just his luck, she wanted to get married. She wouldn't sleep with him.

I had visited him in the hospital. He had gone in for a simple hip injury, had some complications, and then stayed a very long time. Time dragged. I was jealous that he was taking drugs and wouldn't miss me the way I missed him. It was Sunday. He got a bad review in the *Times*. "Physical pain is worse than emotional pain," he said. I closed the door. I knelt at the side of the bed. In a second he came in my mouth. I rose. The nurse came in.

I GO INTO Syms. There has been a bad omen. I almost closed my hand inside the door as I left my apartment. I choose a fabulous heavy tweed pants suit. The jacket fits. The pants are way too long. I return the slacks to a rack outside the dressing room. I am wearing the jacket as if it belonged to me. Suddenly, I see a female security guard watching me. She is blond with a putty face. The hanger is completely naked on top without the jacket. It is the only pair of slacks without a jacket. I have put it in among jackets. The jacket cannot be sold separately, I have already removed the price tag. My heart pounds. Then I see there is a woman talking to the security guard, who is her friend. The security guard's eyes glaze over. They wear a polite blue enamel glaze. She nods her head. She talks back to the woman. I am safe. It is a miracle. I leave the store.

IT WAS SPRING, I was with Carl. We sat in his black Jeep, facing away from the Hudson River. Facing the traffic. Like Gertrude Stein on a picnic, we did not face the view. We sat in silence. My mouth was dry. My tongue cut out. "Just a lot of soulful looks," he commented. "And I have to sit around all day thinking of things to say to you that I don't want to say." He wouldn't let me smoke because there were federal agents in the next car.

I WALK UPSTAIRS on the broken escalator to evening dresses. Patterned silk. Dancing couples on a long skirt with a slit and a shirred top. They are tied together with floss joined with metal. Without anyone noticing, I put the skirt on under my own long skirt. I try on the evening top. I don't like it. I take it off. I start to leave the crowded dressing room. "Where are you going?" the attendant asks. "Where's the pants to that?"

Pants? She means skirt.

"I put them outside on the rack," I say, corroborating her error. I am caught. Terrified. I imagine my humiliation in front of these twenty or so women.

She grabs the silk blouse out of my hands. She studies the tag. Some of the women look up with mild interest. "Oh, they're sold separately. That's all right, then," she says.

IT WAS RIGHT at the beginning of our affair. "You look just like a whore," Carl said softly. "But that's all right, I always liked whores." Then, walking to his house, he added: "Maybe I'll pay for it someday." "It" meant the four women he was sleeping with at once, or maybe five by then, including Jerri-the-maid.

Now sleep is the only subway to him. I dreamed I went to his new studio. He wasn't there. I sat in a chair and rested. I had a headache. I was wearing a big winter coat, high heels. Suddenly, Carl came in. He was carrying a rolled-up rug, the kind Cleopatra came in. He saw me and gave me a grunted hello. We went to his house. I met his sons. They had smooth round brown faces. "They look like you," I said, seeing their dark skin. "What beautiful teeth you have," I said to them. They smiled and wanted to sing. They vied for attention. Their mother had come home on another floor. "Didn't you hear her come home?" they asked. Carl walked me to the door. We had passed the kitchen where the maid was preparing dinner. "That smells so good," I said. "Why don't you learn how to cook?" he said. He indicated that he couldn't kiss me at the door. "Will I ever see you again?" I asked sadly. "Early, very early," he replied. The corners of my mouth turned up. He wanted to see me. Then I was out in the snow, in high heels, on Second Avenue.

I GO BACK to Syms. It is summer again. I am wearing a beautiful stolen dress. A thin dress, coffee-colored, with sandals. My mother's antique coral beads around my neck. They are showing leather suits. I want one. I take several into the dressing room. I am thin. I have stopped smoking grass for several weeks. I am a size six. The purple leather skirt hugs my hips, fits like a glove, like my own skin. It is a very long skirt. I nonchalantly put my thin dress on over it. I am mildly surprised that it covers it. When I am standing still, the purple hem doesn't show. It doesn't stick out. I leave the dressing room wearing it, wander over to bathing suits. I earnestly go through a rack, searching carefully. The dressing-room attendant comes quietly up to me. "Excuse me," she says. "Did you take a leather skirt out with you? Because your card says six and I only found five."

I smile sweetly. "I put it on the rack," I say.

"Oh," she says, glancing at my hem. For all I know, she sees the purple skirt enshrouding me. I walk gently away, amazed at my own audacity. I leave the store.

MY SISTER HEIDI called. I mentioned Carl Vaggio. She had had to be carried out of a museum once. His painting affected her badly. The colors made her dizzy.

"You certainly are tenacious," she said.

She was telling me about rolling on two balls. A course in kinesthetic memory. "Remembering was the hardest work I ever did in my life," she said. I vaguely listened. She was always off on some tangent. Pestering my father for her astrological info, for his. She was having an astrological chart made for both of them. There was a pause.

All of a sudden, I heard her say, "You pimped for Grandpa."

"What?"

"You left him alone with me for him to do his number on me."

"Are you crazy?" I shouted. For a moment I thought I was going to have a heart attack. "How could I have known, if I was so surprised when you boasted about it to Mother? I thought I was the only one! I remember feeling betrayed!"

"Did I boast about it?"

"Yes. You were proud. You said, 'Grandpa touched me in my puupy.' "

"Then I didn't even have the right emotion."

"Mother was going to hit you. I stopped her."

"I suppose I should be grateful to you for that."

I didn't want gratitude. I just wanted sanity. But she went on: "I'm sorry, Joy, but in my heart and mind you're very much involved in this. You lay in your bed next to mine while I was sleeping and—I remember your hair was in two coils of braids over your ears. I remember what a voluptuous look you had on your face. How could you think I wouldn't see, that I wouldn't want to do it too?"

The answer is perfectly obvious.

"Because you were sleeping!" I say.

I GO BACK to Syms. As soon as I enter the store, I see the same saleslady. She sees me. There is dark electricity between us. Like when I first heard Heather's voice, and I knew my doom. Still, I think nothing can harm me. I put on a leather jacket. I put my bag on over my shoulder, and walk around the store, shopping, with my raincoat over my arm. I find nothing I like better, nothing I want to try on. I glance at my watch. I put on my raincoat, and approach the door. The saleslady runs lightly ahead of me, and whispers in the guard's ear. In an instant, he stops me. It is the single instant I have feared most, and it has happened.

He wants to look in my bag.

"There's nothing in it," I say.

"We just want back what is ours," he says. "Is that unreasonable?"

They took me to a little room. The saleslady took me behind a curtain and asked me to remove my coat. I was surprised by her neutrality. She didn't play the scene. The stolen jacket I was wearing appeared. She took it from me and went away. The manager was called. I pleaded to be allowed to pay. He refused. The security guard had to write up the report. He couldn't type. "Do you want me to type it for you?" I suggested. "No, that would look bad," he said. He crumpled the paper and started over.

Deponent states that he observed the defendant knowingly in possession of stolen property, to wit, a leather jacket, without paying or accounting for the same and without permission or authority to do so, and with the intent to benefit herself or a person other than the owner thereof and to impede the recovery by an owner thereof in that deponent recovered said jacket from underneath defendant's raincoat.

We waited for the police. I was allowed to make one phone call.

I called my father.

"I'm at Syms, arrested," I said.

"You're kidding!" he said.

The police came and put handcuffs on me behind my back. I laughed. "I'm hardly violent," I said. My wrists were damp. They wriggled out easily. I had one handcuff on only, I showed them. They were angry. They made the handcuffs tight and led me out of the store.

People looked shocked.

At the precinct, they took my fingerprints. They put me in the cage. The security guard guarded me. I recited poems for him. "Don't you have one about—this?" he said. "No," I said. "I never did this before," I lied. They took my picture, three times. "She's modeling in there," I heard them say. He wrote my description. "Hair: salt and pepper," he read aloud. I was a little startled. I thought it was still black, or smoky.

"I don't like this line of work," he said.

"Which?"

"Retail security."

"You seemed to be enjoying it when you arrested me."

"That was because it had been so boring," he said.

I had to go to court. "They'll just give you a slap on the wrists," I was told.

I would have had to clean the subway every Saturday for a year; but the subway and parks department person was absent. My father pleaded my case. "She's a college teacher, Judge, and she hasn't been paid in ten years." His hands trembled from Parkinson's. The judge was a wiry, redheaded man. "Take your hands out of your pockets," I was told. "Speak up." Tears came. "I would fine her, but then you would just pay it," the judge said to my father.

I was let go scot-free.

Outside, my father spoke to me sternly.

"Do you know what prison is like?" he said. "Especially women's prison!"

"Maybe I just did it to see you," I said.

"If there is a next time, don't call me," he said. "Forget you know me!"

I'M TRYING TO decide whether to go to the new Carl Vaggio show at the Whitney. I'm sitting on the edge of the bed dangling a boot. The left boot has a small tear in the leather. If the seam along the toes of my Calvin Klein Daytime Sheer is not exactly in place I may suffer excruciating pain with every step on the way there. I suffer unbearably from any wrinkle, or crumb. This may be the last chance I get. It closes very soon. Dressing, I know I am putting on my clothes not to have a good time, the way I used to do. Putting on my clothes to take them off. The subway route seems very complicated suddenly. Walk to City Hall and take the 6? I forget where Central Park is. And can I walk east if I take the number 1 from Carlton Street.

Sitting on the edge of the bed, I have been reading the reviews. It is another dramatic departure, another attempt to capture the critics' attention. They had been pointing to a peculiar aura of privacy surrounding Carl's personal life as if he were some kind of Bluebeard. Now he is making art of his person. He has thrown open the doors to the castle. More aspersions are cast. My heart starts to beat faster. Will the truth come to light? There is a chilling, a repugnant, side to his success, critics suggest, even to the artworks themselves. They are called hollow, inhuman, repellent. The museum itself is criticized for glorifying this work. He is compared unfavorably with a much younger artist showing simultaneously at the Modern, whose new wife is his muse. They say Carl Vaggio is running out of gas. That he is a prostitute servicing his own fame. One critic says that the work is diverse because the artist is torn apart by suffering. The sculptures are eviscerated by sorrow. The others all agree that the work is exuberant and full of joy. I have to see for myself.

I leave the house. A rare occurrence. I get there.

A huge flag with his name on it hangs the length of the building.

He has covered the walls with blown-up photomurals of himself, he is playing tennis without an opponent, he is swimming naked in alabaster pools, he is sitting alone in his studio playing chess with a robot, he is holding aloft a shaggy Canadian trout, he is astride a camel in Egypt in front of a pyramid.

The artist as Renaissance sportsman.

In the center of the gleaming rooms are stainless-steel tennis balls. They are piled opulently in stainless-steel pails. They flex automatically in the glass biceps of Carl Vaggio figurines.

All the minute love I lavished on him, he has lavished on himself. He doesn't need me anymore. His success is his mirror and his muse.

I see a stainless-steel-and-polychrome-wood replica of a child's electric train set, in motion, on its way to Auschwitz, the cattle cars packed with tiny Jews. Every detail exact.

In another, larger room there are enormous horses. Carl Vaggio is among them, in ceramic, or porcelain, his arm deep inside a "phantom mare," removing the valuable pouch of sperm a hoodwinked thoroughbred has deposited there.

There is no woman anywhere. Then I see her. In one

corner of a photo, as if the camera slipped and she was accidentally included, a frizzy-haired figure on her knees injects his bare buttocks with a needle.

Among the artworks, a woman hanging on the arm of a tall, wealthy gentleman says, "I must admit, I find it very attractive, I don't know why. . . ." She sounds apologetic. Her dress is sequined in a design reminiscent of Carl's earlier work. Fashion follows in his footsteps. In a corner, leaning against a wall, a drab woman in slacks takes notes. Two young men, students, study a gigantic jutting penis. "Look at the veins!" one says. "Incredible!" says the other. I feel at home. Even among the trample of stallions, the stampede of Carl Vaggio everywhere, the hooves of his great artistic daring overhead. Once his art seemed to me the image of my joy, like the angel-hair ceiling of Bendel's at Christmas.

I do not shout or moan or talk to strangers. I leave quickly. I limp home.

I REMEMBER THE time Dorothy Black from upstairs dropped into our apartment. Douglas and I were sitting in the dining room, light streaming in from the south and east, Persian sun patterns at our feet. Tears were streaming down my face. I was a weeping statue. Dorothy was a beautiful young redhead, a potter, who lived right above us—until her separation. She was married to André Black directly over us. Our mail got mixed up because our last names were the same. A little lace rosebud showed on her black lace bra. Her breasts were buoyant and white. At the sight of her, my tears increased. Then I saw a way out. She was going downtown.

"Can I say I'm going with you?"

"Yes."

She and I could leave together. I had found a way out of the house! Without her I could invent no destination. I was paralyzed with sorrow. A pillar of salt, Lot's wife. She was a supple conspirator. We said goodbye to Douglas. Immediately, I called Carl from a pay phone on B'way. Yes! I could come down. I threw my jacket up into the air. It was like a movie, it turned plaid cartwheels. It was a triumphant kite. My flag.

How can I put away this love?

I've got to go back to the show. This is the last day. I've got to see the flag one more time, with his name on it that reaches from sidewalk to sky. The photos of him.

But I decide not to go. It is like missing my last great date with him. I am standing him up. This excites me, and then I am sad that he won't be there. That's it, the message. Even if I go. *"He's* just not there." What Nicole tried to tell me.

But to deprive me of his friendship, of even a farewell . . .

LATER MY FATHER drops in to make sure I'm all right. It is a thrill to see him. He is such a good father to me. He looks at my Dior raincoat on the hook. I wore it out of the store on top of a smaller, paler raincoat I had stolen the week before but didn't like as much. He looks at the smaller raincoat on the hook next to it.

"My two nutsy daughters," he says.

12

HEIDI'S COMPLAINT

/ / / / / / / /

The day before Thanksgiving, my father called me. "Did you know that Heidi was going to sue me?" he said.

"What? Sue you! For what?"

"Child abuse. I was served with a summons in my office. There was a long complaint. Forty pages. It's the worst thing I ever read," he said.

There was an explosion of darkness. In it I remembered the time I wet my bed. My mother never came in the night. She sent my father. He put a scratchy woolen blue blanket over the wet spot under me. I felt exquisite relief. The loathsome cold spot had prevented sleep. My gruff father had fixed it without anger, awkwardly, lovingly, and suddenly I could go back to sleep. My wonderful father had made it possible. I vaguely realized it was not a solution of which my mother would have approved. It was a cover-up. She would have remade the whole bed. All my faults were tucked in in a jiffy.

"I didn't know Heidi was crazy," he said.

She had impugned the whole family. She claimed everyone had abused her. He would not tell me the details. It was too disgusting. I couldn't have grasped them anyway. My mind was blanketed with darkness.

"Do you know if Heidi ever had an abortion?" my father asked.

"Of course she didn't. Not that I know of. What's a 'complaint'?"

"It's a kind of story. With allegations."

DAZZLING DARKNESS. I went to Washington Square Park and scored a nickel bag of grass. It was a gyp. Oregano. I had never been more desperate, or poorer. And I was ripped off. I tried again on a nearby corner. This time, it was the real stuff.

I inhaled, and saw the red tip emerge like a dog's penis.

My sister and I were in bed, our twin beds, in our large bedroom. (Our parents slept in the smaller bedroom, really the dinette, with a swinging door to the kitchen.) I came into my sister's bed. I had taken off my pajama bottoms but decided cautiously to leave on my tops. I was the girl, it was my turn. She fingered me, I liked it. Suddenly, we heard my father's footstep. I bolted into my own bed. The wedge of light sliced our room. He came in. I was in my own bed with my arms out of the covers, buttoned up in my long-sleeved pajamas. He hadn't seen. "Go to sleep," he said, unsuspecting.

HEIDI'S LAWYER CALLED me from Vermont. He questioned me for an hour.

"Your sister wanted to sue you too, but I want you to know, I will not prosecute another abused child."

"You couldn't sue me, I was only a child."

"Oh yes, another lawyer would. But I will not prosecute another rape victim."

"But I'm not a rape victim."

"Yes, you are. You may have forgotten. Your father raped you also."

It was the most preposterous thing I had ever heard.

At the end of the hour I said, "You mean my sister is suing my father for rape?"

"Yes."

SHE WAS MY father's favorite. Weekends we went house hunting. She sat between my mother and father in the front seat and rubbed my father's earlobe till it bled. The "satin" border on her blanket was frayed to lace. Her brow was always furrowed with some hidden agenda.

I was my mother's favorite.

My mother stood in the kitchen peeling grapes, putting them flayed, shimmering, into champagne goblets, putting them halved into my mouth. She cut them in half and took the pits out. Flayed them alive, painlessly. One for me, one for the goblet. The tip of her ear was transparent, a red grape.

There must have been two goblets. One for me and one for Heidi.

Four years younger, in the shadows, forgotten.

She told all the neighbors she had twelve brothers. "I have a muzen brothers," she said.

A grade school teacher said she had a "sharp tongue."

When the ball rolled under the radiator in our room, Heidi stood there and watched it. She didn't want to put her arm under and reach. It was too short anyway. She twirled her braid. But she knew she should be looking for the missing ball. She decided to look in the corner where there was no radiator. She got down on her hands and knees and searched, her chin touching the rug. Nothing.

My mother beat my sister in her bed on her birthday.
On my birthday my presents were heaped on my bed.

DENNIS BERG TOOK me to see Maillol's *Four Seasons* at the Museum of Modern Art. I only liked "Spring." I didn't like fullness, or ripeness, only girlish slenderness. I shuddered at the breasts of "Autumn," the hips of "Summer." I don't even remember "Winter."

Heidi was thin but dark and my mother didn't love her.

When she went to college, she told me a man came out of the woods and tried to rape her. "Not here," she told him. "Come back to my room with me." And he fled.

It had never occurred to me not to believe her.

AS SOON AS she moved back to New York from Minneapolis, I went to see Heidi dance.

She rented a church in Hell's Kitchen for three days. She had a company of dancers. I sat in the empty church. It was like visiting our childhood. Only darker. She was my mother. Wearing a fancy ball gown. Dancing with my father. The tango. At the end of the dance, her breast came out. It was a long red velvet snake. It was sensational! What a prop!

Then my father picked up a golf club and left her.

She was accusing my father of abandoning my mother. Probably nobody got it but me. Afterwards, Heidi wasn't happy with the reviews. She didn't like having her own company.

"It just isn't doing it for me," she said.

Heidi did not start dancing till she was forty. She rehearsed in my dining room. I helped her. She did a piece based on my father's snores. She set up a tape recorder in his bedroom. His snores were the music. But every time I saw her perform, it somehow got worse. Slipped from coherence. It lost the point.

BEFORE MY MOTHER died, Heidi sat on a white wrought-iron chair in my mother's living room, a figure of dejection, a brown study. Mute and twisted on the metal chair, she was like a lover, worshiping my mother. I lost all patience with her. My mother had deteriorated into a crazy woman. It had been easy for her to comfort my mother on the phone. "Why would you want such a man back?" is all Heidi would say. She worshiped the carpet of garbage my mother walked on.

On the street, some red tomatoes rolled loose from a bag Heidi carried. The image stayed in my mind. The family jewels. Ripe tomatoes barely bruised on the sidewalk.

"Leave them, leave them. Throw them away—they're contaminated," Heidi cried.

Right before my mother died, Heidi flew back again from Minneapolis. "Walk like a dancer," my mother said, as Heidi approached her bed. "Don't slouch." These were my mother's last words to her.

ONE DAY, LONELY, in graduate school, I called home and nobody answered. I called all day. Finally, my father answered.

"Where *were* you? I've been calling!"

"Oh, we were—driving around," my father said uncomfortably.

"Why?"

"We were—looking for a—place."

He was being tactful. It was a disgrace for the younger daughter to marry before the older. He didn't want to hurt my feelings. He didn't want to tell me Heidi was engaged.

They were looking for the right wedding emporium, I later found out, for Heidi and Jeff to be married in.

Heidi married a mathematician, in the same wedding emporium, exactly three weeks before my wedding to Douglas took place.

After her divorce, Heidi put her teenage son, Jeremiah, on a plane, without telling anyone, and sent him to live with my father for six months. She didn't mention it to my father until the boy was already in the air. After six months, he returned to Minneapolis. His father sued for custody and won.

As soon as my father married Ruth, Heidi told me she felt vibes telling her her father needed her. She flew to New York and moved in with them. It didn't work out. She slipped on the rug on their polished bedroom floor and blamed Ruth. Then she came to live with me. She became violently ill. She felt bad vibes from her former husband, aimed at her womb. I nursed her. She was hospitalized. Her ovaries were infected. An IUD had been inserted in her womb years before, the Dalkon Shield. She had forgotten that she was still wearing an intrauterine device that had been removed from the market.

MY FATHER AND I went to federal court. Twice. Heidi's lawyer had made it the court of original jurisdiction, claiming the parties were from diverse states. Once, my father was his own lawyer, once, he defended his brother. Heidi was also suing my uncle, who is rich.

I went to court with my father to comfort him, to be with him, and because I knew that if anyone saw us together they would know he was innocent.

I TURNED ON television and saw her on Dan Rather. It lasted four minutes. She sauntered along the edge of Central Park, a victim, blending in with New York.

Then, one morning, I was rushing to my first aerobics class, when Isabelle called out to me. Heidi was on a talk show. I stopped dead in my tracks, sat down on Isabelle's bed. I watched, mesmerized.

Heidi sat in a row with other women whose fathers had abused them. One woman said she wanted money from her father because he had just won the lottery in New Jersey. He had millions now, she said, and she needed help raising his child, whom she had borne through rape, through incest. I was tempted to believe it wasn't true. But maybe it was. Heidi was plugging a dance performance she was about to do. That weekend. She looked very satisfied to get that advertisement in.

Saturday night, I went by myself to see Heidi dance. You

had to walk up seven floors. Everybody paid twelve dollars. Outside, on the landing, were her paintings from the Art Students League. Thick impasto babies with pins sticking out of them and penises in their mouths.

She had rented a space. Somebody's huge loft. Amelia, Heidi's friend, who lived on Carlton Street, came over to the cushion on which I was sitting. She was dead white, and blond. The opposite of Heidi. I had always thought they were a nice pair, dark and light, like chiaroscuro. Amelia asked me to leave. My presence was disturbing Heidi, she said. My heart was beating violently. There seemed to be hundreds of people. I refused to go. "Get your face out of my face," I said. Amelia said they were calling the police. But I stayed put. I heard thumping backstage. It was Heidi. I could picture the choreography of her anger. She was horizontal. Bare feet, gnashing teeth, fists.

I just sat and waited. After forty-five minutes, Heidi came on stage. She was wearing an outfit my grandmother had brought us from Florida, a turquoise taffeta skirt and white lace off-the-shoulder blouse. The audience clapped. She began the performance. She announced that she was Little Miss Matching Outfit, sent to her grandmother's house, going down the hill and up the hill in Riverdale. She had been told to wait seven minutes at the door. She checked her watch. The young man who played my grandfather came to the door, naked. The big bad wolf. He raped her.

She has the wrong grandfather, I thought. This was my "good" grandfather, my mother's father.

Then my grandmother raped her.

My grandmother? My mother's mother, whom she loved so much?

Then my father. This was the most evocative movement, almost beautiful. With his back to the audience, he thrust a naked doll between his legs. Then he passed the doll to my mother. Who also raped her.

Two dancers wearing jeweled sweaters came on stage. I

recognized my beige sweater with coral trim, which had been my mother's. Then I recognized my mother's black sequined sweater, which I had given Heidi.

These were our two aunts, my mother's sisters.

"Why are you telling us now?" the dancer wearing my sweater with coral trim asked.

The dancer wearing my mother's sequined sweater asked the same.

"Dear, you're not well, it's a dream," my sweater said.

Almost a lesbian love interlude followed between this aunt and my sister.

"Is she right? Am I crazy? Can I not tell a dream from reality?" Heidi asked herself out loud.

Behind her, our family photographs flashed on a screen, my parents, Heidi and me, grandparents, aunts, interspersed with shots of the Holocaust and Hiroshima.

At the end she lay on the floor, recited a poem, twined daisies and black-eyed Susans between her toes. A group discussion followed. This was the main attraction. I was suddenly aware that everyone in the audience had been sexually abused.

She had found her theme, her niche. It was a career move, suing my father. She had become the spokesperson for Incest Survivors, Inc.

"Incest is not about sex—it's about violence. Those females who are now remembering that their fathers raped them—now also remember that their mothers raped them also," Heidi said.

"I wanted my mind back. Adults who aren't raped as children don't dream of genitals being cut up," she argued.

"Why do whole families sacrifice children to protect criminals?"

"I have the right to my body and to my mind. I have the right to remember."

I stood up. I spoke out. "I am her sister," I shouted. "I was in the bed next to hers. I was there. And this is not true, it never happened."

"Bitch!" a woman said loudly, turning around to me.

But I was not the sole dissenter. Someone questioned her use of the Holocaust and Hiroshima.

"Historical atrocities were for me the most important part, because the world is heading for nuclear war. If we don't stop domestic violence, we will have nuclear war," Heidi said.

In the dark, another woman rose. "There's something that doesn't feel exactly right to me," she began. "I found the piece depressing. The road to healing has to be taken with a lot of smiles," she said. "The survivor's glee is missing from this dance."

MY MOTHER WAS famous for her hyena laugh. It instilled gaiety, obliviousness. It meant "fins," time off from all the ordinary rules. When she laughed, no one was in trouble—not my father, not my little sister, not me. When she laughed, the chairs and table laughed. The food laughed on the plates.

No one could talk to my mother before her morning coffee. Three cups of coffee, three portions of cottage cheese. She had hazel eyes, unlike mine, and fine, plucked eyebrows, unlike mine, and thin lips, unlike mine. She had had her nose fixed. My nose was my best feature, she said. "I want to put you back in my belly," she threatened.

She served baked potato mashed with cooked carrots every night for dinner. In a large soup bowl, the white and orange-spotted meal. One night I protested. "I don't want to eat any more measles," I said. I went to bed hungry, and I never complained again.

I HAVE TO meet my father at Supreme Court at nine-thirty. It is freezing. I go to the appointed room. I am early. He isn't there. By nine-thirty the room has filled. I see Heidi's lawyer. He has on the same clubfooted shoes, the same pinstripe suit, he wore in the summer, the same beard. He is a twerp from Vermont. Then I see Heidi. Her mousy hair looks jet black.

Her face is dark. Her lips bright red. She wears earrings. She is laughing, standing when the lawyers stand, listening, frowning. Now that my face has softened with age, we look more alike than ever, furrowed, grimacing.

Her hair was oily, mine normal. We had one good joke in childhood. "My hair has already peaked," she said, still in the shower giving herself a shampoo.

I thought she was a lesbian. Once, she arrived from Minneapolis at my father's office with a tall blond girl with a cold sore on her lip, her traveling companion. They acted like lovers. The tall blond girl made hats for Heidi. My father winced when he saw Heidi in one. "You know those *Esquire* cartoons, with the sugar daddy and the tall, sexy blond?" Heidi said. "I always wanted to be the sugar daddy."

She said, "I only feel happy when I have a Slinky between my legs."

There is a handsome young silver-haired man at her side. I can't tell if he is a lawyer or a friend.

Our case is called, *Frankel* v. *Frankel*. "My dad isn't here yet," I tell the judge. "He's the defendant." He comes in. I sit at the table with him, facing the judge. He rises. He speaks. "Laches," he says. "Statute of limitations. I move that the case be dismissed." The judge is a woman. "You'll have to raise your voice," the judge tells my father. "I can't hear you."

My father speaks in his young, steadfast, ebullient voice.

The young twerp from Vermont says he wants to prosecute this case in New York because he is the only specialist in this new field of child abuse. Because of the severity of the tortures his client endured, she suffered from amnesia until she was forty-three, two years ago.

It is a miracle that the cold that morning has not killed my father. May 12 he will be eighty. He has angina. He is having trouble breathing. Some hairs at the back of his head are standing up straight. I smooth them down. I see her looking at me.

* * *

MY FATHER LOOKED like Clark Gable, like Rhett Butler. Once, he took me down the hill on a sled, holding me from behind. Once, I stood outside with him at night during a blackout, the only child my age. Once, at eleven at night, I couldn't sleep, it was too hot. "Why don't you go for a walk?" he said. I went into my room and put on shorts and a halter. I was just going to stand outside the door and get some air. I came out again into the foyer. "Where do you think you're going?" he yelled. He slammed me across the room with his hand.

ONCE I EXERCISED my strength. I wrestled with a boy and beat him. He was red-haired. It was in the circular driveway of the James Madison in Riverdale. I felt a curious exaltation all through me. It was as if I had sinned, done the forbidden. Girls were the weaker sex.

On the same day, my sister bit me. I was the recipient of welcome pity. All the children felt sorry for me. My sister's teeth marks were in my arm.

They felt sorry for me because I had to take care of her. I was always nice to her, but when I turned thirteen and my mother gave me an ermine collar to commemorate my womanliness, I protested at Heidi's matching one. My dad had had two made. Many of his clients were furriers. They took it immediately away from her.

WHEN WE GREW up, Heidi studied French because I wasn't good at it. I didn't like verbs. I never read Colette, her favorite novelist. She wrote her master's thesis on her. Later I read somewhere that Colette's husband chained her to the desk. This physically excited me.

I didn't know then that he forced her to write so that he could sign his name to it.

I wanted to be forced. I got hot in *Gone With the Wind* when Rhett Butler carried Scarlett up the stairs.

I daydreamed about a boy who practiced the violin at night in the yellow window, the only planet across from me.

Once in the lobby a new boy in the building said, "Why pay for a cow when you can get the milk free?" I knew that he was talking about girls and petting.

One day I was home sick and my mother was sitting near my bed, keeping me company. I put a pillow between my legs and it felt good, I wanted to keep it there. I devised a method. "Look at this," I said, "I've made a sliding pond."

"Don't you ever, ever, put anything between your legs again," my mother said.

EVERY SUMMER WE went to the Takanassee, where my father taught me to rumba. My mother took two weeks off from staying in bed, having headaches and rheumatism, talking to her friend Millie, an interior decorator, on the phone, making our little Beatrix Potter meals, entertaining. She took a vacation from her flannel pajamas, her woollies fastened at the waist with a safety pin, her droopy drawers, her at-home outfits, and dressed up. She tortured Heidi's lanky hair into ribbons and curls. She dressed us in matching dresses. On the dance floor in the early evening, my father held me, and my hips moved without instruction as he taught my feet the box step.

I was in love with a boy there, who had a handsome father, named Chesty, with hair on his chest. The boy liked Heidi. My mother was angry. She made Heidi go to our room immediately after dinner so that the boy would be alone on the porch with me.

AFTER THE TRIAL, at a party, I met the handsome silver-haired man who had been in court with Heidi. His mother had raped him. He taught anger seminars. He was with another woman, a poet I knew. He tried to shake my hand. I shuddered and recoiled. Then he disappeared.

"I'm sorry if I upset your evening," I apologized to the

young poetess wandering lost in the crowded room. She had written poems about incest. "Oh, that's all right," she answered somewhat frantically, "but where is he?" He had fled.

I saw an article about my sister in a New Age magazine. A large picture of her dancing. Her face tragic, her limbs hobbled. A picture of the handsome silver-haired man, once her lover. He claimed to be impotent. She reported indignantly that shrink after shrink actually said to her, "Haven't you gotten it through your head yet that your father is not going to sleep with you?" Two items in particular shocked me. She had converted to Christianity, and she had had her first orgasmic experience with her father. "Frankel had her first orgasm with her father." At eight in the morning, I called my father. I told him about the infuriating article. "She says you're a lawyer practicing in New York!"

"She should have given my address. I might have gotten some business out of it."

"Would you like me to come to your office and bring it to you?" I asked.

"Not really," he said. "It sounds like a big nothing. But I *would* like to see what's gotten *you* so riled up!"

"It's the orgasm!" I told him in no uncertain terms.

THEN HEIDI HAD an art show in a women's gallery on Carlton Street. I forced myself to go. The walls were lined with her "reconstructed" child's drawings. Her re-created drawings from grade school, with typed accounts of how the teachers had suppressed them, had ignored her broken bones. There were twin beds. I was her sister, Betsy. She had a dozen brothers, all murdered in satanic rituals. There was a huge book of all the babies murdered in Riverdale. I was responsible for making sure one baby brother didn't cry. He cried. When I, Betsy, was forced to admit that he cried, I was killed by my mother in my own little bed.

There was one moving sculpture. An unwanted child upside down in a plastic bag, with one elongated arm reaching out of the opening in the bag, the arm going on and on endlessly like longing, like loneliness, like a child's sorrowful years.

MARLENA RAN INTO her on Broadway. "What did she look like?" I asked.

"Heavier. All wrong. A lot of gray hair. No makeup. How much older is she than you?"

"She's four years younger."

"No! Really?"

I HAVE JUST thrown out two ugli fruit, uneaten, because they just got too unattractive to keep in the house. I had bought them for the name and because one reminded me of my sister. The browner one.

Now I have no sister.

When she lost in court, Heidi sent everyone in the family a copy of the following letter:

Dear Father:

I came into this world with my spine covered with black-and-blue marks. You had abused me even before I was born. Now that it is time for you to die, I want you to apologize for the constant rapes and beatings with which you bruised and tormented my childhood. I am sending a copy of this letter to the whole family, so that you will be forced to read it. So that you won't crumple it, unread. I want you to know that every day of my life I am forced to deal with your abuse of me.

Mother hated your snoring. But all through the long nights of my childhood, your thunderous snores were the only peace I had. Silence meant rape. The minute the snores stopped, you would come to my bed and rape me. Starting with kindergarten, you forced your penis into my rectum. Even before that, when I was in diapers, you would jab me with the safety pins and force me to perform oral sex on you. As an infant, your penis was my bottle. I had no other. I was starved for being ugly.

I was told I looked Ethiopian and was reduced to a skeleton. You used me for an ashtray, putting out your cigarettes on my scalp and nipples and vagina. I was made to sleep all night in the bathtub. I was forced to urinate on newspapers like a dog. If I disobeyed, mother would bang me against the tiled wall till I was senseless. Every night, she sewed up my vagina with trussing thread, and you cut it with scissors and razor blades and knives to enjoy me even while I suffered from infections. I was taught that I was less than the family mongrel. I was taught to keep low. I was your cur, your concubine.

You told me it was my fault that you abused me, because I was "irresistible." If I didn't want to be a sex slave, I would have to stop being so cute, you said. You took away my childhood from me. You took away my identity, my self. My brain stopped working. I could not think or feel or know or remember. I want you to apologize.

I have thought very carefully about why you did what you did. Yes, there is a reason why you are a perpetrator. You take after your ancestors. They raped too. They raped not only me; they raped you. That is why you are the criminal you are. The perpetrator is a victim too. But there is no excuse for what you did to me.

Still, you were the kinder parent. The kinder parent! You who watched Mother beat me to a pulp, and after, to comfort me, raped and sodomized. One night, after a particularly violent beating in which I lost the hearing in my right ear, you took me to the hospital but first stopped the car, spread my thin little legs, and abused me so savagely that there was blood on the car seat. You told mother that it was menstrual blood, and I was punished for menstruating.

Though incest was enforced on me my whole life, I

thought I deserved it. Because Mother did not think I was beautiful, I believed I was bad. When I went out into the world and found people who looked up to me and admired me, I thought they must be wrong. I could not allow myself to succeed, because I had been trained to think of myself as a pauper. I could not endure respect, because I was conditioned to expect only contempt. Still, I would not succumb to what you and Mother wanted. I would not slit my wrists.

It is not surprising that I wanted to end my life. While other children said their bedtime prayers and hoped to wake up in the morning, I would beg to die so I could escape from your nightly visits and daily persecutions. For I was raped not only nightly but also during naps. Every single day of my life, I experienced terror so acute that even now I can only dimly remember it.

You raped me even after I was adult, and even then, in my thirties, I was too traumatized to admit to myself what was happening. You forced me down on my childhood bed and, holding your hand over my mouth, squeezed my nostrils shut until I fainted and you were able to have your way with me. When I woke up, I had no memory of the abuse. This amnesia persisted until a year ago.

Slowly, one by one, I remembered all the perpetrators in the family. Lastly, I remembered you, because you were the worst Judas. I remembered the incest, and then only after that did I remember the beatings. The casts and slings that I had to wear to school, the black eyes that caused other children to call me "black-eyed Susan."

Now I want my apology. Before it is too late and you die. It is the very least you can do. Even though you deny your actions, expertly lying even to yourself, I think that, in your heart of hearts, you know the truth. It may be only for an instant in the middle of the night when you awaken from a bad dream. A dream of me. But you know. Some iota of honesty and lucidity exists in you. You know that *you tortured me all through my childhood, that you beat and raped and sodomized me my whole life. And I want you to apologize. I am writing this letter to that pinpoint of truthfulness in you.* Apologize!

There is a certain commercial in which I imagine I see my sister. I always look for her, and there she is, looking her best, her bright-red lips, not parted, smiling. Citizen watches, Citizen watches. My pulse quickens when it comes on. I am starved for every flash of her. She has never looked better. Elegant dress, bracelets, a spit curl on her cheek. All too soon she is gone.

But lately there is another. I haven't identified it, the product, yet. Maybe orphan children. She is brown-skinned, laughing, some age I remember as a place, Florida. I am like a moth against the screen, beating, futile. In tears.

Now I go into the bathroom for a late-evening joint. Since Thanksgiving two years ago, I have been smoking more than ever. I turn on the fan and look in the mirror.

I only get beautiful when I smoke grass.

I pull up the skin at the corners of my eyes in a mini face-lift, and I see Heidi, her almond eyes, collagen lips. I look like my sister. And yet my mother liked the way I looked and not the way my sister looked. That was the whole message of childhood. When I moved downtown, Heidi saw the framed photograph of my mother and me in matching net gowns covered with rosebuds and said, "That picture ruined my childhood." When we sold my mother's jewelry to divide the money, I kissed her cheek on the corner of Forty-seventh Street and Sixth Avenue (we had done well!) and she screamed. A crowd gathered. "That was a very intrusive kiss," she declared.

She told our aunt in California, "I would rather be crazy than have what happened to me happened to me."

But still I can't forgive her for wanting to harm my father. He would have given his life to protect her from harm.

I love my father. I love his voice. I called him last night and he was home, Saturday night. He had a cold, but his voice sounded ebullient and jubilant and young. This is because he doesn't do drugs. He doesn't smoke, he doesn't drink. He has Ruth. "Thank you for taking care of my father," I said to her. She obviously loves him. "Oh, Joy," she said, choked with emotion.

THIS HAS GOT to stop. I can't go on smoking. My lungs can't bear it. Black, tattered, like my shoes. Dear God, please let this be my last joint. My lungs are speaking again. My lungs, two angels. Visitors, warning me. Mama, help me. I am burning holes in these gentlemen, my lungs.

I GO TO an AA meeting. "Hello, I'm Joy, I'm a pothead." Half the people there are furious. I'm not an alcoholic. My sponsor thinks that I was in a state of denial about it. Every day she waits for me to tell her I also drank. I never drank. The other half welcome me warmly, they say all forms of intoxication are the same.

All the clichés I loathed from my mother's tongue become my survival kit. One day at a time. Keep it simple. The serenity prayer. I am no longer locked in the bathroom with the fan on. The ashtray with roaches is no longer the first thing I see in the morning, the last thing I see at night. Like Auschwitz, the piled emaciated charred corpses.

Then I get my first reward.

I meet someone who has worked for Carl Vaggio.

"Hi, I'm Sabrina. I'm an alcoholic."

Sabrina is "qualifying," telling her story, how she came to be an alcoholic, and she mentions a great job she had. She worked for an artist who was never home. He and his wife were always away. She had the run of the house. She had a woman lover at the time. The pay was great. When he was there, she fancied she was in love with him. Their "two diseases interlocked," she said. They flirted but never made love, Sabrina said, wearing a long cardigan like Nicole. Like Nicole in an at-home outfit when she was sick. She looked a little like Nicole, I thought. She was an artist too, and she asked him to come see her work at a gallery. "No," he said. "I'm going to play handball and have some real fun." He gave her paintings, which she had sold to live on. I knew at once she was talking about Carl Vaggio. I recognized his style.

During the coffee break, we speak.

Sabrina was there when I called! She remembers talking to me. When she answered the phone at Carl's house, I asked: "Are you Jerri?"

"No, I'm Sabrina the bookkeeper," she had said.

"There are certainly a lot of women in that house!"

"Now I'm getting nervous about this conversation," she had said.

After the meeting, she came to my house. We looked at a Carl Vaggio picture book together. There was the picture of Heather and Carl in Machu Picchu on their premature honeymoon. "I'd like to put my hands around her scrawny neck," she said, "and strangle her—I hate Heather so much. She polishes the furniture with Preparation H. . . .

"I would have gone to bed with him too," Sabrina said, "but for one afternoon when we were having a great discussion, a great time. Suddenly he got up and said, 'I have an appointment,' and left, just like that. He was sleeping with Jerri, the maid," she said. "They had a place right near the gym where Carl played handball. The no-perks club he joined. She was the perk. He slept with her every time he played handball. His wife was in such a state of denial about it. They had the most squalid, disgusting little marriage," she said.

I couldn't believe he had been sleeping with Jerri-the-maid while he was promising to marry me.

"I like to pretend that the little black ball is your head," I remembered him saying. At the time, no words could have seemed more romantic.

When he left me to play handball, he was sleeping with

her? A nice helpful hippie with a bare midriff. When he jilted me, he played handball and then went across the street to her?

I thought he had made some dire Catholic vow behind my back. God, grant me this one wish, this child, and I will be faithful and monogamous for the rest of my life. But he had been sleeping with the maid all along.

"He is still sleeping with her," Sabrina said.

We drank tea. Sabrina mentioned Gloria, who had worked for Carl too. "She was really great. A feminist. We all felt sorry for you," she said. "We didn't think you got a fair deal. He probably did really love you," she said. "You have such a sweet nature."

Before she left, she offered me another crumb of information. "Once, just before his third son was born, he said to me, 'I feel so jaded. I've had everything.' "

13

MOUNTAIN GRASS

/ / / / / / /

"You are not the center of the universe!" my mother said. She was on her deathbed when she told me this. It was close to the end. She told me her dream. "We are both in open coffins and Carl Vaggio is in the dream and we get up from our coffins and go toward life—and Carl Vaggio is my 'little daddy.'"

She said, "Get up out of your coffin and move your feet!" I moved my feet.

At an art opening on Wooster Street, a young woman turned to me suddenly. "Joy Frankel?" I didn't recognize her at all. She had kinky hair, a pretty, angular face; she was flat-chested, chic, wearing something black. I had no idea of her age. "I'm Orso's wife," she said. "Orso?" I said. "Orso Lombroso?" I was slow. I had to go back a long time. I had not spoken to him in about ten years. I forgot her name entirely. He had married her when Nicole died. "Kiki," she said.

"Yes, Kiki," I remembered. Kiki had been Nicole's friend too.

"Orso died, you know."

My eyes closed in disbelief.

"You didn't know?" she said. "I assumed everyone read it in the newspaper. There was quite a nice obituary. He just died two weeks ago."

"Why?" I said, stricken. I could only get out that monosyllable, because to me he seemed indestructible.

"Why?" she repeated sarcastically. As if I were asking maliciously what wonderfully irking thing caused his demise. What had triggered his heart attack.

"Did he have a heart attack or something?" I said. Tears wet my cheeks. A huge mountain of a man. An oppressor. It was like thinking that death could die.

"Oh yes," she said, shrugging.

And then I remembered everything. My past. The last time she and I had met. I had brought my new boyfriend to meet Orso. I had rung the bell. She had come to the door.

"Yeah," Kiki said. "It was exactly ten years ago. Orso freaked. 'We don't take drop-ins,' he said."

"I met Dimitri ten and a half years ago," I said. "We're still together." I proudly pointed out a man standing across the room in a plaid flannel shirt, more handsome than ever.

"No, it wasn't that man," she said, "it was some other."

"There was no other, unless it was my former husband," I said, confused.

"No, it wasn't your husband," she said.

It was as if my whole past were dying again. She stood there with a supportive friend at her side. Probably she was still in shock. "Orso was so horrible to me," I blurted out.

"I don't want to hear this," she said.

And then I ridiculously invited her to my house. To visit! She turned away in the middle of my sentence.

*　　*　　*

I AM DOWNTOWN, walking west on Twelfth Street. I am full of myself; I have just seen the shrink. I had not wanted to follow in my mother's footsteps, and yet I had. I had held on to my husband because she had lost hers. Then I had been jilted, like her, and held on to my sorrow. I feel centered, immersed in my own story, my self. Purposeful, even young. About to get my whole, concise life into a sentence.

For some reason I have put on my makeup carefully this morning. First a ring of copper eyeliner, then a trace of black eyeliner, and black mascara. Red lipstick from Borghese. Gilded bronze rouge. I have discovered that if I pull my hair back with my bronze turtle barrette, it hides the roots where my hair parts in the middle. Those gray roots down the middle like a zipper. I am wearing my daughter's tight jeans, which I have never worn before, with buttons instead of a zipper for a fly.

Dimitri had been standing on a ladder on the street, installing an air conditioner for the living room when I left. It had been a cool summer, but now we really needed it. He was looking so handsome as he worked that I went back, though I was late, to say goodbye again. Dimitri was brusque. He hates public displays. He hates to be stared at. He was unshaven. His three-day beard reminded me of Carl's when I would arrive at his house, a married woman from the Upper West Side.

"You're a horrible oppressive person," Dimitri said.

I WAS WALKING along when suddenly a man, whom I didn't notice, a man on the edge of the sidewalk, an uninteresting workman, said something to me. I didn't quite catch the words. Something not quite rude; something cautionary. I kept walking. Then I wondered if my fly was open. I turned around. He had kept walking. He turned around. At some distance, he stood looking at me.

I looked at him for a long moment. He was short, he had

white hair, cropped, with a bohemian tennis band around his head. His skin was brown and leathery, his face stubbled with white. He looked like a little old Jewish man from the garment district. Like Rumpelstiltskin. His pants were speckled. Paint-spattered.

"Wait!" I cried out.

It was Carl Vaggio.

For eleven years I had seen him only in dreams, or on television, or in the Arts & Leisure section, or on the cover of art magazines.

I ran to him and put my arms around him, as if he were a shade that might vanish. "Is it really you?" I said.

I could not believe how small he had grown. In my mind he had not aged a day.

"I didn't hear what you said. What did you say?"

"I don't know," he said.

"But what were the words?" I said, still amazed that he had spoken, that I had turned around.

"I said, 'Watch out, lady.' " He gazed at me with his mute admiration. "There must be something in the air," he said, gesturing with his mutilated hand. I was surprised the missing fingers had not grown back, since his hair had. The three stumps hung there limply. "I just had dinner with Dennis and Ghislaine."

I looked at him blankly.

"You remember Dennis and his wife, Ghislaine?" he prompted. "You look good," he said.

I was anointed with his approval. It was like having my roots newly dyed. He had overcome his instinct to run, his low profile, because I still looked good to him. I felt as good as new. As good as when I used to go to him in jeans and little leather gloves, every part of me an accessory. When I used to feel so expensive and young.

"I do?" I said.

I couldn't say he looked good back. He looked leathery, like his conscience. He looked reduced to his true size and importance. He looked shorn of his youthful mane, his glitter, his greatness.

Slung over my shoulder, I was carrying a denim jacket he had liked. "This is the jacket you told me to buy!" I reminded him, overwhelmed by the coincidence.

"Isn't that a little out-of-date?"

He had said that many times before. All his phrases had been used before. They were like used contraceptives. Limp, hanging condoms.

This was the most important moment of my life.

"I'm wearing the chain you bought me," I said, holding my amber pendant, garish, two-sided like one of his canvases. "I stopped wearing the amber rose years ago," I admitted.

"I feel honored," he mumbled.

"Did you know that Orso died?" I asked bluntly. To hurt him. I am glad that Orso is dead.

"Yes! I'm very angry at him. He didn't tell me." Carl laughed. "I had to read it in the paper. I wasn't invited to the funeral."

"Can we have a Coke?" I asked. The street was eternity. There were giant cameras dangling from the sky. It was Judgment Day. "I've waited for this for so long."

"This 'chance encounter'?" he said with his familiar irony. "Okay." And he steered me into a nearby luncheonette. There were two stools free at the counter. "Let's sit here," he said. It wasn't what I had pictured. I had pictured a booth.

"Can we be honest?" I said, at the counter.

"You were always honest," he said, "and I have no objection to honesty."

I was nervous. This was my one chance to say what needed to be said. To ask why he had jilted me. I was afraid I would not be able to find the right words, that I would not be able to do justice to my own suffering.

One image came back to me. Géricault's life raft. I am

drowning in an enormous sea holding on to the splintery edge; Carl Vaggio stands above me laughing and, as if it were a game, pries my fingers loose.

There was a sea of aging women customers around us, dyed-blond ladies in hats. The waitress appeared behind the counter. He ordered a grilled cheese and Coke; I carefully ordered a diet Coke with lime.

I had called his number three times a week for ten years and hung up when his wife answered.

I wanted to be an example of the cleverness of woman, but I was thwarted at every turn. I could not even arrange an accidental meeting such as the heroine of nearly every movie enjoys. Even at the movies, seeing *The Accidental Tourist*, I was unable to escape a sense of my own failure.

Now I sucked sweet medicinal caffeine through a straw. I felt his admiration alight on my bronzed cheeks and eyelids, my nicely colored subtly black hair. Hair that was not too, too black.

"You said you would marry me," I reminded him. "And you didn't. How could you have done that to me?" I said. "I was made for you."

I noticed that he didn't want to challenge my last statement. It flattered him still; there was some future in the phrase.

"It ruined my life," I said. "I almost died—and my children almost died." I was talking wildly, horrified by my own clichés.

I only looked at him in little sips. He ate quickly.

"I had to go to AA to stop smoking pot," I continued, "and I met a friend of yours. Someone who worked for you."

"Who?"

"Sabrina-the-bookkeeper. She told me that all the while I was wooing you, you were sleeping with Jerri-the-maid."

He seemed to grow nostalgic at the thought of Sabrina. "She didn't say that we did it, did she?"

"No, she said you almost did it. She's not too attractive," I added.

"A lot of men find her very attractive," Carl insisted.

"Not anymore," I persisted. "She's prematurely wrinkled."

The conversation returned to Jerri-the-maid.

"She's married now and living happily with her husband, an art critic, and their child, in . . ."

I was surprised. Even that eternal debauch had ended. I had no interest in her new address.

"I saw Dawn recently," he said.

"Did you sleep with her?"

"Yes. But she's become rather mannish. A dyke."

"Are you sleeping with her now?"

"No. She's crossed over the line."

I raised my arm in triumph over my head. "The sisters are doing it for themselves," I said, quoting from a movie I had just seen (*Without You I'm Nothing*).

"It made *me* rather sad."

I suddenly didn't care what made him sad. His sadness was not important to me. It was deserved. It was well-earned sadness. It was his due. I remembered my own sadness, the hourglass of it emptying inside me for years. I remembered Nicole's, as she was bravely dying. "He is the same with all of us. He does treat us all the same. All four of us!"

"Do you still have your horses?" I asked.

"Yes! We did very well this year. Heather hates the horse farm," he added intimately.

As if I would care what Heather hates!

"Who are you sleeping with now?"

"No one. Only my wife," he said with prurient piety.

"How is she?" I asked politely.

"Fine. She's an attorney, a J.D.," he answered nonsensically.

So he had really weighed my Ph.D. against her J.D. and found me lacking. I was amazed by his conservativeness, his conventionality. He thought a business attorney was better than a poet. I wondered if my father would agree. "And your new sons?"

"They're very nice," he mumbled.

"How old are they now?"

"Four, six, and eight."

"That young?" The years had dragged so. "You should have helped me," I said. "You should have at least given me a credit card. At least if Isabelle and I could have gone shopping together and I could have pretended I was Mrs. Carl Vaggio . . ."

Smiling, he said, "I would almost feel bad, but you look too good for that. I can't feel guilty."

I was pleased. I forgot I was poor, I felt rich.

He looked at the check. I couldn't at all see what it said without glasses.

He started anxiously checking his pockets.

"You look worried," I said. "Do you want me to chip in?"

He laughed his helpless laugh. "You're making me nervous," he admitted.

"But why did you do it?" I asked.

"Do what?"

"Jilt me?"

"I never said I would marry you."

All the dates were fresh in my mind. On Veterans Day he had said he would marry me. I had been chastely wooing him for two years. I had looked at him with reproach, not believing my good fortune. "At first I thought it was . . . unlikely," he had said. "But now it seems like a better idea." He had leaned towards me, and we kissed. Our short interview was over. I ran down the ballroom stairs, like Cinderella at midnight, and out into the street. I was carrying Nicole Lombroso's green Chinese parasol.

"Yes, you did," I protested. "It was after my mother died. My mother died on January 19 . . ." I stumbled, searching for the year.

"You're a little confused," he mocked.

"I loved you so much, it was a religious experience for me.

More than AA," I added ironically. "I know you loved me too, because you said so. And you didn't usually say that."

"I say it much more often now. I found it was very popular, and so I say it all the time."

Somehow his brutal honesty was not as charming as it once had been.

"I did love you," he whined. "You were very nice. But I never had any idea of marrying you. I never even hinted," he said.

That wasn't true. I could prove it wasn't true. "I have countless examples of verbatim dialogue."

He was laughing.

Had I made it all up? I wondered. No. It had been said. It had been promised. Now he was lying to my face; still he was lying. He was a liar. I found that unpleasant. Damning.

"Then why did you never see me again?"

"Because you were a horrible oppressive person," he answered fiercely.

It was my turn to laugh. I was surprised by the coincidence.

"That's what my current boyfriend just said."

"Well, we both didn't make it up out of thin air."

Again, male triumph. He was ready to leave.

"Can I tell you about my boyfriend?" I said.

"Yes. Go ahead."

"Well, he's gorgeous and a great artist." I was surprised at my own warmth, at the words tumbling out like love. To cover it up a little I said, "His work is like yours, only his materials are different, they're not slick and impersonal, they're personal and shabby, like a bit of his flannel shirt."

"Yeah, yeah," he said, dismissing my art criticism. "Does he support you?" He got right to business, to the heart of the matter. The Artist as Great Businessman.

"No. I support him, with money I got selling your painting. But it's all gone now," I added.

"That's amazing," he said. "Now, with all the artists doing

so well, you managed to find the one that was unsuccessful."

As if we were making love, his words touched all the bases. "Do you like him?" he said.

"Yes," I answered immediately, "but I can't have an orgasm."

"I find that very difficult to believe," he said in a subdued voice.

"It's true, though," I said. "That's why I'm seeing a shrink. I have not had an orgasm practically since the day my mother died." That day in the flying cab, Carl Vaggio had stolen them from me.

When we said goodbye, he leaned his forehead against mine. He kissed my lips. He hadn't changed at all. I had. It was all exactly as it was. His forehead bumped mine at exactly the same height. But now I wondered how I had ever liked him. His little narrow lips like scars, which used to thrill me barely brushing mine, now made no impression. No cigar rings puffed from them like a magic billboard. "Call me," they said. They had no breath. No meadows of mown watermelon grass, no sweet stirring breath of Eden. They were inert. "I will give you a number where you can reach me," they said.

"No," I said, laughing. "As Nicole said, 'I'm not going to call *you* anymore, you can call *me*.' "

The very air reverberated with echoes from the past.

"All right. I'll call you. I like to be the aggressor in sex."

All of a sudden, it occurred to me that he didn't. Always I had taken his words at face value, but he had said the opposite of what he meant. He liked to play it safe. He liked the woman to make the first move, come to him on the subway, take her clothes off, climb into bed. He was afraid of rejection. It was no wonder, I thought, looking at him.

"Bring your number in a sealed envelope to my studio," he continued. "You know where it is."

"I'll give you my number."

"Okay."

I removed my gold Cross pen very deliberately from its loop

on my black leather organizer. I began slowly leafing through the scribbled days of the year, looking for a scrap of day that didn't have things written on it. Fumbling in my bag, "I have nothing to write it on," I said.

"Here." He got out a yellow duplicate receipt from a pocket.

I wrote "Joy" self-consciously on the flimsy paper. Wouldn't Heather see it? I wanted to see the amount, the item he had paid for. But I couldn't. I was moving in slow motion, fascinated by every second.

"Hurry up," he said, with his familiar brusqueness, as he had Tuesdays and Thursdays for five years, waiting for me to come. "Hurry up," he repeated, embarrassed, afraid he had offended me. "Hurry up, that's a good way to come," he mocked himself.

I slowly wrote the number leaning on nothing, going over individual digits, making them darker. Gave it to him.

"I may not call you for a long time." He was suddenly worried, considerate. "I'm leaving today for the country. For the horse farm."

IT IS AS if they are making a movie on Carlton Street.

My happiness throws a spotlight on the colors of the brick of all the downtown buildings, on the China Brilliance Corp across the street. Words leap to life at the Korean grocery store. "All flowers pay outside."

When I get home, Dimitri is outside in the backyard, admiring his work. The garden. The pool. The sculptures and rocks. The cemented-over windows of the CIA building that he has painted white. The new light that visits, that invites more light all afternoon, till dusk. He sits on the stoop, the barn-red door behind him.

"I met Carl Vaggio on the street," I blurt out. He barely reacts. But he is interested, I can tell. "He liked me, but I didn't like him anymore."

"Did you talk?"

"Yes."

"Did you two kiss goodbye?" he asks (he is clairvoyant).

"Yes."

"Did you kiss on the lips?"

"Yes."

"There you are, there it is," he says. "Mrs. Blackball gets her wish." He calls me that because my married name was Black, though I was always Joy Frankel.

"But I don't like him anymore."

"Oh, you will if you get a dose of the power."

We go inside and sit in a triumphantly cool room, the walls covered with his paintings. He sits on one of the paired blue velvet theater chairs. I sit at the glass table so as not to crowd him. The stubble of his beard looks so much more like Carl in his glorious youth than Carl's own stubble did, I worship every hair.

A MONTH LATER, I saw Dennis again. He was hunched, nearly bald, plumper, especially from behind, wearing tinted glasses, bustling. His wife was with him. Ghislaine. Her straw-colored hair, which he had written so many poems about, was now the same color as mine. Only it had the texture of straw. Her eyes were bright blue. She too wore tinted glasses, perhaps over tinted contact lenses. Her "boy hips" that he had fallen in love with, had celebrated in verse, were square and matronly now. She wore black leggings and silver flats, more like Humpty-Dumpty than a sylvan nymph. Her accent was wearying and oppressive.

It was at an artists' colony. We came into the first stall and were shaking hands, unimpressive art on the walls, when he appeared. I had an enormous advantage. I had seen his picture, with his name beside it, in a brochure. He had been the visiting critic the summer before. Dimitri had pointed it out to me. "But it can't be," I said. "I don't know any other Dennis Berg who's an art critic," Dimitri said. Carefully I studied the photograph, until finally I recognized his stance, his body. When he saw me, his gibbous face fell in amazement. Now, even more than in the picture from the year before, he looked like some Dr. Botwinick, some dentist from the suburbs. I smiled coolly. I introduced Dimitri and our two young friends.

He made his apple-polishing way across the vast pastures of the usurped farm as if he were back at Yale, working a room of professors at a faculty tea. He held forth in small groups or singled out a sculptor to bestow himself upon. His wife too appeared in silhouette, talking to a puny artist her husband might write about. It was stultifyingly small. Juvenile. "Should I talk to him?" I said before we left.

"If you have to," Dimitri said, so young and handsome and slightly jealous. It was his thirty-eighth birthday.

I didn't have to. I didn't want to tell him I had just seen Carl Vaggio. I was more than content to leave without speaking further to Dennis Berg.

REASONS I CAN'T have an orgasm:
1: (Yeats)

> Because the mountain grass
> Cannot but keep the form
> Where the mountain hare has lain.

I am the mountain grass; Carl Vaggio the mountain hare.
2: (Dimitri)
During sex, his balls disappear, like landing wheels when the plane leaves the ground. I miss them. Where are they? I wonder. God, I can't fly. I need them to swing against me. To swing against my bottom. I am like a man with a flat-chested woman, who likes big breasts.

WE MET AT Bard ten years before. In the cafeteria, as I was carrying my tray, I saw a very handsome stranger in a faded plaid flannel shirt. He was the handsomest man I had ever seen. I was pinned by the boulders of his eyes. I could not lower my tray. His name was Dimitri Dorogovich. "I am an artist in residence," he said, "they pay me to do nothing." He was twenty-seven. "Sometimes I'm so afraid," he said. "That's so manly of you to admit," I said. We were walking in the dark, crossing the greensward. He put his head down and his mouth closed over me. His sensual Buddha lips, his Gentile breath. His shoulders were like the mountains behind us. "Everyone will see," I said. We went to my room for a joint. He took off his shirt. He had hair on his chest. He was wearing a cross. "I have three children," I said. He took off his pants. Marble legs. A little pouting belly like Bacchus. He entered me. I tried to show my excitement. "What's wrong?" he said. "Why are you acting so spastic?"

Afterwards, we went to a bar. "I think it's so clever of you to have gray hairs," he said. "Cunt-face."

I felt it swell. "What does that mean?"

"It means when you look at your face, you see what your cunt is doing."

We listened to "Maggie Mae" playing on the jukebox. It was the era of the older woman. *"Tout est possible,"* he said, like a foreign film. *"Tout est possible."* He came to New York to live with me.

His small hands are not beautiful. They are squat, the knuckles are not shapely, and his closed fist is strangely square. His fingers are tiny iron crowbars that massage.

He says, "Your kisses are becoming warmer, like stuffed cabbage." I am piping hot.

His aggression stirs desire in me that is as sharp as a knife. My vagina sings. My useless womb. My ovulating head. He rides over me chin-first. His muscular arms, his huge shoulders, his back, are satin. I kiss his Adam's apple with little popping kisses. When I lick it I feel like a bitch, and my thighs spread. His mouth comes down from time to time and wets mine, or brushes it. It is a little like Carl's no-kiss.

My mouth drinks long-necked at the bowl of his mouth. I want his pleasure. It comes. His silence grows deeper. He is still.

He calls us the Blackballs. "Mrs. Blackball was up all night counting her children," he says. We ride down in the elevator with a young father holding his infant. "All the men in this building have a tit."

"I think you only smile so you can close your eyes," Dimitri says.

"Why do you like me?" I ask him.

"You're like Nefertiti," he answers. "I liked her first. . . . I once saw a slut that looked like you on Fifth Avenue."

But once, a Russian taxi driver, a Jew, said. "The Russians don't *know* sex."

"I can't come," I say. It is our big fight over sex.

"I don't care," Dimitri says. "Isn't that what a nymphomaniac is all about? Being dissatisfied?" Then, his answer to everything: "I'm not Jewish," he says.

ONCE, WHEN I was with Dimitri, I nearly broke my back because I thought I saw Carl. It was at a huge art show at a defunct train terminal in Brooklyn—Dimitri was in it—I was wearing a mink jacket he had bought in college for five dollars, with a Canadian V sewn over the sleeve where a dog's teeth had torn it.

I saw Carl walking with a small blond boy. His new child.

It was so right—his appearing at this enormous avant-garde show, turning up where you'd least expect him. It was so right—my mink, my jeans, my high heels. I saw his ponytail, his walk. I thought his behind looked fatter. I ran after him. My back snapped. He turned around, a stranger.

WE MOVED DOWNTOWN; Dimitri built me a house. A garden. Our big fight about sex continued.

"Why do I feel that I'm about to be served with a summons every time we make love?" Dimitri said.

"I'm sorry." I tried to laugh.

"Why isn't it fun anymore?" he said.

You had fun, I thought. I still couldn't come. It had been

years. With Carl, I came first. Then he came. The correct etiquette of sex. He'd lean on one elbow and hang around, waiting. "C'mon," he'd say. I'd clench myself around him, and it would happen. The lapping of pleasure. The reward. Or I faked it.

I said, "I wish nature were kinder that way."

"Nature *is* kinder!" Dimitri said. "If I gave you money, you'd be popping with orgasms."

"No, I wouldn't," I said.

Then my dad was the lawyer for a new discotheque. He was a ten percent owner. The disco was opening in a month very near us. He wanted to know if Dimitri would paint the mural. Dimitri was watching Spanish news on television when I asked him. When I mentioned a job he got angry. "Why won't you help my father?" I said. "Are you afraid of earning money?"

"You've ruined my day for no reason," Dimitri said, violently getting up, turning off the set. He left the house in a rage.

In a practical, businesslike way, I called Carl.

Roy answered. I asked for Carl. He was in. Roy came back to the phone. "He said, 'What do you want?' "

"Just to have lunch," I answered, somewhat indignantly.

Then Carl got on the phone. "What do you want?" he said, in a harsh voice that belied his vulnerability. His susceptibility to me.

"To see you, if you want to see me."

"Why?"

"To be friends."

"We are friends."

"No, we're not, not at this distance."

He laughed.

His flirting back, his even coming to the phone, produced a massive excitement in me.

"When?"

"Today."

"I can't, because I have to be at a little League game at three o'clock and at the circus at five."

It had been so long since I had heard the apologetic details of his life, the glamorous details that excluded me.

"Tomorrow, then?"

"I can't. I have to work. I'm sorry."

"The day after tomorrow?" By now I sounded tortured.

"I can't, because I'm leaving for Europe. What can I do?" he asked helplessly. Then he was challenging, aggressive again. "What do you want?"

"I don't know."

"You don't know?"

It was the old torture: desire, love. He understood what happened to my voice.

"What do you want?"

"I want you to tell me when to call you."

"Call me next Wednesday at ten."

ONE DAY OF incredible excitement. At Walker's, I realize I can bring him to Isabelle's apartment. She has just left me— moved in with a man. At first I cried, and was nauseated, for a week, just at the thought of a chapter closing—my children gone (Benjamin, who is six feet four, and Penelope, are away at college). But now Isabelle and I are more inseparable than ever. It is more an expansion than a separation. "Like gold to airy thinness beat." We found the great, mint apartment to- gether. A penthouse with dazzling views. There is even a small Vaggio on the wall inscribed with the words *for Isabelle and Benjamin, my solid favorites.* "Dennis thought it was tacky, my using words," Carl told me. I picture going up in the elevator together, getting out my key.

I walk home from the restaurant, past the firehouse where *Ghostbusters* was filmed, down the street where David Letter- man lives, glorified, at one with the neighborhood.

Dimitri returns from making the rounds of the galleries

like Douglas, drained of reality. Muttering. He even says, "Indeed."

But then at night we are close. I think I will never go back to Carl, when suddenly on TV there is a MasterCard commercial. A man is standing next to a woman in an elevator when suddenly her pocketbook emits flames. Only *he* notices. The wrong charge card is burning a hole in her pocketbook. She stands there on fire, oblivious.

I register the alarm. My own pocketbook is on fire. I realize I will have to call Carl. My pocketbook is nearly empty. It isn't love, it isn't sex. It's money. Wednesday morning, I call. Carl is in Italy.

THE FOLLOWING WEDNESDAY I call again. I am afraid Dimitri might pick up the phone in the bedroom if I call from the living room, might hear the word "Carl," might hear Roy, or the new guy, Antony, say "Carl isn't in," or hear Carl's voice. One syllable could be fatal. But I close the door to the bedroom ostensibly because of the loud German—he is studying foreign languages incessantly on Channel 13 and cable, watching "Deutschland, Germany Live," before French and Italian and Spanish—I go to the front of the house, my studio, and call. I call anyway, my heart thumping. It isn't money, it's sex.

I have come alive, he is my lifeline. It's sexual fulfillment.

Someone answers and says Carl hasn't come in yet. I am afraid that he is avoiding me. I relive the past. That pain that I will feel even after death . . . When Dimitri leaves to go to Job Lot, I call again. I ask for Roy. Roy says Carl is in Europe, actually. Whoever had spoken to me earlier had been confused.

I WANTED TO go to the new downtown circus, the Cirque du Soleil, because Carl had seen it. It was in Battery Park City, fairly near me. I wanted to see what he had seen, be where he had been. But Dimitri didn't want to spend the money on tickets. The front-row seats were expensive, because the people in them could participate in the show. But even the back row was expensive.

Finally, I decided to go with Isabelle and her friend Portia. On Friday, May 31, the last night of the season, we got tickets. At the last minute, Dimitri wanted to go. Isabelle went to the phone. She is so thoughtful and considerate. "There are no tickets left, but I'm sure we can scalp one," she said to him sweetly.

Dimitri felt welcome and joined us.

As soon as we got there, a Chinese woman and a man were selling one ticket. I bought it. We went to the big tent, prepared to separate. Dimitri's one seat would be far from us, I realized. But to our amazement, his ticket was for the seat directly behind me. Next to the Chinese woman and the man.

The whole tent is filled with dazzling specks like childhood. The clowns blow smoke rings that circle in the air, reminding me of Carl Vaggio. My thoughts of Carl Vaggio fill the whole tent. The aerialist, Vladimir, dives through the smoke rings. He is Russian like Dimitri, his body voluptuous. Only he is vain, narcissistic, a porn star. I like Dimitri more.

During the intermission I am in raptures. It is so magical. The clowns are rudely borrowing a camera from a man in the front row on the other side of the tent. Dimitri leans forward. "Who is that man in the blue shirt next to the man with the camera?" he says.

Far away, almost on another planet, I see Carl Vaggio.

He is the man in the blue shirt next to the man with the camera. But it can't be. He's already been to this circus. It can't be. I look to the left. A boy is leaning towards him. In the next seat is a smaller boy. Heather is sprawled with the smallest boy in her lap. The smallest boy's seat is empty next to her. The boys have dark hair. Heather is wearing glasses. Heather's legs are stuck out straight, her feet pigeon-toed. "Carl Vaggio?" I answer.

"I think so," Dimitri says.

I look harder than I have ever looked at anything. I see Carl hide his face in pleasure, bending over the boy, embarrassed and delighted by the limelight. He is a good father. He is white-haired. He looks average. He is enormously happy. He is in love with his life.

"Heather is not at *all* pretty," Dimitri says. I can hardly see; Dimitri has amazing eyes. I turn to Dimitri, interested. "But she is his base, and he fucks everyone else on the side."

When I search for Carl again, I think I have made a mistake. The man in his place is older, fatter, the man in his place is wearing a white shirt, he is a different man.

I panic, as if I have lost something valuable, something irreplaceable. The intermission is almost over. I have made a terrible mistake. Then suddenly I see Carl coming down the stairs, carrying refreshments like a good family man, Mr. Ordinary.

He sits down. As in the fall, when you gain an hour, the flattened rows fill out again. The different man in the white shirt is sitting in the row behind Carl Vaggio.

All through the second half of the circus I sit with my head tilted upward, for Dimitri's sake, while I stare straight ahead in awe, watching Carl Vaggio and his family watching the high-wire acts.

"I saw you Friday night," I said.

"Oh yeah?" he said, intrigued. "Where?"

"At the circus. Did you like it? You must like it. You went twice."

"I don't, actually. But the kids do."

"Do you want to have lunch?"

"Yes," he said.

"When?"

"Tomorrow."

"Tomorrow isn't absolutely perfect," I said.

"What would be 'absolutely perfect'?" he asked.

"Today."

"I can't," he said, "I have to go to the foundry."

"Oh well," I said, "it's as if I was out with you, and your whole family, on Friday night. It's like I just saw you."

"Oh yeah? What's wrong with tomorrow?"

Then I knew he wanted me.

"The day after tomorrow?" I suggested happily.

"I can't, I'm leaving for Europe. But I think I can do something tomorrow. Have a sandwich."

THE NO PARKING sign is shaking like my father on this affluent street. The Carlton Street subway is marbled like St. Petersburg. A movie star has opened a restaurant on the corner. Carlton Street Grill. Limousines line the block three deep. I have never been to this restaurant, I have always been on the outside looking in. This is where I wanted us to meet.

"Okay," he said.

"Are you sure?" I asked.

"Well, I'd much rather meet there than in my neighborhood," he said. Well, I won't have to travel far, I thought.

I sat at the bar and waited for him. Then I saw him a half block away, lost. He was wearing all white. "Artist for Amnesty" was on his T-shirt. I was wearing a leather jacket painted with Frida Kahlo's *Diego on Her Mind*, which Isabelle's friend had just given me.

As soon as he came in he hated the restaurant.

"I couldn't find the entrance."

"I know, I saw you looking for it."

"Why didn't you help?"

"I couldn't risk it."

"This is so tacky and pretentious," he said. "Let's go someplace else."

"This is the only place where people don't know me." It was the place where I had never been, where we had never gone for a bowl of soup.

I had requested a table in the private room in the back, away from the windows. It had a skylight, a few tables. Paintings on the wall. It was entirely empty.

I thought that if Dimitri passed by on the street, on the way to the video store, say, he wouldn't see me. I was completely wrong. Under the skylight, I was illumined as if from within. I was like a stained-glass window. Brilliantly visible. I was nervous. I kept looking towards the front windows for Dimitri.

"How did he know what I looked like—how did he recognize me?" Carl said.

"Everyone knows what you look like. You've been on the covers of art magazines."

"Well, I don't know what *he* looks like," Carl said, motioning toward the front windows. He looks like Adam on the ceiling of the Sistine Chapel, I think, only better.

"But he knows what *I* look like," I said, "and I'm very noticeable." I was thinking of my black hair, my gold cuffs, my painted jacket. "Isn't it wonderful how noticeable I am?"

"Yes," he agreed, and I could tell that he thought I was still beautiful.

THERE WERE ABSOLUTELY no answers.

"Three miscarriages in five years, and one to term. It was *gruesome*," he said.

"When she lost the baby, why didn't you leave?"

"I'm not the leaving type," he laughed.

"Yes, you are," I laughed, "you left me."

We left it at that.

HE ASKED ABOUT Dimitri. "Where is he from? How long has he been here? How did he get out?"

"You mean from Russia? He was born here," I said.

"Why isn't he at work, anyway?" he said.

"All he does is lie on the bed and study foreign languages on television," I complained.

"I saw some of his work in a magazine. I was impressed."

In my bag, I carried a sentence on a scrap of paper: "That pain that I will feel even after death—a pain deep enough to reach through an ocean and cleave the tail of a mermaid in half." But I never showed it to him. I said, "I thought of one sentence to say."

"What?"

"It has a few different versions."

"What is it?"

"It goes, roughly: 'I have listened to your detractors and been comforted.' "

He laughed. "What do they say?"

"They say you are the most highly paid artist in the world."

"I'm not. Do they also say that I'm the most highly over-rated?"

"No," I lied.

"I was such a terrible druggie," he said. "It's a miracle I survived."

"Me too." I mentioned my shrink, complained of the expense. "Even at a clinic, I have to pay her twenty-five dollars a week."

"I don't want to stress the distance between us," Carl said. I was saddened by the word "distance," thinking he had grown away from me, there was some spiritual gulf between us. "But I pay mine three hundred."

I laughed and felt better. It was only money.

"Why doesn't Heather like the horse farm?"

"Oh, it's so expensive, and I have all the grass mown."

"I thought lawyers liked things very tidy."

"No, she's very messy. She's the bookkeeper now."

We both thought of Sabrina. We talked about her again. "She got a Guggenheim," he said. "I gave her a recommendation. They didn't believe it. They called me up. 'No, I think that she's good,' I said."

"How is Cara?"

"The wedding cost me eighty-nine thousand dollars, and that didn't include the extras," he said. "I'm a grandfather—can't you tell?"

Yes! Suddenly I saw the resemblance—the ugly European look: my grandfather who molested me.

*   *   *

HE DENIED THAT he had just slept with Dawn. "That may have been what I told you—to upset you," he said, "but it's not true."

I told him what Dimitri had said. " 'Heather is not at *all* pretty, but she's his base and he sleeps with everyone else on the side.' "

He didn't defend Heather's looks. He shrugged helplessly. "When you have that reputation . . ."

I told him that a very tall woman I knew said that he had made a pass at her. But she didn't like him. She said, "He's so small—and commercial."

He flinched from the blow. He sat there and took it.

I decided to mention my one-night stand with his daughter's new husband.

"I slept with Frank Wood."

"That's the most disgusting thing I've heard in a long time," he said.

"It was only once. He borrowed money from me and never returned it. I was shocked. I was going to tell Cara it's not a good deal."

He sat there and took whatever I said.

"How could you give up what we had?"

"Sex isn't that important," Carl Vaggio said.

I ordered the same dish as his. He ate nothing. I ate the entire rare, practically raw, grilled tuna steak. The waiter didn't speak English. "Please don't take my bread," I said. He smiled and took away my roll and butter.

"What time is it? Do you have a watch on under all that?" I had bought a new blouse in Greenwich Village the night before. It was white, ruffled, off the shoulder. Under the jacket, it looked like a huge tablecloth.

I slid my Swatch watch down below my painted gold cuff. "Three o'clock."

"I can stay here till three-fifteen," he said, as if he were granting me three hundred years of mermaid life. I was meeting Isabelle at my house at three-thirty—it was my alibi, we were shopping for curtains for her new apartment together— but I got confused.

"I have to go *now*," I said, and jumped up.

He paid the check with a charge card and left a fifty-dollar bill for the tip. I looked at it hungrily. It was so long since I had seen a fifty-dollar bill. I thought with a pang of his rolls of fifties near the bed, which were just there for decoration. It suddenly occurred to me that he was willing to hurt me again but not to help me.

On the street, I felt forlorn. A look of anguish on my face. "Don't worry," Carl said, like my dad at my mother's death- bed, and he blew me an old familiar kiss.

STILL, AS HEIDI says, I am "tenacious." I call the studio a hundred times. He is in Canada once, then Europe, then Asia, then Europe again. I like it when he is out of the coun- try; I feel as if I'm on holiday. I relax with Dimitri. I rejoice that I have a life.

But I still think Carl will help me. I still believe in his magnanimity. "They that have power to hurt and will do none . . ." There are so many ways available for him to help. He could help me by helping Dimitri, for example. He had liked Dimitri's work, he was "impressed." Typing Dimitri's Guggenheim application, I gamble on Carl's good will, on his benevolence. I put down Carl Vaggio for a recommendation, without telling Dimitri. Dimitri has already signed the form; he would say no if I asked him. Carl had recommended Sa- brina, and she had gotten one.

I keep calling the studio. I finally reach Carl, after months.

"I've called you a hundred times," I say.

He acquiesces silently. I tell him about the Guggenheim application. "It's too late," he says. "I already mailed it."

My heart has almost stopped beating. "What did you say?"

"I said I didn't know him or his art."

It is a death sentence. I can think only of Dimitri, of his

disappointment, which I will have caused. There is no chance of a Guggenheim now. "That's terrible. Now we won't be able to live."

"You can't *live* without grants?" Carl says with deep sarcasm.

"No."

Then I ask him for a painting. "I need some help," I say.

"It wouldn't help. You wouldn't be able to sell it. You shouldn't have sold the one I gave you. No, you were right," he laughed. "You made a 'killing on the market.' "

I ask for money.

"I'm not going to give you any money. On the principle of it. And because—I have enough responsibilities," he whines.

I have just read about his daughter's visit to him in New York, Charlotte the cocktail waitress's baby, how she's going to the best schools. I suppose that's what he means by responsibilities. I am not moved.

But it ends well. He tells me to call him on Wednesday. I still feel he will help me. I have stood the test of time. I am still beautiful.

ON WEDNESDAY, ROY answers. "Uh, Carl isn't here. He's away. He's out of the country."

I have been talking to Roy, briefly, for years. I know his voice. Recently he volunteered that he didn't see Carl much anymore. "I'm just here trying to scrape together a living," he said. Strangely, in Carlton Grill, Carl and I had talked about the fatal moment when he broke our date, our day-after-Christmas rendezvous, and Roy broke the news to me. "I never knew why exactly," I declared, "it was left vague." Carl nodded in satisfaction. As if he were checking up on Roy and I had given the right answer.

Now I say, "Roy, are you just saying that because Carl told you to?"

"Yep. That's right. That's what he told me to say."

The eagerness with which he tells me the truth! Gallantly,

like a man helping a woman into a carriage, knowing she is tired and needs assistance.

Probably Carl Vaggio is standing right there beside him. Even Roy is disgusted. I see myself through his eyes, shopworn and weary, ridiculous after all these years. He has risked losing his job to warn me. His telling me the truth has changed everything.

Carl and I marry and divorce in an instant. Instantly, I detest him.

I thank Roy and say goodbye to Carl forever.

I laugh out loud. Still cruel after all these years. But the same mean trick. Not to have changed even in that! How heartless and mechanical he is. How stunted, like Rumpelstiltskin. I have no further interest in this man. He is not my father. He is not a provider, a protector. He is not a friend.

On my honeymoon, I saw an opera from a velvet balcony in Italy. It ended with the heroine buried alive with a corpse. I have just been released from one. The dead body of Carl Vaggio is no longer with me in bed.

I am very happy. Something in me is released. For the first time in eleven years, I am blessed. I feel the sweetness of life. I am restored to myself. It is as my mother said. Nothing is lost.

IT IS MORNING. Dimitri has just gotten out of the shower —a beautiful, pearly room with iridescent tiles from Sri Lanka. I bought them myself, by mistake, in SoHo, thinking they were standard white tiles, but they were the most expensive.

"I'm the wrong dickhead for this job," Dimitri says. "The only people who like me are my underwear."

Russian poetry pours out of his lips.

His big head is wet and dripping. He dries himself with a tiny towel. Gets into his underwear wet. I try to kiss him, but he pulls in his head like a big male turtle.

"Leftover kisses from the fifties," he protests, and comes back to bed.

We make love. My legs open wider. I feel his balls lightly touch the clenched cheeks of my buttocks. "Pinball," I think, and feel it again. I come with Dimitri. I am making contact with him like Lotto, the balls coming in. The right numbers. I come again.

"Say something nice," I say. It occurs to me that Dimitri never says he loves me.

"I'm going to squirt," he answers.

"No, really. Tell me you love me."

"I think I'm more a doer than a sayer," he says.

I am satisfied. I am more than satisfied. Just to look at him is uplifting. His egregious beauty. His lion gaze.

When I look in my mother's journal, I read: "*Effervescence* means youth—means how I used to feel. It means responding It means enthusiasm—It means you can do anything It means a happy tiredness Nothing can faze you. You will find a way. It means twilight orgasm—or an early morning one. How can you effervesce without one? How can one stand life?"

It is like winning the lottery. I come again and again.